Necropolis

Bethan Evans

Bethan Evans ✱

NECROPOLIS

First published in 2021
by Wallace Publishing, United Kingdom
www.wallacepublishing.co.uk

Typesetting courtesy of Wallace Author Services
www.wallaceauthorservices.weebly.com

Cover design by Steve Williams
http://saa.co.uk/art/stevewilliamsart

Chapter 1

It was nearly time.

They were in the final preparations and the countdown had begun.

Everyone said this was a suicide mission; they were either going to come out heroes, having done the impossible, or they wouldn't be seen again. Weathered troops had gone before and few had returned; those that had come back were shadows of the people that had left—apparently two of them still hadn't said a word—and now the next platoon was heading towards the abattoir. With so few people left in the city eligible to recruit, it was no secret that everyone thought this would be their last chance to win this.

She watched them go into the main part of Necropolis, the giant warehouse that stood proudly above the mismatched buildings of the City of Suthchester; a landscape that had been irreversibly changed by The Breakdown. The warehouse was the hub of the army base of The Southern Company. It was really called The August Centre but nobody saw it as noble anymore; Necropolis seemed far more fitting and now there were very few who didn't refer to the entire base as such. She had always wanted to know what was inside but civilians were forbidden unless employed directly, and even then, they were sworn to secrecy. The troops were rarely allowed to fraternise outside of the base, so there was no one to ask. It was a constant tease. She lived below the city and the entrance to her home was tucked into the city walls, just far enough up the hill that it required her to walk past the gates that gave her a view straight in. Every day she watched the soldiers walk in, coming up from the barracks at the bottom of the hill on the other side, each day looking a little more beaten. Most of the cadets left were only a little older than her, completing their initial training. She sighed and stood up from her perch on a bollard, knowing she couldn't put off going home any longer—there was no way she'd get away with being late for supper again.

She skulked back towards home and the ornate metal gate built into the crumbling brickwork; behind it was a thin, winding staircase that you'd miss if you didn't know it was there. She scurried down the stairs as quickly as her legs would allow, pausing at the front entrance to undo the catch as gently as possible and pushing delicately. She opened the door just enough to slip through, any further and she knew it would creak—she'd made that mistake too many times. She slipped along the hall and tried to dash across the kitchen doorway; thinking she had made it.

"Terrwyn. You're late. Don't you dare pretend that you weren't outside of the gates! It is not proper for a young lady to be out on her own during the evening." Oh great, Sister Cariad. Why was it never Sister Astrid who caught her?

"Sorry Sister, the troops went in late tonight…"

"You and those boys. If I didn't know any better, Wyn, I'd think you wanted to be one!" Brother Aster chuckled, walking into the kitchen, squeezing her shoulder gently as he passed.

"You really need to keep away—it isn't right for a young lady. The General wouldn't like it." Sister Astrid followed him in, but had a gentle smile lingering behind her words.

Wyn sighed with relief at being able to use the Brother and Sister as a buffer; she was safe from Sister Cariad's wrath, for now at least.

"Exactly! Enough nonsense, it's supper time—a Collectioner caught a rabbit, so we're having rabbit stew," Sister Cariad snapped, rolling her eyes. She gestured to the pot bubbling on the stove and the smell that rolled over to Wyn was ridiculously inviting as she realised she hadn't eaten since breakfast.

Without being asked, she hurried round to set the rustic oak table that took pride of place in the centre of the kitchen. It was modest in design but the strength and weight behind it was a luxury compared to any other she'd seen in the city and it screamed 'home' to her. As she straightened the fourth place setting she looked up and saw Brother Aster had moved to the head of the table and was tracing the veins in the wood with his finger.

"Are any of the others joining us tonight, Brother?"

He jumped slightly, and looked at her flustered.

"Sorry, I was lost in thought, a conversation I had today just keeps playing on my mind... But anyway, enough about that. No, it will just be the four of us tonight, there are talks in the city that we must have representatives attend." He chewed his lip and couldn't stop the concern from casting a shadow over his face.

She smiled softly at him and continued in her task. The Retreat where they lived was split into two, and her end was generally reserved for taking in those in crisis—which is how she'd ended up being raised there, although she had rarely seen anyone else come in from the community. She always thought it was a shame that the Collections Children from the other end so rarely came to see them and she could tell that her Brothers and Sisters wished that they were more included.

It wasn't long before she was called to collect a bowl and took her spot, taking in the scent of the rich broth that was rising up to warm her. The day had been rainy and miserable and she couldn't have thought of anything better than a hearty casserole, especially Sister Cariad's—she may be stern but she was a fantastic cook.

"Brother Aster, did today's engagements go to plan?" Sister Astrid asked, briefly pausing to look at him.

"I cannot say that they were positive. Things across the water have gotten increasingly difficult, and the last company to deploy has suffered greatly. They're saying that this will no longer be the final deployment; all bases will have to sign up another tour." Brother Aster looked lost in the gravity of what he was saying. "General Baudin described what they are contending with as nothing but a massacre, bodies lining the..."

"Not in front of Terrwyn, Brother!" Sister Cariad barked, furious at such an inappropriate conversation being brought up at the dinner table. They finished the meal in silence.

Wyn was sent straight to her room once they were finished—she wasn't even allowed to stay and clear away from dinner. Not that she argued about it, she hated washing up—especially the stew pot that was coated a deep brown from years of use—but she resented the reprimand nonetheless. She was sixteen and far too old to be treated like a child, but that was the 'joy' of the Collection.

She sighed as she sat on her bed and looked around the room; it was modest with a basic metal bed frame, wooden desk, and minimal belongings. Living with the Brothers and Sisters of the Old

Collection, affectionately known as the Collections Children, meant that since she had been in their care she had lived in line with their lifestyle. Too many personal items were considered selfish and shallow but they had been lenient as she grew up, never completely denying her toys or art materials, and books were readily encouraged. She'd lost her parents when she was a baby and had no family that she knew of, they'd lived as workers in a countryside estate and that had left nowhere for her to go. She knew she should be grateful that they had taken her in but there was still a part of her that wished she could live out in the city. Much of it had been lost and restricted through the conflict that had been going on since before she was born, but there was still technology and a modern life that she had never been allowed to explore properly. She had only seen glimpses of the outside world through the odd day at a friend's house and what little they could afford at school. It was all worlds' away from how The Old Collection lived and even further away from what her life would have been before that.

Wyn turned out the light, lent back and stared at the ceiling; a thin shaft of moonlight was creeping into the room and casting shadows across the floor. She had often climbed onto the bed frame when she was younger to look out of the small, barred window, but had been disappointed to see nothing but the coastline, although it was soothing to her now—the sea breeze whispering of freedom and peace to pierce the containment of her room, and the lapping of the waves lulling her to sleep. Despite this, her sleep was always restless, full of words she could never quite understand and implausible stories that she couldn't quite remember being told. And tonight was no different.

At school the next day, the new updates on the troops was all anyone could talk about. Kiara's dad was on the council, the General's right-hand man, so she got all the gossip first.

"So, daddy said that the new selection will be in the next few weeks. He told mother that the enemy had brought in new people that had taken them by surprise and that they were working to retaliate. Some of what they saw was gruesome and daddy thinks they've been doing genetic experiments on people. They've got logistics coming in from another base to bring new technology and training – out of all the bases, they've chosen Necropolis to be the next base of the Special Forces recruitment!" She sounded excited at the prospect, but none of them really knew who Special Forces were.

"Daddy didn't know I was listening so I don't think we're supposed to know anything yet!" Kiara smirked at the congregation of her classmates, satisfied at her insider knowledge; there was nothing Kiara loved more than holding an audience and being the centre of attention.

"So, when are they signing up? We're old enough now, right?" Carter pushed past Wyn to get closer to Kiara, not even glancing in her direction as she stumbled away from his elbow.

"They just said 'soon', but it can't be long, they're absolutely desperate. But yeah, seventeen is the limit, so most of you are fine." Her eyes scanned the rest of the boys in the huddle. "I didn't know you were so desperate to sign up, Carter? I'd miss you..." Her voice had gone all girly and high-pitched as she flirted shamelessly. Wyn didn't even try to hide her contempt as she rolled her eyes.

"It's a man's job to protect the community and be a hero. My eldest brother went, and Cole's just finished his training so he will be going out on the next tour too. But we shall just have to make sure I have a girl to go out and fight for... and to come back to..." he winked at Kiara and sauntered off; she flushed pink and fanned herself dramatically.

"Isn't he amazing, Wyn?" she gushed. Wyn stared at her in disbelief.

"Amazing? He's so arrogant! I don't know what you see in him Kiara, let's hope he buggers off to war and we can find you someone better!"

Kiara did an unattractive squawk and looked at her best friend with disgust; beside her, the other girls giggled. The boys had already dispersed, following their arrogant leader, and Kiara turned on her heels with a huff and stalked off with her nose in the air. Wyn chuckled to herself; she knew she'd be over it by first break. Kiara was one of the few people Wyn had always had in her life; their parents had grown up together and Kiara was one final connection to a world she couldn't remember. As such, she would never lose faith in the strength of that bond.

"She looks like one of those birds on the canteen roof when she walks like that, doesn't she?" Wyn commented to Isabella and Cleo, who had fallen in step beside her, watching Kiara swing her hips as she stalked across the schoolyard. The girls giggled and chatted as they followed her into the tired-looking building.

Wyn couldn't concentrate during class. Customer-facing roles of modern banking just didn't hold her interest and instead, she was thinking about what Kiara had been saying. Special Forces; it sounded exciting. She wondered whether the cadets would look any different. They were running out of people to sign up so maybe all the strong ones were already gone and they'd only get the wimpy guys. Maybe there would be new things to watch with Special Forces coming in. What would the logistics experts even be like? She sighed. She knew she didn't have much chance of knowing; if only she could get onto the other side of the fence.

"Okay ladies, so remember, if you do follow a career in finance, it is important to always check the customers' credentials but also approach each individual with great caution. We don't want you to get into a situation you can't get yourself out of." Even Mrs Clay sounded bored by her lesson, probably fed up with the patronising drivel that she had to cite. She was always so distant from her class. Her teaching style was strict and although there was the odd occasion when she was in the mood to laugh and joke, she generally kept them at arm's length. Wyn could never decide if this was because she just didn't like them or if there was something more to it.

The boy-girl segregation that came into effect due to The Breakdown was frustrating. It was justified as a requirement to prepare the boys for life in the forces, to help them understand the different roles and coordination, and whatever else they could get away with teaching in schools. However, according to Kiara, General Baudin had said the boys' syllabus was pointless. The teachers didn't have any idea what they were doing, or know anything about the army, and they had to be completely rewired when they got into training. Meanwhile, the girls were taught the basics of the roles they would have to fill to keep the city going.

"Okay girls, fifteen-minute break and then back in here for some Modern History with the boys." Mrs Clay grabbed her coffee mug off the desk and scurried out of the room in search of a caffeine fix.

"I don't think I'd mind working in a bank," Isabella said as Wyn spun round in her seat to face her friends, "I like dealing with money."

"You like spending it, more like! I think a restaurant would be more interesting, don't know if I could manage in the kitchen though," Cleo mulled thoughtfully.

"Ooh, I know what I want to do! I want to work somewhere in

the Gild District, doing hair or nails or something, like mother used to do before she met father and moved back out to the country. Then I only have to deal with the elite, and I can marry an Officer. I'd get to use all the nice things instead of actually having to work." This was so typically Kiara, she was definitely not naturally humanitarian. "What about you Wyn?"

"Ugh, I don't know... I guess if I had to do something I'd teach, but only if I could teach the boys' stuff... Our classes are so dull."

"Oh Wyn, you're so obsessed with what the boys do, it isn't normal! Why are you so desperate to see what the troops do, it's probably just messy and loud and unsanitary." Kiara cringed at the idea, and something boiled in Wyn as she saw how happily they all just accepted the society standard for women.

"I just want to do something exciting..."

With that, Mrs Clay re-entered the room, joined by Mr Kane; interrupting Wyn from expressing her notion, and distracting the rest of the girls who began primping and pursing their lips, to ensure they were ready when the classes merged. The boys followed and took their seats, giving them the last few minutes of break to flirt across the desks. Once they had all settled down, Mr Kane took a seat at the side as Mrs Clay picked up the tablet and flicked across until a presentation filled the screen at the front of the classroom.

"Okay guys, today we are going to be recapping some stuff we've studied over the last few years and through it, create a timeline of women in history. Back when women were once allowed to actually do something—rule and lead and fight. Before that chauvinistic pig Lint took over the military and government... When women could actually think for themselves." She spat the words out, her eyes misting over in anger.

Mr Kane took the tablet out of her hand in one clean movement that was too quick for Wyn to even notice him leave his chair.

"Enough Lydia," he hushed furiously and moved on with the presentation.

The words rang in Wyn's ears, *'When women could fight'*. Maybe she could fight. What if she put her case forward? If they were as desperate as Kiara made out, then they might just let her. Her head started spinning, but how could she convince them?

Wyn didn't listen to the rest of the lesson, she was mulling and planning and pulling together everything she knew about the military base. Kiara's father—he would be the best place to start, and at least she knew him from her childhood years.

"Kiara, would I be able to come over one day after school – Sister Cariad is driving me mad and I just need an evening away!"

"Sure Wyn, how about tomorrow? I'll get Alana to do something nice for dinner."

Brilliant, step one complete, now to hope that Major MacCulloch was home tomorrow.

By the next day, Wyn's head was buzzing with ideas of what she could say and what reasons she could give. Should she ask him straight? The Major didn't appear to be particularly fond of any female except his daughter, who he kept on a diamond-encrusted pedestal, and his wife, who he could simply keep happy with an endless shopping fund and glamorous lifestyle. He had only ever given Wyn the odd contemptuous sideways glance, apart from that one evening when he'd had a few too many glasses of brandy at a Majors' retirement party and started to slur at her about how much he appreciated the female form, and that she would grow into a "fine young lady". She had tried to keep out of his way since.

She spent the next day nervously shaking her leg in class—driving anyone near her crazy—as she stressed about how to tackle the topic with a man she hadn't spoken to properly in years. But, all too soon, it was the end of the day and Kiara was waiting at the door to walk back to hers. It wasn't too far, about a fifteen-minute walk if she was on her own, but with the girls gossiping about the day, it was more like thirty.

"Did you see the way Carter looked at me today? Do you reckon he does like me? There isn't long left until we leave so if he does, then he'd better make a move and quick!" Kiara raved.

Cleo and Isabella clucked obediently about his obvious infatuation and how he must just be too scared to do anything about it because he thought she was out of his league.

"Well, what was it that Mrs Clay said yesterday about women doing their own thing? Maybe tomorrow I'll speak to him about it!" Kiara stated triumphantly, but Wyn could detect the tiny wobble beneath the surface. Kiara's confidence was hard to knock but the thought of going against the society-defined female roles clearly did just that. Wyn felt a nervous lump rise into her throat as she contemplated the conversation she was about to have, and how it was doing that tenfold.

They couldn't have arrived at Kiara's soon enough, as Wyn's

nerves snowballed with each step towards the house. By the time she'd reached the front door, she had trepidation fluttering all through her. They said goodbye to the other girls and went in.

Kiara's house was grand and stood proudly on the edge of the city. They were a rich family and one of the few that seemed to still live well despite The Breakdown. They could still afford nice things, still had a housekeeper that they had brought with them from their country estate and who doubled as a maid and a cook, and Kiara had always been utterly spoilt. Standing in the hallway was always a reminder of the differences between the humble home she had with the Collection, with its plain walls and threadbare rugs, and that of Kiara's house, with the strong, carpeted staircase that rose in front of her, encased by shelves full of the delicate statuettes and historical artefacts that Major MacCulloch collected. They were things from the wars they'd learnt about in history, and reminders of the world before The Breakdown started.

"Alana? Where are you?" Kiara shrilled through the house.

"In the kitchen, Miss Kiara," the soft voice drifted back. Alana was always so polite and welcoming, despite the dismissive tone Kiara always seemed to use – she was definitely taken for granted. "Ah, Miss Wyn, it's so nice to see you, we are well overdue for a catch-up! Are you staying for dinner?"

"If that's okay Alana, you know I never turn down some of your delicious cooking!" Wyn smiled at her warmly.

"Where are my parents?" Kiara demanded before Alana could respond to Wyn.

"The Major is in his office completing paperwork and Mrs MacCulloch is still at The Gild, shopping."

Kiara nodded and turned her back abruptly to flounce off up the stairs. Wyn followed obediently. The Major was in; she was really going to do this. Luckily, as Kiara headed straight for the office, she wouldn't need to come up with a reason to go find the Major by herself. Now she just needed an in to the conversation.

"But daddy, it's the last six weeks of school ever! I need to go out looking amazing!" She whined and pouted at her father.

"Alright, alright, speak to your mother and she can take you to the salon for hair and nails after school tomorrow! Anything to keep my petal happy … and quiet… Now, take Terrwyn to your room, I have work to do."

"Um … Major … before we go, is it okay if I ask you a

question? It was following a query Brother Aster had about the next sign up." She could hear her voice tremble. The Major looked curiously dubious.

"Make it quick, if it's for Brother Aster. But if it's sensitive then you will have to tell him to come to me directly, as it's not like him to get a child to do his errands." His brow furrowed. Panic flashed through Wyn as she feared she could get Brother Aster into trouble.

"It was just about the numbers required in the new sign-up. If there aren't enough eligible males, then what would be the next move? Would you drop the age or just combine with the people from other cities, or could you even train up some hand-picked women?" The words rushed out of her mouth, muddling together. There was no going back now.

The Major was laughing, creasing up all the wrinkles in his face with the strength of his reaction. Wyn had never seen him lose so much composure before as he guffawed at the thought.

"Women? Why would we ever accept women, they are far too weak and too emotional!" He collected himself and continued, forcing his face back into his usual stern expression. "If Brother Aster has concerns over the sign up then he can speak to me directly, although we will not consider options until we know what numbers we have. I am horrified that he would even entertain the thought of women!"

"I must have got what he said wrong; I didn't hear all of the conversation. He doesn't know I'm asking… I was just trying to help. I'm sorry if I intruded, I…" she stammered and backed out the door, taking just long enough to see the flash of irritation and his mouth pursing as he considered how disrespectful and arrogant she was. He had thought leaving her in the care of the Old Collection would have ensured she was not brought up like this.

She knew she'd done that all wrong. She flushed red and breathed hard as she stood outside the doorway with her back against the wall, trying to regain her composure. So, convincing them to sign her up was not an option, but she wasn't ready to give up. Mrs Clay was right; women should be able to do these things and she'd set her mind to it now – she was going to work something out.

"What was that?" Kiara demanded, rushing out of the office looking horrified. "Why would you talk to daddy about that? You know what he's like, and how he feels about children and women getting involved in politics and military matters! You definitely can't stay for dinner now, you need to get away and give him time to calm down."

She escorted Wyn to the front door and waved her off. Self-preservation was completely innate for Kiara and she knew it was the best way to avoid her father's temper.

Wyn felt deflated as she dragged her feet back home, barely looking up even as she passed Necropolis. What was she going to do now?

Chapter 2

Mrs Clay looked exhausted by lunchtime the following day. The morning had consisted of more discussions on the appropriate customer service techniques in any customer-facing roles, and she was clearly no more passionate about this than she had been about banking. Whilst watching her, Wyn often wondered what she had wanted to do with her life—because teaching the inane life skills that she was obliged to do, clearly wasn't it. Once the class had been dismissed for lunch, Wyn waited behind, shuffling her feet back and forth, trying to look inconspicuous to her classmates.

"Mrs Clay," the words tumbled over each other as she forced them out. If she didn't say it quickly, she wouldn't say it at all. "When you were talking about women the other day … about them being able to fight, did you, um, did you really believe that they should?"

Mrs Clay's eyebrows rose in interest and she peered quizzically at Wyn.

"Yes, things are ludicrous the way they are, although Mr Kane isn't very happy that you heard any of that and he'd be even more furious to hear us talking about it again. Why? Did you have a query about women's roles in past societies?"

"Um, no, not exactly… I… I want to join up. And I need you to help me…" Wyn held her breath; there was no going back now.

Mrs Clay's eyes widened. She looked horrified and inspired in equal measure and there was a gleam behind her eyes that Wyn had never seen before. The corners of her mouth were starting to rise, deepening the dimples in her cheeks, as she couldn't stop the excitement from creeping into her face. She stood and walked to the half-open door, swinging it closed in a jaunty manner before turning back to Wyn. She was grinning now and looking her straight in the eye.

"Wyn, are you serious about this? I've been dreaming of taking a stand for years. Getting women to stand with me against the tyrants that destroyed the rights women spent so much of history fighting for. All I've needed was a catalyst, someone to actually believe in my vision and stand with me, not the fluff-brained puppets that society has created. If you're serious, really serious, I will do everything I can to help you!" Passion buzzed through the words as they poured out.

Mrs Clay had stopped abruptly, doubt flashing across her face as she waited for Wyn's response; her sudden anxiety was clear. She had barely disclosed this dream to anyone, not even her husband knew just how strongly she felt about it. Revealing such a rebellious passion to the wrong person would have guaranteed losing everything. The moment had taken her by surprise, a glimmer of hope of the revolution she was desperate for, and she had lost all sense and clarity. She also knew there was no guarantee they could even achieve it. Was Wyn really able to make a difference or had she just signed away both of their lives to imprisonment and community service or, even worse, disappearing completely like her friend Enya had years ago?

"Mrs Clay... Do you mean it? You'll help me? Please, please do! I don't know how to do it, or what to do, or where to start, or..." Wyn's voice raised an octave as relief and anticipation washed over her and, as she tried to fumble together more words, she found she could only squeak unfinished syllables. The world suddenly seemed brighter as elation set in; someone was on her side, this was really happening!

"Wyn!" Mrs Clay laughed, looking just as thrilled as Wyn felt. "If you mean it, then I will do everything I can to get you there. You can be the first. We will get you in, you will succeed and you can prove to those robots that just follow orders that women can still be great!"

They smiled at each other, both realising that their dreams were finally tangible. Despite two completely different motivations and endgames, they had a parallel journey that drew them together.

"But," Mrs Clay's tone changed suddenly, "this stays between us. No-one else can know or both of our lives will be over, forever. If you try and double-cross me, then you will fall with me." There was a fire behind her eyes now, as the fears that had kept her in line for so long began to burn at the surface. She pushed them back down; she had given her word and she was going to make this happen. "Okay, class starts again in twenty minutes. Go get some lunch, get some air... You might want to freshen up a bit too, you look frazzled."

Mrs Clay smiled gently at Wyn, the previous harshness disappearing as quickly as it had started and Wyn obliged, darting to the door. As she stepped out into the yard, she let out her breath—she had been holding it since Mrs Clay's warning, and the weight of what she had decided to do was settling onto her chest. There was no going back now and she hadn't even thought about the seriousness of what she was asking, the risks of getting caught. It had started out as just some selfish adventure and now she was playing with people's futures. She closed her eyes and pictures of the Sisters and Brothers of The Collection danced into view; how much of an upheaval would she cause them when she left and how much pain would she be inflicting if they ever found out?

Wyn gathered herself and went into the toilets to splash water on her face. Catching her reflection in the mirror, she pulled in her lips and scrunched her face up before finding her resolve and plastering on a neutral, strong expression with a self-assured nod. By the time she returned to the classroom, nearly everyone was back. She made her way to her seat, trying not to catch anyone's eyes.

"Oi, Wyn? Where were you at lunch? Did you even come out at all?" Kiara was leaning across Wyn's desk with a half-whisper.

"I needed to speak to Mrs Clay, about all this job stuff... I just, I don't know what I should do..." She felt like Kiara was looking straight through her and unravelling her plans. But Kiara still looked confused.

"Oh! Does this mean you've stopped obsessing over the boys being more exciting? About time too!" Kiara stated triumphantly and turned back round to her desk.

Mrs Clay was glancing across the room, concerned about this exchange, having heard none of it, and Wyn returned this with a small reassuring smile. Mrs Clay visibly relaxed.

The rest of the day passed in a blur. Wyn and Mrs Clay tried to actively avoid eye contact but couldn't help but glance over at each other whilst Mr Kane banged on about some biological phenomenon.

Both searched for any tiny sign that the other may have changed their mind – but each time they couldn't help but just smirk at one another. As she passed the desk at the end of the day, Mrs Clay reached out and momentarily squeezed Wyn's arm, solidifying the pact between them.

Their exchange danced through Wyn's head for the remainder of the day, as glimmers of ideas and plans danced in and out of view, but anything concrete seemed just out of reach. It was all-encompassing and completely distracting.

"Are you okay Wyn? You've been awfully quiet tonight," Sister Astrid asked concerned, peering over the glasses perched on her nose. "You barely said anything through dinner!"

"I'm fine, Sister. A very tiring day at school, that's all—coming to the end of the year and all that. I think I just need an early night!" Wyn gave her broadest smile and turned back to the dishes in the sink. She couldn't wait for her chores for the evening to be done so she could escape to her room and start planning properly.

"Well, that is understandable, big things to decide for when you leave!" The Sisters were rustling through bits of paper, preparing for prayer group that was held each Thursday night. They would be leaving to meet at the City Hall shortly, and then Wyn would be able to settle into her brainstorming.

"Are you sure you don't want to come to prayer this evening? You haven't been in a few weeks and the Collectioners' are always asking after you!" Sister Cariad was constantly frustrated by Wyn's lack of interest in the Old Collection and the religions from which it developed, but now that she was old enough to make her own decisions, nobody forced her. They were just grateful to have brought up an obedient and intelligent young lady, considering her background.

"No, thank you, Sister, I might attend next week—and I'll be at Sunday service—but I'm just so tired!" Wyn did her best to imitate a weary smile at the Sisters and put the rest of her focus on the remaining dishes, turning her back so she couldn't be engaged any further.

Once all of the Collections' Children had left, Wyn gathered up her papers from the table where she had been feigning doing homework, and retired to her room. She set up camp at her desk, put the lamp on and set about making notes.

She didn't know where to start, so started her scrawlings at the beginning; right at the top, with a line through it, the first idea she'd had that had failed:

\#

Ask the Major to allow women to sign up.

\#

Below it, she set about writing what she could do next, but she couldn't work out anything substantial. Words scattered the page: the things that a soldier needed to be; strong, fearless, courageous, and as many other adjectives as she could muster. Below it all, written in pure frustration, in big bold letters which just made her heart drop every time she looked at them, she wrote:

\#

BE A BOY!

\#

It was pathetic, she knew. It just made it clear that she was aiming for the impossible. Maybe her excitement had been for nothing; there was no way for her to sign-up and be accepted. She turned off the light and sank under the covers, completely deflated as she fell asleep.

On Friday morning, she got to school early in the hopes of catching Mrs Clay before class started. She peered around the doorframe and frowned as she saw Mrs Clay and Mr Kane stood there. Their voices were raised and she paused a minute to see if she could hear what they were discussing.

"Lewis, I just want to see what the boy's classes are about—I've seen the syllabus, yes, but I want a better understanding. It'll help us tailor the joint lessons if we know what all the students learn day-to-day!"

"Lydia, it is not appropriate for a woman to be involved in the discussions and demonstrations of the male students! You know that just as well as I do!"

"It would benefit everyone! Imagine I take a history lesson and teach about some war and the tactics used—like the storming tactics used at the beginning of The Breakdown—and it completely contradicts what you're teaching the boys!"

"How do you know anything about the tactics? Only people on the August Centre Council know the details of the tactics?" Mrs Clay pulled her lips in tight, her eyes wide as she'd been caught out. "But you do have a good point. Fine, we will draw up a rota of when the girls are doing something, meaning you can then sit in … but only on the vital stuff! And only if you don't tell anyone that we're doing it, as the General would kill me… Or maybe he wouldn't, maybe he would think it was intuitive to ensure the boys were appropriately trained... Either way, don't tell anyone – leave the decision to me!" He sounded triumphant, having already decided to take the credit for the idea—if it worked—and abruptly turned away from her, striding towards the door

Even from the doorway, Wyn could see Mrs Clay's entire body relax as she released the breath she'd been holding. She really thought she'd been caught out for a moment but, with the realisation that he could use the situation to bolster his own image, Mr Kane had clearly forgotten all about her gender inappropriate knowledge of war. Wyn rushed in as Mr Kane walked out and stood eagerly in front of Mrs Clay.

"What was that about? The boys' lessons? Is that to help us?" she gushed but then stopped, realising how rude she had been to eavesdrop on their conversation. She blushed in embarrassment.

"Ah, yes, Wyn, we need a chance to talk about this and what we are going to do. I've worked on Mr Kane to infiltrate enemy camp and find out what we need to know—that's what he was agreeing to then. So, now we need a plan of action. I'll think of a reason for you to stay behind at lunch and we can start?" She sounded contemplative, as if there was a whole world of ideas hanging in the air, waiting to be said, and she was frustrated she couldn't say them yet.

Wyn grinned at her in agreement and slipped back out of the classroom to take her place in the yard, so that nothing seemed out of place to her friends. She arrived just in time for registration.

The morning dragged on as Wyn waited eagerly for lunchtime and, when Mrs Clay reprimanded her for the poor quality of some fictitious homework and instructed her to stay in at lunch to redo it, she couldn't help but smile. She regretted it immediately and a bolt of fear flooded through her as Kiara looked round. She was a picture of confusion as she caught the jubilant expression on Wyn's face but Wyn forced her grin into a grimace, with dramatic eye-rolling to accompany it. She relaxed as Kiara turned back to the front, seemingly satisfied by the reaction but still concerned that her normally conscientious friend was in trouble.

The girls all shot her sympathetic looks as they filed out to lunch. Wyn made sure to look miserable at her desk in an attempt to be more believable; she avoided any eye contact that might risk giving her away. The second they were gone she leapt up and rushed to the front of the class, standing in front of Mrs Clay, who looked up from the screen in front of her and gestured for Wyn to pull up a chair.

"So, Wyn, where are we going to start? When you asked for my help, what were you thinking?"

"Well, Mrs Clay, I..."

"Call me Lydia," Mrs Clay cut in. "But only when it's just us, of course."

"Ah, okay, well, *Lydia.*" She grinned as she said it. "I don't really know where to start. I tried to write down some ideas but I didn't really get anywhere."

She pulled the piece of crumpled paper from her pocket and handed it over. Mrs Clay looked at it carefully, taking every word in. She smiled when she got to the bottom.

"I think you've hit the nail on the head there!" She pointed at the standout statement on the page. "You need to be a boy!" She chuckled to herself, her mind whirring.

Wyn's mouth was open in confused disappointment. What was funny? That was all she could come up with and it was stupid! Mrs Clay saw the look on her face and gave her a reassuring smile; she looked Wyn slowly up and down and pursed her lips, narrowing her eyes as she contemplated her words.

"So ... this could work!" Wyn looked at her in bewilderment. "We need to get them to believe you're a boy, get you signed-up and on the inside. Prove to them you can do just as good a job as the rest of them—maybe even better—and then, once you've fought and proven yourself, we reveal who you are. Then they can never again deny that women can do just as well as men! So, how do we make them believe that you're a boy?"

She wasn't really asking, just airing her internal dialogue, so

Wyn sat statue-like with her eyes fixed on Mrs Clay's face, waiting and hoping for some sort of epiphany.

"Well, firstly, I've finally got access to what the boys get taught in preparation – so we can get you clued up on that. And in the past, I may have had a few, ahem… dates…" She blushed slightly and cleared her throat, trying to make her wording appropriate for the audience, "…with a Major, so I have some knowledge of the initial process of joining up. Next, you're pretty scrawny really; we'll have to get you built up a bit so you can match the strength of some of the boys. Some of them are pretty weedy anyway so it shouldn't be too hard and I know someone who will be more than happy to help! And finally, it'll just be appearance. We'll have to do your hair, work out how to bind your chest—at least you're not too heavy-chested—and sort out some clothes. But let's put the groundwork in first and get you fighting ready!"

Wyn nodded but doubt still shrouded her mind and read clearly on her face. She didn't think she could ever pass for a boy; she could barely open a bottle of water much less prove herself to be fit enough to be a soldier. Mrs Clay could see the concern on Wyn's face and softened her smile.

"We can do this, Wyn. I've spent years looking for a way to break down the barriers of the military, I am not going to let this fail! But that is enough for now—I will arrange what we need for step one and will let you know when we can start."

Mrs Clay smiled broadly and it was clear that the conversation was over. But, as Wyn turned and left the room, concern shadowed Mrs Clay's face. She sat in thought, her mind casting back to her best friend Enya, the only person she knew who had ever stood up to the city leaders and demanded a return to equality. She had disappeared shortly after and they declared her 'missing assumed dead' a few weeks later. If they caught Wyn, then the same fate would be theirs. She gathered herself as she felt tears begin to sting behind her eyes. She took a deep breath and set about preparing for the afternoon's lessons.

Chapter 3

The next few days passed slowly. Nothing had happened and, even though she was desperate to ask, Wyn tried not to bother Mrs Clay as it had been made perfectly clear that she would let her know when things were sorted. Instead, Wyn brainstormed constantly, starting with the little things she would need to do to convince people she was a boy. She started studying the boys closely: how they walked, how they talked, little movements they made—the way Marcus cracked his knuckles (she'd tried, she couldn't do it), the way Jed rubbed his fingers along the stubble on his jawline when he got stressed, or even the way Carter ran his fingers through his hair whenever he thought one of the girls was looking at him. More than once the boys had caught her staring, and the girls had questioned why she suddenly seemed to fancy them all. But Wyn brushed it off, vowing to be more subtle, and just kept making her notes, building a blueprint for what sort of boy she was going to be.

The preparations didn't stop at school; when she got home and was in her room she would stand in front of the jagged-edged mirror and try to emulate the stance of whoever had last been in her sights that day. Once she had worked out a rough standing position, she would saunter towards the mirror trying to get the swagger right. She'd tried to copy some of the more popular boys because she figured that the more she came across as an alpha male, the more people would take her seriously, but it made it even harder to do. The only way she could look even remotely masculine was if she pretended she had a box between her legs, and then she couldn't concentrate on what she was doing because she found she laughed at herself. She just thought she looked ridiculous—it was like one of those silly games you play at parties where you pass a balloon from one person to the next using just your knees. After a week of trying she had, at least, settled on a pose—legs far further apart than she found comfortable, shoulders back, chest up, hands in her pockets with her thumbs hanging out. If she squinted enough to get rid of the long, dark blonde hair and what little chest she had, then she could sort of pass for a gangly boy that was still a bit cocky. And that was pretty much the aim. She would have to keep working on the walking.

Ten days after their first conversation, Mrs Clay asked Wyn to wait as she passed her on her way out of the classroom for lunch. Kiara looked round and questioned with her eyes, checking if her friend wanted her to stay, but Wyn smiled softly, motioning with her head for Kiara to go on without her.

"Yes Lydia?" she questioned, feeling her heart rate quicken as she hoped for progress.

"I have spoken to my friend who owns a gym and runs some closed sessions and he's willing to train you up personally every night after school so we can get you into some sort of shape. Not everything that goes on in the gym is entirely legal—none of our business of course—but it means we can be sure he won't spill our secrets and he won't let anyone else who might be there to rat on us either!" She sounded confident and although nerves shuddered down Wyn's spine, she didn't let fear take over. "If we start next Monday, then we can sort out some sort of regime with him; when to go and what else we need to do outside of training. And once I've done some of the boys' lessons, we can factor that into the times. How does that sound?"

"Okay, yes, that's fine! You really think I can do this? I've never even been in a gym. I'll need to think of something to tell the Sisters when they ask why I'm home late." She was screwing up her face as she contemplated the time and effort this was going to take, and if she was even up for the job. She hadn't anticipated this much commitment and was annoyed at her own naivety, but she was still hopeful that it would all be worth it.

"You'll be fine, Wyn! Snapper will make sure you get the training you need, but don't expect anything too fancy – it most certainly isn't like the membership gyms you see in The Gild!" She paused a moment, thinking, before she continued, "Tell the Sisters that we've started a study session after school that you want to stay on for—that it's in preparation for the end of your formal education and will run for the last four weeks of term."

Wyn physically relaxed at this suggestion, although the idea of the gym left a knot of fear deep in her stomach. Who had a name like Snapper? But she had a week to get her head around it and break it to the Sisters, so that they would really believe she'd be staying after school; she'd avoided extra-curricular activity her entire life so she knew it would take a lot to convince them now, but it was the only way to make the plan happen.

"I'll speak to the Sisters tonight," she stated with a determined nod and set her mouth in a tight line. This had to work.

She broached the subject over dinner, deciding that mentioning it in passing and not making a fuss was probably the best and least suspicious plan. There were four of them today – Sisters Cariad and Astrid, Brother Aster and Brother Dane. Brother Dane rarely joined them as he was senior to the others and was often busy with official duties, but he did try and meet with them for supper once a week. He had always had a soft spot for Wyn.

Wyn looked down at the bowl of vegetable soup in front of her, focussing on the carrots sinking under the thick blend as she dragged her spoon through it; as a child, she'd always pretended they were boats bobbing in the sea and she found it soothing. She drew in a deep breath, ready to make a throwaway comment and start the conversation off, but it caught at the back of her throat and the words didn't come out. She couldn't understand why she was so nervous – these were the people that had raised her since she was one and a half, they had been there through all the childish tantrums and teenage rebellions, how could she be so worried about telling them something that they would actually be happy about, even if it was a lie? She closed her eyes and drew another breath.

"Just to let you know, Sisters,'" she looked up and caught Sister Astrid's gaze, directing it at the women who were her primary caretakers, "I'll be staying after school most days until the end of term – Mrs Clay has put in some extra study sessions to prepare us for the outside world."

She shovelled a spoonful into her mouth slightly too quickly, to buy her time to answer any questions that came her way.

"Okay Terrwyn, that sounds like a very good idea – I'm glad you're finally taking this seriously. Only five weeks left until you decide the direction of the rest of your life!" Sister Cariad looked delighted at her, a rare sight that was reserved only for things she thought were especially pleasing. She rarely showed her emotions, day-to-day she would deliver a weak smile at best, and Wyn could count on one hand the number of times she'd seen Sister Cariad seem excited by anything. Sister Astrid and the Brothers nodded at her in agreement and smiled encouragingly.

Wyn smiled back, relieved but, although she knew it was the reaction she needed, she was still slightly disappointed. She had spent all afternoon building up to this moment, with a speech worked out about how she was truly committing to her last chance to study and to her future, and how she had finally realised it was time to take her head out of the clouds and take control. She didn't get to say a word of it and although she had achieved her objective, she still felt slightly deflated.

The rest of the week leading up to her first gym session was fairly uneventful. More practicing standing and walking like a man – taking longer strides had definitely helped and she was feeling more comfortable with it. But she had no more chances to talk to Mrs Clay, except to tell her that the Collections Children were fine with her 'extra lessons' and there was nothing else for them to prepare. Her nerves grew as she over-thought everything. Who was training her? Who else would be there? What illegal things were they involved with – what if they got her involved? Where was she even going? By Sunday night, her breathing sped up and her palms got sweaty just thinking about it; she felt physically sick.

On Monday afternoon, the numbers on the clock in class flipped over to 15:00 and everyone started to move and get ready for home. Wyn took her time packing up her stuff and watched as her friends sloped out of class, having told them earlier that Mrs Clay was giving her some extra tuition so they wouldn't expect her to walk home with them. They had accepted it with only a little more questioning than the Sisters. People seemed far too accepting of the fact she was claiming that wasn't ready to leave school and she was realising just how little she had thought about coping in the real world before, but now it wouldn't matter because she would barely have to see it.

"Ready for this? Grab your stuff and we'll head over to the gym, it's only a five-minute walk so the exercise will be a good start. And that means once you've settled into it, you will be able to walk over on your own after school."

"What? You won't be coming with me?" Wyn interjected, fear radiating through her voice.

"Well, no, not every time. I will be using that time to sort out other things for us. It'll work well that way – we can each be the other's alibi!" She sounded bright, absolutely positive that this plan would work. "Come on then, time to get started!"

Mrs Clay swung her handbag onto her shoulder and started out of the classroom; Wyn scrambled to pick up her school bag and gym kit and stumbled out after her, tripping over her own feet in the process. From the moment they left the school, they were walking along backstreets to avoid the risk of passers-by, with both of them on the avid lookout for anyone they recognised.

The walk passed in no time with Mrs Clay striding along with a new bounce in her step; putting everything into motion had reinvigorated her passion and had given her a reason to be excited by life. Wyn kept up and by the time they reached the gym, she could feel her heart beating through her chest, her mouth was dry and her throat tight. She stared at the building in front of her: a square brick building that looked like a weed growing up in the middle of the garden of quaint, brick offices; it was painted a dark purple that made it look dingy and uninviting. Wyn swallowed heavily, a new level of fear gnawing at her but Mrs Clay didn't notice and pushed the heavy black door open with ease, walking straight in with confidence. Wyn hurried behind.

Inside wasn't much better. The walls were covered in peeling paint and wallpaper; Wyn could see there had once been murals of boxers and weightlifters on them, but they were now tired and looked more like torn-apart bodies. Scattered around the edge of the gym were machines, racks of weights, hooks with skipping ropes, punch bags, and the floor was covered with a soft rubber matting that had a slight give under her feet. Straight ahead of them was a reception desk. Behind it stood a tall man with bulging muscles and veins; he was huge without a shred of fat on him, dark stubble lined his face, his long hair was pulled back into a ponytail and his bushy black eyebrows made him look serious and angry. Wyn took an involuntary step back when she saw him – he looked like the sort of person she associated with crime and violence.

"Okay Wyn, this is Snapper, he's going to be looking after you here."

"Hello Wyn!" His voice was deep and rough and his accent was lazy, but he sounded happier than she expected, although his angry expression didn't change. "You and Lydia come with me and we will talk through what we're going to do with you."

Snapper led them through a door behind reception and into an office, then gestured for them to pull one of the mismatched tatty chairs up to the desk that sat slightly off-centre. It had an ancient computer sat on top, surrounded by unfiled paperwork and as Snapper sat down, he carelessly swept the ink-smudged papers directly in front of him to the side, scrunching them all together in the process.

"So, ladies, what is it you want from me?" He looked from one to the other expectantly. Mrs Clay initially looked to give Wyn an opportunity to speak; but her eyes jumped back and forth between the adults, unsure of what she was expected to say.

"Okay, I guess it's up to me then?" Mrs Clay laughed. "Well, Snapper, I've given you the basic run-down—on a strictly need-to-know basis—we are going to get Wyn into the next sign-up for The Southern Company. She is going to prove to all those military bastards that women can do just as good a job as men, but to do that they need to believe she's a boy or else we'll never get her past the gates. They are opening up the next intake in eight weeks and we need to get Wyn's strength up by then, so she can pass the physical tests and keep up with the training. But nobody can find out about this, which I believe we already have an agreement about." Mrs Clay's eyes narrowed at him slightly in threat before returning to normal. "And we will need your advice on what else she needs to do to get to the best and most convincing place possible. Anything else you can think of, Wyn?"

Both of them were staring at her and she shook her head slowly, her face scrunched up as she tried to show them an anxious smile.

"Let's make a start then, shall we. I'll run you through a couple of tests today, Wyn, and see where your strength and general fitness is at. And then I'll put a training regime together for us to work through. How is your diet generally? Lots of protein?"

"Um, well, I don't know… The Sisters cook with whatever has been grown or caught by the Collectioners', so it's stews and soup and meat and vegetables. I don't really have a lot of control over what I eat." Her voice wavered as she was put on the spot, losing confidence in what she was saying and feeling pathetic and young for how little control she had over her life.

"Okay, well at least you're getting a healthy diet. I'll get you some supplement bars, mainly protein and extra calories. You're going to need a lot more food if we're going to get you some muscle, and that'll help us bulk you up – I'll give it to Lydia." He nodded towards Mrs Clay, "You can take some home and she'll keep some at school for you. You'll have to keep them quiet though; we have our own suppliers who don't do things quite by the book... Nothing to worry about though!"

He flushed red briefly as he tried to brush over one of the clearly dodgy aspects of the gym but gathered himself and stood up abruptly. He led them out of the office and directed Wyn into the changing rooms to the left of the door, before re-joining Mrs Clay. Wyn was about to follow the directions but paused as she realised that from the other side of the doorway, she could just about get the gist of what was being said, although it was faint.

"So, what do you think of her?" Mrs Clay asked expectantly.

"She's small, I don't think she'll build muscle easily – you'll have to do a lot more prep than just spending time with me, but I'll do what I can. Then we're even! You can't blackmail me anymore or I'll just throw this back at you twice as hard!"

His demeanour had changed and his voice was now dripping with malice but Mrs Clay sounded completely unfazed as she responded.

"Snapper, you know me better than that. I've not once blackmailed you, just reminded you that you owe me a favour. And it is just time for me to cash that favour in!"

As they continued, Wyn knew she'd heard enough; scared of what she might discover, she rushed down the corridor to change before returning to the office. On seeing her open the door, Mrs Clay smiled innocently; giving Snapper a clear signal that Wyn was back in the room and that meant that their conversation was over.

"Ah Wyn, there you are, let's get started! Goodbye Lydia, we will be done in an hour."

Snapper navigated Wyn towards the back wall of the gym before she could even acknowledge Mrs Clay, and anxiety flushed down her spine as she realised she no longer had anyone to hide behind.

Wyn tried her best to relax as they ran through the test, despite knowing how appallingly weak she was coming across. She was out of breath after two minutes of skipping, could barely lift the smallest weights they had, and didn't even get as far as bending her arms before she collapsed into a heap when attempting a press-up. Snapper looked pained watching her and seemed more exasperated after each exercise Wyn tried. By the time Lydia returned he looked ready to give up, but composed himself as he greeted her. Wyn stood just behind him, deflated and exhausted.

"How did it go then?" Mrs Clay queried, brightly.

"We've got a starting point. I'll draw up a plan tonight and we'll go through it tomorrow. It's going to take some hard work, but I reckon we can get there." He gave Wyn a gentle, reassuring smile.

By the time she got home, Wyn felt like every part of her body was turning to jelly; her legs were wobbling, her eyes were crossing and her muscles felt like they were seizing up. She'd never felt so physically drained, but she had to keep it together in front of the Sisters or else they'd know something was wrong. It took every last drop of focus she had not to fall asleep in her supper and she excused herself as soon as possible.

Once she'd escaped and was alone in her room, she collapsed onto the bed and burst into tears—she'd never felt so hopeless. It was like every ounce of positivity had ebbed out of her and the excited butterflies that had risen up with every step forward had broken free and flown away; she was both heartbreakingly empty and totally devastated all at once. She felt stupid for ever letting herself believe that she could do this, that she could ever achieve the impossible. Maybe it was just a pathetic dream that she should let go of; women weren't meant to be in the military, or the government, or anywhere else that gave them an inch of power, and she might as well just accept that. At some point she fell asleep and, on waking in the pitch black of night and traipsing to the bathroom, she found that her eyes were puffy and her head was pounding from sobbing so much. Completely defeated, she climbed back into bed and resigned herself to failure.

Chapter 4

Wyn woke up dreading the afternoon's session. Last night had been hard enough and today Snapper would have some proper, supposedly productive, programme in place. She stared at the ceiling for a while, thinking of ways to get out of it, wondering if she should just tell Mrs Clay that she couldn't do it and didn't want to anymore. She jumped at a frantic knocking on her bedroom door.

"Terrwyn! Are you awake? You're going to be late, breakfast is waiting!" Sister Cariad cawed, her annoyance resonating around Wyn's room.

In a scramble, Wyn sat up and looked at the clock—she needed to leave for school in nine minutes. She flung on her uniform and splashed some cold water on the dark circles under her puffed-up eyes. Her mind wandered, wishing that the Old Collection would let her wear makeup like Kiara did so that she could at least look half human, but then she felt ashamed for wishing it.

After shovelling a massive spoonful of porridge into her mouth and racing out of the door, Wyn half ran and half skipped until she got part-way to school, but the momentum was hard to keep up as the pulsing ache that seemed to radiate through her entire body was making her feel stiff and wobbly. If this was how exercise made you feel then why did people seem to love doing it so much? She then remembered her feelings of failure. Her mood plummeted back down and she gave up trying to rush, dragging her feet the rest of the way. The longer she could put off getting to school the better; there was nothing she wanted to do less than face Mrs Clay after her devastatingly poor performance the previous evening.

As she skulked into class late, begging the ground to swallow her whole, she felt everyone's eyes on her. Kiara and Isabella looked concerned, Cleo looked oddly impressed, and Mrs Clay just watched her quizzically. Everyone knew this wasn't normal for Wyn.

"Wyn, I would like to talk to you at the beginning of lunch, we cannot tolerate late arrivals so close to the end of term." There was sternness to her voice, but her expression did not reflect the tone. She was never usually bothered if the girls were late unless Mr Kane and the boys were in the class, so Wyn knew this could only be about the plan. Her chest felt heavy as she anticipated the conversation ahead.

The morning's classes were domestic: cooking, sewing, and other menial gender-stereotyped jobs. The groans that resonated around the class at each new topic spoke volumes about how even the girls that readily accepted their place in society were still disgusted by the lack of control and ambition they were allowed. It briefly reminded Wyn of Mrs Clay's passion for rebalancing the culture, and a small spark of motivation returned, but this was short-lived as, during the textiles lesson, she managed to sew the cushion cover she was making to her cardigan, renewing her mind-set that she would never achieve anything. She stared at her sleeve numbly whilst Cleo giggled, unpicking the stitches for her. She couldn't do anything right.

By lunchtime, she had worked herself up so much she felt like her head was going to explode. A barrage of criticism assaulted her thoughts at everything she tried to do, meaning she mentally gave up on every task before she had even started and it all became a self-fulfilling prophecy. Each failed attempt just added to her negativity and she ended up deciding that she would just have to join the Collections Children and live the rest of her life as a Sister—there weren't nearly so many things she could get wrong then.

"Okay girls, lunchtime, and after lunch we're being joined by the boys to work on interview techniques and job applications! Don't forget I need to talk to you, Wyn!" Mrs Clay sang out over the class, breaking Wyn out of her preoccupations.

Wyn avoided standing up for as long as possible, partly because the searing in her inner thighs was making it seem like a dangerous move to make, but soon it was just the two of them left in the room and Mrs Clay was walking towards her. Wyn put her head in her hands and covered her eyes, dragging her hands down her face in agitation before she looked up at the woman stood before her.

"What's up, Wyn? It isn't like you to be late. Are you ready for tonight? I'm sure Snapper is more than ready to work you hard!"

"Lydia, um, Mrs Clay, I can't do it. I can't do this. I'll just let you down and humiliate everyone. I'll probably make the whole situation worse. I think we should just give up." The words tumbled out of her mouth in a muddle, cracking as she said them. She felt like she was going to cry all over again.

Mrs Clay's eyes narrowed in frustration and annoyance. She watched the distressed girl in front of her and tried to decipher the situation. She wasn't going to let her run away scared but she bit back the angry words that were pushing at the tip of her tongue, knowing that they wouldn't help.

"Where has this come from? You came to me. You wanted to be equal to the boys and have an adventure. I thought you were fed up with the pressures on you to be a sheep, and understood what we were fighting for. You can't just throw away what we're working for; we could change the shape of the entire city! Maybe even the country!"

As a tear trickled down Wyn's face, Mrs Clay softened. She'd been that girl once, her confidence shattered and her dreams squashed; that's why she'd never done anything to fight for what she believed. She had to get Wyn back on side, invigorate the altruistic nature which she was sure Wyn had; a girl who had been brought up in the Old Collection, whose ultimate aim as an organisation was doing what was best for others, she was sure it was innate in Wyn by now.

"But last night, I was a disaster! I couldn't do even the easy stuff, and what little I did do has made me hurt more than must be normal. I don't see how we can do this in eight weeks? No-one will ever believe I'm a boy! I won't even get as far as joining the queue to be signed-up before they realise and chuck me out. Then my life will be over... They'd never let me get away with that insubordination!"

"Wyn, this is bigger than just us. You could change thousands of lives in the city, not to mention the country. Isn't that worth the risk? You don't need to worry about how we convince them; I'm here to help you do that. I won't let you near them if I don't think you're ready. What have you got to lose in trying?" She was crouched by the side of Wyn's desk, her voice gentle and her hand on Wyn's arm. "Now, do you have your kit and are you coming to the gym after school?"

Wyn looked up at her with a sad and sheepish expression, her face was red from where she had been covering it with her hands and peering through her fingers.

"I didn't have time to pick it up. And I didn't think it was worth bringing. I can't do it." Nothing Mrs Clay could say would change her mind.

"Okay, well, no gym today. I'll ring Snapper and let him know. But I want to show you something instead, maybe it'll give you something to think about and we can talk again tomorrow about what we're going to do."

Wyn agreed reluctantly. If Mrs Clay was going to let her think and make a decision then that was going to make things far easier than the battle that would ensue if she just tried to refuse any further involvement.

She spent the afternoon feeling sick, not through the nerves that had been plaguing her but from watching Kiara and Carter flirting outrageously as they practiced interview techniques. They had been instructed to pair up boy-girl, and Kiara had pretty much jumped the desks and flown across the room to get next to him before anyone else could. Wyn was paired with a geeky guy called Edwin, who was generally pretty quiet, meaning the process was frustratingly painful as he wouldn't do the role play that they had been asked to do. She understood, as it was definitely not her favourite activity either, but she would have preferred it to watching Kiara fluttering her eyelashes at an unnatural speed and sticking her lips out like a fish whilst Carter stood with his chest puffed out, an arrogant smirk on his face.

She was almost grateful when the class was over but she had no idea what Mrs Clay was going to show her and, watching Edwin shuffle out of the room, she felt like she'd lost her protection.

"Ready, Wyn? We can't walk to where we're going but the tram goes near enough. We'll just jump on that."

Twenty-five minutes later, they were stood outside an apartment block in downtown Millston. It was white-washed and old, with rows of run-down windows and vulgar, clashing coloured balconies that created an optic nightmare of a spectrum as you scanned from one end of the block to the other. It was notoriously the poorest district, which was why the upkeep was often overlooked by the city leaders. Other than humanitarian jobs with the Collections Children, Wyn never came to this part of the city. The schools had little to do with each other either, so all she really knew of the area were the stereotypes created by endless gossip and the horror stories that were already ravaging her mind.

Mrs Clay walked in without a word and headed straight to the stairs, she was clearly comfortable here. Wyn followed behind quickly, trying not to leave too much distance between them. Up to the third floor, fourth door along, and Mrs Clay pressed the bell. There was rustling behind the door and it opened to reveal a woman who must have been about fifty, but the dark circles sagging under her eyes made her look older. She looked exhausted; with matted, greasy hair hanging limply around her gaunt face, she could only manage a weak smile as she waved them in.

"Wyn, this is my friend Mara. We've known each other a long time, since before The Breakdown. I've asked her to tell you how much her life has changed since The Breakdown came and the military and the city leaders started to oppress women. Have a seat." Mrs Clay sat down and patted the seat next to her. Wyn obliged, perching uncomfortably on the very edge of the worn-down, yellowing sofa. The room was small with old-fashioned furniture; piles of books lay on every surface and were starting to build up on the floor.

Mara looked Wyn up and down and took a deep breath, pursing her lips. She looked pained as she did it, and was clearly not pleased to be having this discussion. Before Wyn could say anything to her, Mara let out the breath she was holding and closed her eyes briefly.

"Okay, Wyn, is it? Lydia has told me briefly what you're doing. That you want to take a stand against the male domination that's been pushed onto us, starting with the military." She looked at Mrs Clay, her eyes pleading for her to stop the conversation. Mrs Clay nodded encouragingly, willing her to continue her story. "She wants me to tell you why it's so important. You have to appreciate that this is difficult for me – I don't like talking about it, I much prefer being the spinster that stays inside her apartment most of the time and ignores the world outside … it's safer and far less painful that way. But, before The Breakdown, I worked my way up the local government – we were actively linked into the National Government back then as this was before each city was segmented off to try and control the negative powers that were starting to corrupt everyone. I reached all the way up to Head of the City Council. I was only thirty – women were in politics, the military, heading companies… they were seen just the same as men. Back then, we were all—men and women alike—trusted with technology, communication, and a real education. Then they decided that the public were getting out of hand and demanding too much, so they started to plan and implement their ideas to isolate areas of society. To begin with they were doing it gently—they started to fix elections to get the women out, for instance. Then they came down hard on those of us they couldn't shift. Men would come to my house in the middle of the night and threaten to hurt me. They threatened my husband at work and harassed him on his way home, it got so bad that he left me because he couldn't take it anymore and didn't understand why I wouldn't concede. Even then, I still refused to give up my position. Without Simon, I didn't see what else I could possibly lose by defying them. They made life impossible, the threats got worse, they drained my bank account so I couldn't even afford to eat and they manipulated my work so that all my proposals, interviews and campaigns failed. The council lost all faith in me. Eventually, no one took me seriously and I had to give up my post because it was doing so much damage to the city. Not that the role mattered much by then; the few men at the top controlled everything and democracy had all but disappeared, just like it has now. On that last day, packing up my office, General Baudin came in and told me that he had made sure I would never find work again and that he was glad I had finally learnt my place. I had to give up my beautiful four-bedroom home just outside the city perimeters and move here. I can barely afford to keep the lights on; they give me just enough money to scrape by but it still doesn't cover everything. I tried telling people when it first happened, but people either didn't believe me or thought that it was too much of a risk to take my side. As such, I lost most of my friends. Lydia's one of the few that stuck with me." She smiled gently at Mrs Clay across the room, welling up. "That's why I love my books; it's the only way I can escape. Worst thing is, I supposedly had it lucky; several of my friends in high-powered or high-risk jobs disappeared completely. Lydia and I had a close friend called Enya who tried to stand up for herself and defy the changes they were making and she went missing from under our noses. One day here, the next gone. I must have not posed enough of a threat. But I still wish every day that I could have been one of the ones to go missing, as this is not a life."

Mara had stopped, her quivering lip and the breaks in her voice showing how hard it was for her not to let her emotions take over. She looked at Wyn, hopelessness exuding from her face and her dull eyes shining with the held back tears. They didn't stay much longer. Mara had clearly had too much and was desperately trying to keep it together. Mrs Clay made their excuses and hurried Wyn out of the door, pausing to give Mara a hug and to whisper in her ear once Wyn had left the apartment.

Mrs Clay accompanied Wyn to the tram stop closest to her home. As they pulled up to the platform, Mrs Clay looked at Wyn intensely and left her with one final thought. "I hope that gives you something to think about; what the men in charge of our society have done to women and what it is we need to change. Mara is not the only one, I know of women who have taken their own lives to escape what was done to them. I'll see you tomorrow… With your gym kit, I hope." And, with that, she waved Wyn off and the tram doors closed.

Chapter 5

Wyn's head span with the moral dilemma that she was faced with. The first value that the Old Collection had ever instilled in her was to always work for the greater good of the community and the less fortunate, even if this was not in line with your own desires. Selfishness was not acceptable, a lesson she had learnt early on, when Sister Marjorie reprimanded her for taking a doll out of the donation box at the children's hospital; other children needed it more. She had spent nearly every weekend until she was thirteen going on 'Acts of Salvation' with the Collections Children, to wherever their aid was needed most in the city and in whatever form that would take. She remembered they'd spent weeks on end going to a care home to create a sensory garden for the residents and she'd even had to miss Cleo's birthday party as a result. This had devastated her but the pride that she'd experienced when they finished the project had reminded her just how good it felt to do the right thing. After she turned thirteen, her education was seen as of paramount importance and she was allowed every other weekend off from Collection duties to focus on her studies. Part of her missed it, even though she liked having free time—she had spent more of it at Kiara's or Cleo's than doing homework—but she still missed the feeling she got when she saw the gratefulness on someone's face, and she missed knowing that she'd helped change a life, even if it was only in some tiny way. If this plan worked, would she get that feeling? If it worked and she changed the balance of society and benefited thousands of people, how good would it feel then? But what if she failed and humiliated herself, destroyed any chance of having a future and ruined other people's lives in the process?

She barely slept, kept awake by the thoughts spinning round in her head and making her feel nauseous. One minute she was convinced it was the right thing to do, to be a martyr in pursuit of a fairer world, and the next she thought only of everything she could lose and the pain she would cause the Brothers and Sisters who had raised her. Pain she would cause them regardless of the outcome, purely because of her deception.

She got out of bed two hours before her alarm was due to go off, the tossing and turning was pointless and was doing nothing but frustrate her. Sitting at her desk, she got her notepad out to work out the pros and cons of going ahead with the plan.

Pros

- *Give women back their rights.*
- *Make Mrs Clay Proud and avenge Mara's treatment.*
- *Achieve something worthwhile instead of doing some stupid 'women's' job.*

Cons

- *Might be found out.*
- *It could be humiliating.*
- *Might fail and make everything worse for everyone.*
- *Upset the Collections Children, especially Sisters Astrid and Cariad.*
- *Potential for imprisonment or be made to disappear completely.*
- *Might die fighting.*
- *Will have to cut hair.*
- *Have to train with Snapper.*
- *Would miss the girls and what would I miss out on at home?*

Looking at it, she could barely come up with any reasons to do it. They were big reasons but if things went wrong, then everything would just get worse for her, and maybe the people she loved. She closed her eyes, searching for any inspiration, and ran through how she'd even got into this state in the first place. Where had all this even started? Her eyes shot open and she looked at her list. In bold letters, she wrote the biggest pro of all:

ADVENTURE

That was why she'd gone to Mrs Clay. Not because she wanted to do some moral act to change the shape of society and give future generations a balanced and prosperous world. She'd just been jealous—jealous that the boys got to do something interesting and exciting, jealous that they got to leave the confines of the city, jealous that they got to have an adventure. Her mind was made up.

She turned up at school with her gym kit stuffed in the top of her bag and a bounce in her step, finally feeling positive. This was her life; it was time to start living it. Mrs Clay glanced up as Wyn entered the room and smiled slightly at her demeanour, but avoided looking directly at her; this was far too delicate a situation for her to risk.

By the end of the day, neither of them had mentioned the plan. Wyn was petrified Mrs Clay would be angry about her wobble, Mrs Clay was worried that Wyn would change her mind and it would all be over. With nothing more than a brief questioning look from Mrs Clay and a nod of reassurance from Wyn at the end of registration, they had created an unspoken agreement to carry on as if nothing had happened.

Fear still washed over her as she stood at the door of the gym, but with a deep breath, she pushed the heavy door open, Mrs Clay following in behind her. Snapper stood at reception and smiled down at her.

"Ah, you came back! I was worried that I'd frightened you off. I have a regime all planned out so head back and change and we can get started." He tried to give her a reassuring smile but as he bared his teeth, he looked more like a rabid dog snarling.

Wyn did as instructed, aware that they were discussing her as she went. She paused briefly at the changing room doors to hear what they were saying.

"She's back on board. So full steam ahead, Snaps. Did you get the supplement bars?" Mrs Clay was asking.

"Yeah, but I can't tell you what's in them … it's another underground operation. Don't worry, nothing dangerous…"

Snapper's rough voice faded as she closed the door and got changed.

They sat in the office as Snapper outlined her new regime. She was going to do four days a week of strength training, each session would be an hour to an hour and a half. The goal was to build up her strength so she could keep up with the boys in training, not build muscle because she wouldn't get there quick enough in eight weeks. He reassured her that she would get some definition, just not enough to be considered one of the strong intakes; she'd still be at the back with the weedy cadets until she proved herself.

He ran through what they'd be doing each day:

Monday: Chest and Triceps

Tuesday: Back and Biceps

Wednesday: Rest

Thursday: Shoulders and Abdominals

Friday: Legs and Glutes

Saturday / Sunday: Rest

Then he started on nutrition, making it very clear that she needed to up her calorie and protein intake if she was going to build any muscle, especially doing it quickly. The bars would help but wouldn't do it all, and if she couldn't get extra food at home then Mrs Clay would help and bring high-calorie snacks into school.

It was all a blur and a whole new world to Wyn; it sounded so intense and she was exhausted just thinking about it.

"Okay Wyn, are you ready to start? We won't get into it properly this week – we'll get you familiar with the techniques and equipment today, and run through the different muscles groups tomorrow so you understand exactly what we're doing. It's important you understand the physiology, because then you know what to focus on and how to maximise the impact! And Friday, we'll crack on! We don't need you anymore, Lydia, you are excused."

Wyn shot a pleading glance at Mrs Clay. This was all getting too real, but sure enough, Mrs Clay had removed herself from the room and it was just her and Snapper left, along with a guy doing pull-ups in the corner of the gym. His muscles were rippling and glistening with sweat and Wyn watched him half in horror. As long as Snapper promised that she would never end up looking like that!

The session passed surprisingly quickly and by the end, Wyn was getting into it. He introduced her to the equipment they'd be using but they all had names that fell out of her head as quickly as they went in; he'd seen her confusion and laughed to himself, guaranteeing she'd be an expert in no time. Then he ran through techniques: he taught her the proper way to squat and ran through bench presses and deadlifts. There were some others that she forgot the terms for, but he was good at explaining what to do. For a dingy little gym, she was impressed by how well he knew his stuff and he did make her laugh—maybe this wasn't going to be so bad after all.

Walking home, she was in a really good mood, she guessed it was all those endorphins they'd talked about in science back when they did proper subjects at school and, though she didn't want to admit it, she was looking forward to heading back to the gym. Even the muscly guy in the corner had grunted "Hi" when she'd passed him by, and though she knew it was silly, she'd felt a small tickle of pride in her chest—maybe she could even fit in there.

The next day was muscle groups. A quick-fire anatomy and physiology session that baffled her—there were *how* many muscles in the body? But she was starting to get the idea of what she needed to work, and at least she could now name some of the muscles that felt like they would never stop aching. Snapper threw in the names of different exercises that would work each different muscle as they went, helping her to mentally put things together. He also let her take a copy of the book he'd used, and she scrawled notes of exercises and terms all around the diagrams. If she was going to take this seriously then she needed to get clued up; she would never pass for a boy if she didn't. Plus, if she got in, then she'd have to keep this stuff going by herself.

Friday was more technical stuff and terminology that she knew she wouldn't entirely remember: muscle fatigue, the difference between sets and reps, and how they change depending on the exercise. He made it very clear that good form was everything in order to avoid injury, and that he was going to ensure she was doing things properly.

Then they began. Snapper started at the beginning, building up the reps of squats, lunges, sit-ups and push-ups. She still wasn't any good at them but, adding to her new-found motivation, she was proud that she was already improving and had managed to support her body weight without collapsing. She still got embarrassed when she didn't manage to bend her arms in her attempted push-up, but Snapper looked at her with the corners of his lips lifting, the happiest she'd seen his face so far.

"Progress is progress, Wyn! And that was progress. You're going to do this, girl!" He stated in response to her quizzical expression. She grinned at him involuntarily.

On Saturday morning she was exhausted; every inch of her body was crying out in pain. Why did people go through this voluntarily just to get fit? She was in agony. She got out of bed and had to catch herself on the bed frame before her legs gave in. Eventually she managed to waddle to the bathroom, even though she could barely bend her legs or even lift her arms to brush her teeth.

Sister Marjorie caught her as she was attempting to get back to her room. She looked horrified when she saw the state of Wyn, who looked back at her confused – Sister Marjorie rarely came to this end of The Retreat.

"Wyn, what's wrong? Are you ill? You look awful!" She fussed around. Wyn smiled at her, but the pain turned it into a grimace. "I'll find Sister Cariad, tell her you're sick. Get yourself back into bed."

She didn't argue; maybe lying completely still would help. She wobbled back into her room, fell onto the bed and managed to tug the covers up over her, groaning the whole time.

"Terrwyn, Sister Marjorie says you are unwell? What's wrong? Do I need to get the doctor? Oh, you poor thing!" Sister Cariad rushed through the door and to her bedside. Her edges always softened when Wyn was poorly, and part of her wished she could have this Sister Cariad all the time.

"I just feel achy, Sister. There is a cold going around at school, maybe I've caught that. I think I'll be okay after some sleep." She gave Sister Cariad a weak smile, and coughed meekly. She couldn't tell her the real reason she was in so much pain, so she needed to make this believable.

"Okay, well, call on us if you need us. I'll prepare some soup for you when you're feeling a bit stronger. And I'll put you in the afternoon prayers. Brother Dane is leading them today."

It was a relief to watch Sister Cariad leave, although Wyn couldn't help but feel warmed by the concerned glances that she shot back as she went. There were a lot of things she wished she could do and have that the Old Collection disallowed, but she could never deny that she'd been brought up with love. Once the door was closed, Wyn made the most of her extra time in bed, pulling the covers up over her head and drifting off to sleep.

Chapter 6

On Monday morning Wyn was still in pain; she could walk normally most of the time until it came to stairs, where she still felt a little bit awkward. Snapper had told her that this was to be expected, but the more her muscles got used to it and could keep up with the workouts, the less she'd feel it. She wasn't sure she believed him but she hoped he was right, and over the last week her body did seem to be adjusting to it. Snapper had given her electrolyte-rich drinks to have around training times, which he said would help her recovery, and she had started to eat the supplement bars religiously. Mrs Clay also brought extra portions of lunch in for her, to boost her calories. With all the extra exercise she was completely ravenous, so it wasn't a struggle to keep up with all the food she was given.

More than anything, Wyn couldn't get over how different she felt – more energetic and bouncier, and just generally in a better mood. Maybe she could understand why people did this through choice after all, except for the exhaustion and pain. It was getting difficult to hide from the Sisters how weary she was in the evening, especially since there was no reason for her to be so physically tired and she could only blame a cold for so long. She would have to think about that one.

A couple of weeks into the training and she thought she was starting to see some muscle in her scrawny arms. She was definitely stronger and was keeping up with the goals that they had set; even Snapper was openly proud of her improved techniques and weightlifting skills, showing her off to the regular gym users.

By week four of the eight-week regime, Wyn was settling into it well. She was proud of what she was doing and actually looked forward to each training session and the rush she felt afterwards. She had convinced the Sisters that they were doing physical education at lunchtimes—just games and activities for some light relief and bonding before they all separated—and that was why she was coming home so tired. She was relieved that they accepted this explanation with very few questions.

That week, Mrs Clay pulled Wyn to one side at lunch to ask her how things were going.

"So, Wyn, how are you finding training? Snapper says you're doing really well. We also need to talk more about the background of The Breakdown so you know what to expect. And then we need to work on the rest of the prep we need to do." She quizzed Wyn with a serious expression glued to her face.

"Um, I really enjoy training. Snapper is really good as a personal trainer, and I feel different. I'm definitely stronger: I can pick things up I couldn't before and even unscrew bottle caps on my own! Snapper says he's going to set up some military-style tests to go through, so I know what to expect." Wyn sounded excited over the progress she had made, and smiled at Mrs Clay warmly. "What do I need to know about The Breakdown?"

"Well, what do we teach you in class about The Breakdown? Not a lot really – that there were people that disrupted the country, and that each city was segmented off to ensure that civilians could be accounted for; that this was done to force everyone back into line; that a war then started and unfortunately, due to the new structure that had been created, the enemy was based overseas, making it impossible for us to infiltrate their society and vice versa. However, we never give you details. We aren't allowed. And if you're to enter the military then a bit more background knowledge wouldn't hurt." Mrs Clay gauged Wyn's response to this and, seeing the curiosity on her face, continued. "So, The Breakdown came into place eighteen years ago. But a group of people who didn't agree and felt oppressed tried to fight back. They would stop at no lengths to try and spread their views and get the Government to concede, but it wasn't working, so they fled overseas and that's when they declared war. They still send over agents and soldiers. They've attacked civilians in all sorts of ways, but other than the obvious wreckages we see in the middle of the cities, we are never allowed to know what they are doing or even how they do it. But I did once see someone in hospital who had been completely mauled—like they had been attacked by an animal. The country had to start fighting back properly, and that's where the military bases they had created came into their own. Most cities have a Training Centre, but Necropolis has one of the best and produces some of the most important soldiers. Does that make sense?"

Wyn nodded at her; contemplating the information she'd been given. The people willing to do that must be so vicious and ruthless, and thinking about it sent a wave of fear rushing through her and made her stomach jump. If she succeeded and became a proper soldier, then she would have to face these people

But she also had other things to think about. This was the last ever week of school and whilst her classmates were buzzing over what to do next—the girls were setting up interviews, the boys deciding whether to follow their fathers into their professions or if they should sign-up—Wyn was feeling more and more apprehensive. The schoolyard was a hive of activity—everyone planning, comparing and competing. Wyn had no idea what to say when they asked her what she was going to do. She obviously couldn't tell them the truth but she didn't have any alternative answers ready. What could she spend the next four weeks doing that would be a sufficient cover-up for her real plans?

"Come on Wyn, you have to book in some sort of interview! Isabella and I are going to set some up in the salons in the Gild District. Cleo is going to speak to her mum about being trained up as a nurse." Kiara made a face at Cleo as she said it; she couldn't understand why anyone would want to do any extra studying, but Cleo had always wanted to follow her mother into nursing.

"I will Kiara, but I also want to spend some time with the Collections Children – go out and do some more Acts of Salvation because I haven't been able to do so in a while. I need to prove to them I'm thankful for everything they've done, and that's the best way I can think to do it." Wyn babbled at them, it was the best she could think of.

"Well, come with us when we go to book some interviews anyway – and then you can do both. You don't want to miss out!"

Wyn nodded at Kiara, her eyes dull; she really didn't know if she could keep this up for another four weeks.

They didn't let up until their last day of school. It was a strange day as they spent most of it having a class party. Everyone brought in cakes and snacks, and they sat around chatting, playing stupid games and enjoying the last time they would probably all be together. Carter, Marcus and Jed talked a little too loudly about how they were signing-up in an attempt to show off to the girls and, by the way Kiara swooned, it worked. She confided in the girls that she was still determined to be with Carter exclusively before the end of term – and that gave her three hours left to work her magic.

The girls watched Kiara in horrified fascination as she shamelessly slipped over to where the boys were chatting and sat very obviously between them, a little bit too close to Carter. He shifted in his seat and frowned slightly, before catching himself and smiling at her.

"Kiara, how are you doing babe? Only four weeks left before I'll be gone. Will you miss me?" His voice was deeper than normal as he tried to sound rough and sexy, and his face distorted into the most arrogant expression he could muster. In reality, he just sounded like a desperate teenage boy which, technically, he was.

"Of course I will Carter, I don't know how I'm going to cope not seeing you every day. Maybe we should spend the next few weeks together... You can't deny there's always been something between us!" She cooed and fluttered her eyelashes, leaning towards him so her thigh brushed against his and her chest was thrust under his face. Wyn shuddered at how embarrassing it was, cringing on Kiara's behalf.

Carter agreed to this, and said that he would love to devote the rest of his time to her. It would give him someone to fight for when he was away with the army. Mid-conversation he suddenly looked flustered and said he'd remembered that he needed to speak to Mr Kane, then he sauntered out of the classroom.

Kiara walked back over to the girls with a massive smile on her face and they could practically see the love hearts dancing in her eyes.

"Did you hear that? He said yes. We're official. I officially have a boyfriend!" She gushed, clearly on cloud nine and, whilst Isabella and Cleo congratulated her and encouraged her sappy excitement, Wyn couldn't help but roll her eyes. But this was her best friend, so she put her opinions to the back of her mind and joined in the celebrations. She would miss this, the four of them chatting, gossiping and laughing. She wasn't going to be able to do it much longer.

By the end of the day, most of the class felt sick from too much sugar and too many emotions. They'd had a leaving assembly with the rest of the school and the teachers that had taught them throughout the years—it was one of the few times they associated with the other year groups. There'd been presentations and awards, although Wyn didn't win any, and they each got a memory book with pictures taken at school events. They ran around getting everyone to sign them and giving emotional hugs and goodbyes. It felt silly, as most of the people not signing-up in their class would still see each other—they all lived in the same district—but she was grateful for the chance to say goodbye, considering she would soon be leaving her whole world behind.

After everything had wrapped up and people were reluctantly leaving school, Mrs Clay caught Wyn by the arm and made it clear for her to hang around a bit longer, so Wyn busied herself in sorting out her bag, watching her classmates go. It seemed strange to her how sad everyone seemed, when they'd all spent most of their school lives moaning about how boring it was, bitching about each other, and ruminating on how they couldn't wait to leave. She stared into space for a while, contemplating the fact that school was over for good and feeling nostalgic.

"Okay, Wyn, this will have to work a bit differently from now on." Mrs Clay's words shook Wyn out of her reverie.

"What do you mean?"

"Well, you can't go to the gym straight from school now – we will have to find you a different way to get there. I can speak to Snapper about doing a different time, but I don't know when else he shuts the gym down. And we need to arrange times for us to meet and do the rest of our preparation – get you looking like a boy, and run through the boys' syllabus. What is your plan for the next few weeks?" Mrs Clay had sat on the desk in front of Wyn, watching her pack her bag.

"I haven't really got a plan. I don't know what I can do that'll only last four weeks, but if I don't do anything, then the Sisters will get suspicious. I'm stuck." Wyn scrunched up her face and looked down in self-pity.

"Well, I've got a way round that. Just because the school year stops, my work doesn't; I'll still be here every day making plans for next year, doing the lesson plans and the syllabus. I have to get it ready to send to the council for approval, which is always so hard because I don't want to teach the rubbish they tell me to!" Frustrated anger crept into her voice as she scowled. "Anyway, how about you come help me out – tell them all I needed an assistant and that I hired you. Does that sound like it could work?"

Wyn looked at her incredulously. This could fix everything – the Collections Children would love her to work in education, the girls would stop moaning, she wouldn't have to intentionally fail any interviews to avoid being offered a real job, and she could keep up with the plans.

"The only problem will be paying you. Obviously, the job doesn't really exist and I can't afford to give you anything—I don't earn enough myself. Would you be happy to tell them that it's an internship until the end of the summer? Tell them that we would review and look to hiring you full-time then, just so it looks credible."

"Yes, that would be perfect! Thank you, Lydia! Then, would I continue with Snapper like I am now? What about Wednesday evening? I'd have to come home at the same time every day to make it look realistic."

"Wednesday we can go through everything else we have to do, and we can use some of the daytimes as well. I might get you to do a few odd jobs for me here too; if you help me get my actual work done quicker then we have more time to devote to preparation."

Wyn nodded at her willingly. She couldn't believe that this was going to work out so conveniently; despite her apprehensions, everything was falling into place.

Chapter 7

The Sisters were thrilled when she told them about her internship over dinner; Brother Aster had joined them for food and was beaming at her with pride.

"What an admirable job, Terrwyn." Sister Cariad had responded. She had always been the one to champion the importance of education above all else in Wyn's life and, with the exception of joining the Old Collection, a job in education was the best thing she could have asked for Wyn to do.

Sister Astrid and Brother Aster had complimented her on getting something sorted out so quickly, and they all repeated how pleased and proud they were of her.

By the time she had finished her lamb chops, Wyn was struggling to keep the smile on her face. She couldn't help but focus on the ugly knot of guilt consuming her stomach as she lied to them, and how disappointed they were going to be when they found out the truth; she'd never expected them to react with so much fervour and her deception lay heavy on her heart.

She looked round at their faces and the nostalgia she had felt at the end of school rose up again. The Old Collection had been her home for fifteen years; they had taken her in when she was orphaned. She could have ended up in a children's home but Sister Astrid found out about her when Major MacCulloch approached her at a prayer group, and although it was supposed to be a short-term refuge, she had refused to give her up. They had always accepted her despite the fact she had never fully embraced their faith; even as a child, her imagination and zest for life had kept them on their toes, and she'd never quite managed to conform to the structure and regime that went along with their religion. The Old Collection had been formed not long before The Breakdown started; founded by a man who firmly believed in creating a denomination centred primarily in altruism and humanitarianism. It had started off small and the locals had called it a cult for years, but as they grew to appreciate what the group was trying to achieve, more and more people became involved. The focus was on the community and the good that could be brought to the world. A belief in God became intertwined in this over time, and it was considered fundamental that the member's degree of worship was guided by the individual. That was where the Collections Children came into it – to help the Collectioners' find a comfortable relationship with God. As she'd gotten older Wyn had learned to love the humanitarian side of the faith but could never get her head around the worship and, although she appeased the Collections Children by attending services, they knew that she was not committed to it. But they never resented her for it and for that, Wyn was always indebted to their compassion.

The nostalgia and contemplation wouldn't go away. All weekend—whether she was sitting in her bedroom snuggled into her blanket, attending acts of salvation with Brother Aster, watching Sister Cariad prepare breakfast, or even just when she was walking to school to start her 'internship'—she couldn't stop thinking about all the things in her life that she might soon never do or see again. Four weeks felt far too short for everything they had left to do, and even shorter to say goodbye to all the parts of her life that she would miss. Now that she'd lost the security of school it meant that they were on the home stretch, and reality and apprehension were setting in.

Mrs Clay gave Wyn some simple administrative jobs to get done on the Monday morning, true to her word that she would need some genuine assistance if this was going to work. It was menial jobs to begin with, mainly organising and filing the work and reports from the year. It seemed strange to Wyn that she was going through everything her classmates had done and the sensitive information that she would normally not be privy to. She paused when she saw her school report, glancing through it to see what had been written. One line jumped out at her: *Wyn is capable of great achievements, but she fails to accept this without persuasion.* This was written long before she'd first approached Mrs Clay, but she must have always believed in her abilities to succeed. It made Wyn smile, maybe the faith she had shown in her really was genuine.

Their arrangement was working well. By mid-afternoon they had both completed all the jobs that Mrs Clay had aimed for, and they had a chance to sit down and chat for a while before Wyn was due at the gym. It was the first time they'd had a conversation that wasn't about the plan. Mrs Clay asked about life in the Old Collection and Wyn learnt about Mrs Clay's husband, who managed one of the banks on the high street. She told her how they'd always wanted children but had never been lucky enough, so she had become a teacher to fulfil her maternal side. But she also admitted she hated it now. She had loved being able to teach real subjects that she was passionate about and watch her students flourish, but now she had to prepare them for a reality she had no respect for, and was forced to actively discourage any ambition that fell outside of this. The government's oppression had taken over completely. Wyn felt a pang of sympathy as they discussed it. Even though Wyn had seen a more sensitive side to her over the last few weeks, Mrs Clay still had such a strong front, with her hair tightly pulled back into a bun and her corporate clothing making her look unbreakable. But as they talked, her face softened as though all of her walls had come down; Wyn had never seen Mrs Clay look vulnerable before, it made her look so human.

By the time she walked to the gym that evening she had a new understanding of Mrs Clay. She understood why she threw all of her passion into wanting to change the world; it was because she never got to live the life she wanted.

Their daily routine worked well. Work at school kept her grounded and gave her a base, whilst her training sessions were becoming addictive. Her new motivation for fitness meant that she was much more productive and found herself actually looking forward to going, something she would have scoffed at before she started. And, to match up the hours she was out every day, Wednesday evenings were now devoted to going through the things Mrs Clay had taken from watching the boys' classes and reading their syllabus. This included the basics of discipline and drills, the core values of the military, military history, and lots of terminologies that she had to get Mrs Clay to go through multiple times. It was fascinating, but Wyn knew Kiara's dad thought the school prep was insufficient. She couldn't help but worry that there must be so much more she needed to know.

When she had spare time at school and in the evenings, Wyn

continued to work on her male alter ego. She kept practicing the basics and was getting comfortable with her go-to stance, and with her strength and confidence increasing thanks to the workouts, she was managing to walk with a bit more swagger. She felt that once she'd mastered the walk and also had her appearance transformed, she would be just about passable. Then she'd practiced sitting down, making sure not to cross her legs and fold her arms into herself like she normally would. She had to sit facing straight ahead and upright, legs open, chest open, and sometimes lay one arm on the back of the chair she was sat on. It felt so uncomfortable and vulnerable; her body was begging to hug back into itself so she had to really get into the mind-set to be able to stay sat like that for any length of time. When she was desperate to cross her legs, she would rest her ankle on the knee of the opposite leg like Mr Kane always did. She was starting to feel confident that she could pull it off, but she was worried that when she had to multitask and wasn't just concentrating, she might subconsciously fall back into doing everything with femininity.

Before she knew it, there were only two weeks to go until sign-up and they needed to start thinking about logistics; her appearance, how to leave home without causing a search party, and how to keep up her pretence once she was in the training centre. Mrs Clay set the Friday afternoon aside for them to sit down and discuss it.

"So, enlistment is two weeks today, we've got to get onto the final preparation. You'll keep going to the gym until the Tuesday before, and we'll use the Wednesday and Thursday to sort everything else out. Snapper says you've been doing well and should have no problem keeping up with the average cadets. Also, I've bought you some breast binders – they're ready-made, sort of like a bra, that'll keep everything flat under your uniform."

Wyn snorted at that and Mrs Clay looked at her with concern.

"Sorry, it's just funny – I don't have a lot to keep flat anyway." She blushed as she said it, and Mrs Clay chuckled at her.

"Well, you can't have anything at all so you'll have to have the binder. Also, you'll need to learn to bind yourself with bandages as well – it's better to have options. We'll do your hair the night before … or maybe even that morning… We don't want to raise too many questions. The big problem is, where we say you've gone. I'm sure the Collections Children will notice you're missing, especially when it isn't just a week or two. Any ideas on that?"

Wyn just shook her head. She'd been trying not to think about it as it just made the waves of guilt wash back over her.

"Hmm, okay. It's a tough one, especially when there is so little movement in and out of the city. Let me speak to some contacts over the weekend and I will see what I can come up with. Next, what are we going to do to keep you on top of your persona whilst you're in there?"

Wyn looked at her blankly. She didn't have an answer; she didn't have a clue how any of it was going to work once she was in there on her own, and she had been relying on Mrs Clay for the answers to that. Mrs Clay closed her eyes and took a deep breath, gathering the strength to keep this one-sided conversation going.

"Okay. Well, I learnt a few things about the base when I was seeing one of the Majors—not Major MacCulloch before you jump to conclusions!" She reacted as she saw Wyn's raised eyebrows. "Anyway, in the barracks there's a gym, so if Snapper writes you out a training programme based on what you're doing at the moment, then you can get up early and do that each day. Make sure you keep your consistency up so you don't draw too much attention to yourself. We'll send you in with as many protein bars as possible. And then you just need to work hard to keep everything else up, it will all come down to how well you can play the part."

Mrs Clay smiled softly at Wyn with a hint of sympathy in her eyes. Now it was becoming a reality, they were both realising what a mammoth task this was and how hard it would be to survive the training process. They didn't know how long Wyn would be in training and they hadn't decided when she could come clean, but it had finally dawned on her that convincing them to let her join-up was the smallest part of it, and she wasn't prepared for what might come next. For all their pretences, they were both aware that any idea they had of the training programme was mere guesswork.

They continued to work through what they did know and had planned already, as well as what they still needed to do. Then they came up with a list of things that Mrs Clay needed to find out, whilst Wyn was tasked with continuing to perfect her male persona. As an afterthought, Mrs Clay suggested that she go out and watch the cadets as they walked through the base and see what she could copy from them and, by the time she got to the gym that afternoon, Wyn was feeling the pressure starting to weigh her down. Snapper sensed Wyn's mood and only engaged to correct her form, leaving Wyn to block out the burden she was carrying and throw herself into her workout.

Chapter 8

Wyn did as Mrs Clay suggested and spent time sitting on the wall by the Necropolis gate, watching the cadets walk up from the barracks. It did nothing to calm her nerves; just looking at their stocky builds and cocky swaggers was making her lose all faith that she could emulate it well enough. They looked so tidy and official in their uniforms; dark navy shirts pressed and tucked perfectly, matching creases in every pair of trousers, shoes shined. There were so many things that she could get wrong.

This was the last weekend that this unit would be at Necropolis. She knew from Kiara's gossiping that they were being deployed on Monday, but no one knew where they were going or what they'd be doing when they got there. No-one had returned from the last platoon that was sent out, but it was always 'no news is good news' as far as the city was concerned. Everyone was considered fit and fighting until the reports of the dead came in. She wasn't supposed to know about the reports anyway, but she normally managed to sneak into the Major's office with Kiara to find out. It was one of the few things that Kiara wouldn't gossip about; it could break so many hearts if they found out through idle gossip that they'd lost their loved ones, and even she wasn't so hungry for attention that she'd put people through that.

Once this unit was gone there would be a two week turn around before the new cadets would be moving in and, if all had gone to plan, then that would include her. She'd dreamt for so long about seeing the other side of those gates and the inside of the warehouse that her heart couldn't help but jump in nervous excitement as she thought about it, but that was quickly replaced with the heavy anxiety that lay in her stomach whenever she remembered just how serious this was.

She watched again on Sunday, when they had their passing out ceremony. She'd watched it many times before but this time it felt different, this time it was like watching a snapshot of her future. It was always done in the grounds at the front of Necropolis. The gates were opened and families were allowed to attend, although it was still invitation only and strictly controlled. All she could see from her position were the cadets lined up in full uniform on a decorated stage, with General Baudin stood front and centre pinning a badge on each one as they filed over, pausing only long enough for a photo. Then he made a speech; she could never hear what he said but she knew that, once he'd stopped talking, they were considered soldiers and not just cadets. The ceremony never lasted long; it was always the day before deployment so she reckoned they didn't want to tire the troops out. Families stayed for maybe another hour, having drinks with the new soldiers and all of the other important military personnel in the city. Other than the General and Major MacCulloch, Wyn never recognised any of them, even though she saw the same faces again and again. The Sisters had always kept her from that world, but they couldn't keep her from it much longer.

Mrs Clay delivered as promised on Monday morning, with their list of questions nearly completely answered. She ran through what she'd found out.

"Okay, so, each intake is twenty cadets. The training programme usually lasts around eight to twelve weeks, depending on when they need to deploy. They reckon this will be at least a three month one because of the Special Forces stuff going on, and it might even run longer. I reckon you should keep in until the last minute, only come clean once you're completely signed-off and you've gone through passing out, maybe even during the ceremony. Reveal yourself then. You'll get to choose who your invitations are sent to; every recruit gets two. If you allocate one to me, then I can come and stand up with you and do the talking, show them that they are unjustified in being sexist. Even better if you can get to the top of your intake class! You can't start taking it easy once you're in there though, as not everyone makes it to passing out; some of them get held back to the next intake, and others just get kicked out—though apparently that's only if there's absolutely no hope. You can't be either of them Wyn, or else you've just given them more ammunition to use against us." She'd been serious and focussed throughout her explanation, her eyebrows furrowed as she tried to emphasise the importance of the information she was delivering, but she couldn't avoid the pleading that was creeping into her voice.

Wyn watched her, absorbing what Mrs Clay was saying. Three months seemed like a lifetime, but they'd been doing their preparations for two months and that had seemed like barely long enough. If she kept up the commitment and the training then maybe it could go just as quickly—or at least she hoped it would.

Mrs Clay had brought in all of the boys' clothes that she'd been collecting. Most of them were second-hand and understated so as not to draw attention; there were plenty of suitable shirts and jumpers, but she'd had a problem with finding trousers. Wyn was a slight build and struggled to find clothes as it was, but the shapeless boy's trousers seemed to just hang off of her and flap around her legs even when they fitted at the waist. They contemplated using what she already owned, but her normal trousers were cut to be tight and showed off what little figure she had, especially with the increased tone she'd built up. Out of the pile of clothes Mrs Clay had brought, they found three pairs of trousers and a pair of jeans that were passable. What if there was the same problem with uniforms?

"These are all the smallest men's waist size – if they have that, then you should be okay if you keep the shirts tucked in. If not then you'll have to take the waist in—it isn't unusual for soldiers to have a small sewing kit to do repairs, so no one will think it's odd for you to have one." She paused and half-smirked, half-frowned as she remembered the textiles lessons they'd done during the year's domestic classes. "You'll have to just give it your best shot and not sew yourself to anything."

The only thing left to plan in depth was her cover. It needed to be something that would justify her absence for however long was needed until she could reveal herself. Wyn was still clueless; she didn't think it would be possible to find something that would convince the Brothers and Sisters, and if Mrs Clay didn't come up with something plausible soon, then the whole plan was ruined and they'd have done all of this for nothing.

"I've been thinking about it. Maybe we could convince them you've gone on a humanitarian project. I have a friend, we went to school together, she lives about an hour away and we still have some contact." She saw Wyn look at her quizzically and Mrs Clay understood why: contact between cities was strictly monitored and, for the most part, prohibited. "Well, we both have access to phones at work so we have a scheduled time each week that we ring. They don't pick up on it when you ring school to school, even between cities, because we still coordinate some training and cross-reference the syllabus. Prue is the headteacher at a school for underprivileged children, and they always have volunteers—we've sent our teachers and trainees there before. We could say that I've seen potential in you and that we are working to train you up to be a teacher, and that they've agreed to give you a jump start on training and experience. Prue would cover the back story if they try and check."

Wyn stared at her incredulously, her lips slightly parted and her eyes wide. She couldn't believe it, this sounded perfect.

"What would we need to do? To make it look realistic?" Wyn asked. Her head was buzzing as she tried to comprehend the magnitude of the lie she would have to fabricate for the Sisters. She was astonished that there really could be a way to do this.

"I'll write out a letter, confirming the placement. I'll put an itinerary in it that says you need to leave the day before enlistment so that we can get you to mine and do the final prep. Explain to the Sisters that I will be escorting you out of the city and that you will need to come to school for the allotted time. I'll warn Prue in case anyone contacts her, and we'll just have to hope that there's no reason for anyone to discuss it with the city perimeter staff, because obviously you won't actually be leaving."

By the end of the day there was an official-looking letter, headed with the logos of both their school and Prue's school, outlining the placement and the training it would provide. There was an itinerary of the travel there and it had an open-ended duration: 'dependant on the opportunities available'. Overall, it covered everything needed to convince the Collections Children. Mrs Clay had added in extra emphasis on the prestige of being chosen so they might even be proud, and Wyn felt the pang of guilt and sadness return.

"Good luck. Stick to what we've talked about and there's no reason for them not to believe you. Tell them to speak to me if they want any more details." Mrs Clay waved Wyn off reassuringly at the end of the day, but doubt cast across her face as she watched her walk away. She shook her head to shake out the concern; they were in too deep for her to start doubting Wyn so she just had to have faith that she could pull this off, for both their sakes.

The Sisters read the letter intently. Sister Astrid read through it silently, her brow furrowing. She handed it to Sister Cariad, who made approving noises, especially at the mention of 'highly-esteemed training offered only for hand-picked individuals'. Once she had finished reading it, she beamed at Wyn.

"Terrwyn, this is wonderful news. You have taken so well to the internship with Mrs Clay, but for that to lead to such an opportunity... You're doing so well, and in such an important profession!"

Wyn did her best to simulate the response of someone who had just been given a dream job, but felt that she was falling short. Looking at the pride and enthusiasm that Sister Cariad so scarcely showed felt like the ultimate act of betrayal. Sister Astrid, on the other hand, was still watching Wyn carefully.

"Wyn, are you sure you want to do this? You've not spent more than a night away from us or left the city perimeters since you came to The Retreat, so to move over an hour away on your own... It's not small. It won't be easy to just come back if you miss home..." Sister Astrid sounded meek and pleading. The idea of losing Wyn, who had been her whole world for nearly sixteen years, was heart-breaking. Wyn didn't know whose reaction made her feel worse.

"Sister, this is a marvellous achievement! Show Terrwyn the support she deserves! If this is what she wants to do then we will do whatever we can to support her; beyond a life's work in the Collection, education is the most honourable career we could hope for her to follow." Sister Astrid smiled sheepishly at Sister Cariad, and then directed that smile at Wyn, but there was still anguish in her eyes.

Wyn tried to escape to her room, but Sister Cariad had called Brother Dane; he looked bewildered at the uncharacteristic emotion spilling from the Sister and listened intently as they explained what was going on. Within ten minutes Wyn was being led down the corridor, out of their residential part, and into the other end of The Retreat where he called together all twelve Brothers and Sisters in residence and announced her accomplishment.

Wyn stood in a sea of congratulations, wishing she could disappear. If her guilt had been preying on her before, the shame was now tearing her apart; she was deceiving the most honest and pious people in the city who had always cared for her. She distracted herself by staring above their heads. She'd always found this end of

The Retreat fascinating: where her end was homely with a warming kitchen and small sitting area next to the dorm rooms, this end was elaborate and ornate. Most of the Brothers and Sisters lived down a small corridor in quarters even more sparse than hers that had a tiny kitchen attached, and the rest of the space was for worship. The main hall they were in was spacious, with beautiful carvings on the walls that were interspersed with heavy dark wood beams. Attached to the hall was the chapel with a stunning painting on the ceiling that made you feel as though you were looking straight up at the sky. These were the areas members of the community used; the hallway that led to the main hall from the outside was easily accessible, unlike the entrance she used, and they could use the chapel day or night.

Once she had smiled, and thanked the Collections Children, she could finally escape. She slipped back through the door from the public rooms into her comfort zone. The door was painted to blend into the wall and locked behind them—only the Brothers and Sisters had keys—and the moment the latch clicked back into place, Wyn let her whole body relax. Telling them was always going to be the hardest thing to do, the worst was over.

Chapter 9

Time marched forward with alarming speed and it was soon the Tuesday before enlistment. That evening she got to the gym and found her training session was cancelled. She was disappointed and turned to leave, but Snapper stopped her.

"I said we aren't training, that doesn't mean there isn't something for us to do." Snapper smirked with a mischievous glint in his eye, and from a bag behind the desk he pulled out some of the clothes that Mrs Clay had found. "We are going to see how well you can pass for a boy."

"We?" Wyn questioned, confused, as Mrs Clay had stayed at school.

"Yes, we." Snapper gestured behind him.

Wyn looked as he waved his hand and she saw a row of muscles. The men that used the gym during its shut-down hours were all staring back at her. A lump rose into her throat. She'd gotten used to working out around these men, even started exchanging pleasantries and having the odd chat, but they were built like mountains and always intimidated her with their stern focus and unreadable expressions. Now they were all going to watch her, she had never felt so exposed.

She knew protesting was useless and she was going to have to get used to people seeing her performance, so she took the clothes from Snapper's hand and headed into the changing room. Getting the binder on was a struggle, but once she had wrestled with it, she was surprised at how effective it was and how much better a shirt sat over the top. With the clothes there was also a cap, so she gathered her hair onto the top of her head and stuffed it into the hat. She paused at the mirror before she went out to face them and stared at her reflection; despite it being flat and untameable, she was still going to miss her hair.

Snapper had to stifle a laugh as Wyn came into view, and her face dropped. On seeing this, Snapper's face froze in shame.

"It isn't bad Wyn, it's just funny seeing you dressed like a boy but walking so feminine. I never realised how much like a girl you were until you were trying to be a boy." He flustered, trying to justify his reaction but ending up just making himself laugh all over again.

Wyn felt despondent. They were too far into this to stop now but if she made everyone laugh like Snapper did, then they would never pull this off. Her shoulders drooped as she stared at the ground and tried to avoid any eye contact. Suddenly, she felt a hand tap her arm and she looked round. It was Marty, one of the regular gym users who had always been the nicest to her; he'd come over from where they'd all been sat chatting and gave her a very slight, comforting smile.

"We've seen you in a sweaty heap crying in the middle of the floor – you're past being able to embarrass yourself, so just get on and show us. Ignore Snapper, he's an arse."

Marty didn't wait for an answer—he just went back and sat down, his face returning to its usual passive expression. But he was right, and Wyn walked past Snapper and stood directly in front of all the muscles. She ran through her stance and her walk, then pulled up a chair and sat down in the manliest way she could muster. They watched her silently with their unnerving, unchanging expressions. She said nothing, except to tell them what she was going to do next, and once she was done she sat on the chair comfortably and scanned each face, awaiting their feedback.

She was surprised by how useful they were, if a little insensitive. She was swinging her hips too much so they made her walk behind one of them, copying his movements until they were happy she'd got it. When she stood with her hands on her hips she tilted her head a bit too far to the side, and needed to try and keep looking strong and straight ahead. The list continued but all of the tiny tweaks they made did make her feel more confident with what she was doing, and although she knew she would still look like a weedy boy instead of someone macho, they seemed happy that she could get away with it.

"What about your voice? And your handshake?" Marty asked her when they had exhausted the body language.

"Um, I hadn't really thought about it?" Wyn wobbled. She hadn't even considered how she sounded; she had been far too focussed on how she was moving.

"Let's get on that then."

The nerves she'd originally felt had long gone by now, she just felt indebted to their input.

They ran through voice with her, making her copy them. It was a disaster. With their deep husky voices, her attempts were obviously unnatural; her speech was stilted and if she tried for longer than a single sentence, it just made her throat scratch. They kept working and eventually found a few tips that helped enough to get rid of the highest part of her vocal range. She needed to focus on making her words blunt and sharp, not dragging them out like she normally did, and try and talk from her chest not her throat. If she spoke so she could feel her chest moving, then her voice naturally dropped. They agreed it wasn't perfect, but set a rule that, unless it was around people who couldn't know anything, she was going to talk like a boy constantly and practice. The longer she did it then the more natural it would get.

Finally, her handshake. It didn't take long for her pathetically feminine grip to insight some laughter.

"It's called a hand*shake*… You actually have to move your hand." It was the first thing the biggest muscles had said since she had arrived for the session, and the humour to his voice took her by surprise.

After they directed the strength of her grip and the range of her movement, they were content she would come across as a boy that just wasn't that confident, which fit in perfectly with everything else she'd managed; she was never going to be the alpha male that was for sure.

Wyn thanked the muscles and they all wished her luck. She still wasn't sure how much they knew about what she was doing, but they seemed sure that she would succeed and a small part of her was thriving off of their reassurances and their confidence in her. As she walked out the door Snapper caught her, and took her aback as he bent down and wrapped her up into a tight hug. His arms were strong and he smelt musty and sweaty from a day's work, but it made her feel protected; a far cry from the fear she felt when she'd first met him.

"Go smash it, Wyn!" he whispered in her ear and as he pulled away, he was looking at her with soft, caring eyes. Wyn smiled at him gingerly and ran out the door before he made her cry.

She stood in the street and closed her eyes; everything around her was a reminder of what she was leaving behind. She couldn't believe how much this place and its people had come to mean to her in the space of two months, and how hard it was going to be to give it all up.

She spent the next day practising everything they had worked on with her, speaking only with her new voice if she was anywhere other than home, and wishing that time would stop rushing ahead. She got home that evening to find an aromatic and hearty casserole with homemade bread. Casserole had always been her favourite. Sisters Astrid and Cariad, Brothers Aster and Dane, were all waiting in the kitchen for her, and she noticed a decanter of wine on the kitchen table. Wine was only brought out for special celebrations and worship.

"We're all going to miss you Wyn, and we can't wait to have you home again. You've been an integral light in The Retreat since we got to keep you all those years ago. And as it is such an important celebration—of the faith and joy you've brought to us—I think you're now old enough to be allowed a small toast with us." Brother Dane was pouring her a glass of the wine. He had always been strong with his words and she could see the glisten of tears behind Sister Astrid's eyes.

They fussed around her, making a toast about her promising future, saying how proud they were and how important she would always be to them. Even Sister Cariad—who normally declined any toasts—took a glass, although she only sipped half of it before setting it to one side. Over dinner they chatted aimlessly and it was obvious they were all avoiding the subject of Wyn's impending departure. She lapped the casserole up, appreciating every mouthful; she was going to miss Sister Cariad's cooking, she doubted that military food was anywhere near this good.

Once they had finished eating, Wyn went to her usual spot at the kitchen sink, ready to do the washing up, but Brother Aster stopped her.

"Don't worry about that now, Wyn, the others want to say goodbye to you."

She turned around and saw the rest of the Collections Children filing into the kitchen and another round of toasts were made. Wyn was left out of this one, and she couldn't say she was disappointed – the first had gone to her head and she felt a bit woozy. With more rounds of goodbyes and hugs from everyone, Wyn felt emotionally exhausted. They'd even given her a leather-bound notebook to start off her training, which, when possessions were considered so unimportant and unnecessary by the Collections Children, meant the world to her. By the time they had all returned to the other end of The Retreat for evening worship, Wyn was more than ready to slip away to bed.

Of course, the worst goodbyes came the next morning. She'd arranged with Mrs Clay to get to school mid-morning to maintain the pretence that they were spending the day travelling, which meant she had time to have breakfast with the Sisters—time that she knew she'd treasure in the weeks to come, when she would be almost touching distance from them and they could never know. Brothers Dane and Aster joined them whilst they ate, and both gave her tight hugs and heartfelt goodbyes before they left for a meeting in the city. Wyn's bag was packed and by the stairs. She'd made sure to include all the things she thought would be essential for a trainee teacher; everything she knew they'd notice if she left behind, even though she wouldn't really be taking any of it with her

Sister Cariad and Sister Astrid both walked her to school; Mrs Clay met them at the door and took Wyn's suitcase inside.

"We can come with you to the city perimeter if you want, Wyn?" Sister Astrid asked almost desperately. Wyn looked panicked.

"Oh, I have some paperwork I need to go through here first, so I'm not sure what time we'll be leaving. There's no point us keeping you. I'll leave you to say your goodbyes." Mrs Clay walked back into the school with authority.

"She's right, Sister. Let us say our goodbyes here. Then we can do it properly." Sister Cariad looked sad as she said it, and turned to Wyn. "Well, Terrwyn, go and make us proud. You know we will pray for you every day and you will be dearly missed."

Sister Cariad wrapped her arms around Wyn and hugged her tightly. There was a haze across her eyes as if she was trying not to cry, but she held it back. Wyn had never seen her quite so emotional and felt tears prickling at the back of her own eyes. By comparison, Sister Astrid was already sobbing and, as soon as Sister Cariad had finished, she grabbed hold of Wyn as if she was never going to let her go.

"We love you, Wyn. You can come home whenever you want, and it would make us so happy to have you back. Why can't we have our little girl back who would never leave us?"

Sister Astrid's despair meant Wyn could no longer control her own emotions, and tears were glistening on her cheeks by the time Sister Cariad prised Sister Astrid off. With only a few more words, Sister Cariad took a still tearful Sister Astrid firmly by the arm and led her away, both of them turning back with heartbreak on their faces to get a last glimpse of Wyn.

Once they had gone Wyn ran into the school and let the emotions flood out. She had tried to hold it together for the Sisters, but now she sat on the floor in the hallway and sobbed. She'd left them and it was all through a lie; it would break their hearts twice over when they knew the truth. Nearly sixteen years and she'd never spent longer than a night away from them. She knew, in that moment, that she was going to succeed and make that mammoth change in culture, because she couldn't betray them like this for nothing.

Twenty-four hours to go until enlistment. Mrs Clay had packed everything she'd got for Wyn, which didn't look like a lot when it was all put into one small holdall; just the clothes and as many supplement bars as they could fit, and a few things she couldn't cope without. Toiletries were all provided. They ran through the enlistment process so she knew what to expect, but it was a vague mismatch of what Mrs Clay had heard from others. She had pieced together what she'd been told and from that, she had guessed at the process once the gates were closed. However, there was no way to know for sure.

Once they'd got to Mrs Clay's flat in the afternoon it was time to take that last step. The real point of no return: her hair. Wyn sat on a chair in the middle of Mrs Clay's kitchen, her eyes squeezed as tightly closed as she could. She held her breath in tight and shivers went down her spine when she heard the buzz of the clippers. She could feel her long hair tumbling around her; she couldn't remember it ever being shorter than just below her shoulders, it was like they were cutting away the last part of the girl she was used to being.

"It's done." Mrs Clay's voice was steady but inexpressive, anticipating Wyn's reaction. "Be prepared, it's short! They would have shaved it off before they put you in barracks so I've tried to keep it at the longest we could get away with, hopefully they won't touch it now."

Wyn looked in the hand-held mirror she was holding and tried not to scream. Instead, a single solitary tear ran down her face; she knew there were more to come but she was too in shock to let them out. It was practically a buzz cut. She didn't look like Wyn; she looked like some sort of alien replacement and she could barely recognise herself.

From that moment onwards, she was living as a boy. Mrs Clay wouldn't respond if Wyn said or did anything feminine. It was the longest night she had ever known as she tossed and turned on a camp bed in Mrs Clay's front room. She hadn't had to worry about Mrs Clay's husband because he was on a business trip—some national conference about the financial state of the country due to the cost of the war—but every noise she heard still made her panic that she was about to be found out. By the time it was getting light outside she was too exhausted to move; she just stared at the ceiling, unsure if she'd slept at all. But Mrs Clay came bounding in with a slice of toast and a hot coffee, thrusting it towards Wyn.

"Okay, enlistment day, let's get you ready and down to the gates. It opens at nine so that gives us two hours."

Wyn scowled at her enthusiasm, she certainly wasn't sharing the sentiment. The coffee in her hand smelt strong and overpowering; she'd never had coffee before, they didn't have it at The Retreat and as she sipped on it she found it bitter. She screwed her face up in disgust but kept on sipping, hoping that it would shock her system into moving, knowing that caffeine was probably the answer to get her through the morning. After half a mug she was finding it bearable, and by the end, the taste was slightly more than tolerable. If this made the morning easier then maybe she would give it another go; she was going to need all the help she could get in the next few months.

Chapter 10

Stood at the gates in front of Necropolis Wyn felt like the whole world was watching her and laughing; whispering about the fraud who was so obviously just pretending to be a boy. Mrs Clay had left her at the tram stop, saying it would be too suspicious to her classmates that were signing up if they saw their teacher there with a random stranger. She had prepped Wyn to just follow the instructions, head to a table and go through the questions. Take her bag and keep it with her. The only reason they'd turn her away was if she didn't fit the criteria, so she only had to answer the questions in the right way and she'd be in. It was once she was in that she'd have to start proving herself. They were so desperate for cadets that getting in was easy.

All of the sign-up tables were set up in rows behind the entrance. The uniformed personnel sat behind the nearest one got up and opened the ornate metal gates, which had the August Centre emblem emblazoned across them. Just in front of her Wyn could see Jed, so she followed where he went and found herself in the queue. It slowly moved forward, each candidate being directed to a desk and standing awkwardly as they answered questions before being sent to stand at a marker set up at the far end of the tables. She was nearly at the front of the line.

"Table three," barked the Officer at the front of the line.

Wyn located the table and walked across to it; it was at the furthest end and she felt like she was on a catwalk as she moved along the row. It was the first time her walk had been on show and she was expecting someone to catch her out and tell her to leave at any second. Behind the table sat an older Officer with greying hair; even with her limited military knowledge, she guessed that this gentleman was no longer operational.

"Name?" he asked.

"Terrw…" Oh no, panic tore through her, they'd never even thought about names. How could they miss something so blatantly obvious? How idiotic had they been to have not even considered something so crucial to her persona? They had been so focussed on her cover in the real world they hadn't even considered it, and she definitely couldn't use her real name. She felt the fear radiate. "ah … um … Terrell. It's Terrell." She looked at him, panic spreading across her features, eyes wide and unblinking, waiting for him to call her out.

He just rolled his eyes. "Surname?"

"Um… Rigg?" She sounded doubtful, but he didn't seem to care. She was kicking herself, how could they miss something so simple? What else had they missed? And why had she used Sister Astrid's surname – she wasn't even supposed to know it. They had given their surnames up when they joined the Collections Children, but Wyn had found it when she and Kiara were sneaking a look through some records in the Collection library. Still, she thought, at least it was a small way to keep a connection with the Sisters.

The rest of the questions were simple in comparison. She didn't know her height or weight, but he said it didn't matter because they'd be double-checking that in the medical anyway. She didn't have any allergies or illnesses to note, but pretended she had hayfever to explain away the tablets that Mrs Clay had given her to stop her periods while she was on base. As she was an orphan, there was no next of kin to inform. At least that bit was technically the truth, even though it broke her heart to deny the Sisters their part in her life.

Once the questions were over, she was sent to the waiting area to stand with the other sign-ups. She scanned their faces quickly, trying to avoid eye contact. Jed and Marcus were there, a couple of the other boys from her class, but no sign of Carter yet. She was pleased about that, and was hoping he wouldn't turn up at all – she wasn't sure she could survive her pretence whilst also pretending to be his comrade.

After an hour of standing there, they were collected and taken to a small break-out room in the run-down hut that sat just to the side of the entrance grounds where they'd signed up. She hadn't even noticed the building before; it was clearly meant to have been a temporary structure when it was first put there, but now it had been left to just fall apart. They all sat awkwardly on the wooden chairs, more joining them each hour. The boys who knew each other sat together and joked and chatted. Wyn sat in the corner trying to make herself invisible.

After six hours, with minimal food and drink provisions, it was nearly the end of sign-up and there was still no sign of Carter. Wyn was pleased; maybe he had been all talk and didn't have the guts to go through with it, which would be satisfying proof that he was the arrogant idiot she'd always thought he was. But as the last group of intakes were brought over he came sauntering through the door. Her heart sank.

"Marcus, Jed! Did you miss me?"

"We were starting to think you'd bottled it!" Jed laughed, but there was a sliver of truth to his tone.

"Nah, mate! You know this is all I've wanted, but I wasn't going to rush and get here first thing. I'm not desperate! The world waits for me!" Carter's next-level arrogance astounded even Wyn, his conceited chortle made her shudder.

They were rounded up quickly and silently, instructed to stand in line in front of the hut, and barked at to stand straight, shoulders back, and look straight ahead. Wyn was near the back of the line and was satisfied to see Carter's shoulders droop just slightly as an Officer walked beside him. He marched the length of the line-up and back, eyeing each of them up. Wyn avoided his eye contact and held her breath as he neared, puffing up her chest and straightening her spine to try and emulate that tiny bit more manliness. Every second was another second they might figure her out, and being under scrutiny was only going to increase the chances.

The line-up passed without incident, except for a tall, lanky guy with glasses leaning out to look along the line and getting reprimanded immediately. The Officer marched across to him and demanded his name before telling him he was going to be watching him closely. Wyn couldn't hear the whole exchange from where she was, but all of her muscles tensed as the stern, harsh tone carried over to her. If anyone spoke to her like that, she was sure she would cry and give the game away.

They were walked down to the barracks, and given numbers as

they were sent in. There were twenty of them in total, and each had their own identification. Doors were pointed out in the corridor—toilets and showers, and the common room with a small kitchen—they were then led through the door straight ahead and into the dorm. They were told to stand in front of the bed that displayed their four-digit number. Wyn found hers and stood awkwardly. She glanced around to see the rest of the boys fall into place, and was dismayed to see that the person on the next bed along was Carter. She chastised herself for choosing a name so close to his in the alphabet. There was no avoiding him now.

She dropped her head and closed her eyes. She was already in way too deep. She'd never even considered that she would be sharing the dorm with the rest of them; her identity would be even harder to hide. When she heard footsteps, she snapped her head back up to see the Officer walking past each of them, checking everyone was at their assigned number. Wyn took the opportunity to look around the room. It was plain, with white-washed walls, and four rows of beds. They looked like the camp beds they slept on when they had sleepovers at Isabella's house, made up with green blankets and insanely neat. On top of each sat what she assumed must be their uniform. There was a small wooden bedside table with a lamp on one side of the beds, and a chest of drawers on the other. It looked so sterile, cold and impersonal.

"Okay, listen up. I am Training Officer Baird and this is Training Officer Reece. We will be leading your training and in charge of this platoon."

From the corner of her eye, Wyn saw Carter's head snap up and he looked tense as recognition read on his face. She furrowed her brow before she realised… Reece, that was his surname too. She knew his brothers had joined up before, so could it be that this was one of them? If it was then Carter was clearly not prepared for that fact, and Wyn was definitely not sure she could survive being around another Carter.

"You have fifteen minutes to unpack your personal belongings. Your bed-space should look no different once you've finished to how it does right now – pay close attention: you will be expected to return your space to this level of order every morning by 07:00 sharp, or else there will be consequences." He turned quickly, and swiftly left the dorm with Reece close behind him.

The room was silent and still for a moment as it sunk in. It was as if you could see the reality dropping down onto each one of them as they realised that this world of orders was theirs from now on. They did as instructed. Wyn was done quickly – she hadn't brought much so there wasn't a lot to pack away. She hovered by her drawers and listened to the humdrum of voices as the confidence in the room rose, and neighbouring bunks introduced each other. She held her breath, she tried to make herself invisible; she wanted to put off having to be 'one of the boys' for as long as possible.

"So, mate, we're neighbours." The voice sent a shudder down her spine and she spun round to see him looming in front of her. "The name's Carter."

He thrust his hand towards her and she looked at it as if he had offered her the head of some deep-sea monster. But she took it and channelled all of her energy into imitating the handshakes she had practiced at the gym.

"Terrell, nice to meet you." She could tell the lack of sincerity in her voice, and it dropped an octave halfway through the sentence as she realised she was speaking in her normal voice. Carter raised his eyebrow, but turned away and went to the bunk the other side, far too self-obsessed to pay the inconsistency any attention. She breathed a side of relief.

The bunk on the other side of her, Dorian, went through the same introduction. She kept her composure but had to force herself not to hold his gaze for too long, as she noticed just how green his eyes were—she'd never seen eyes like it. She kept the exchange short so that she could escape looking at them and was relieved when she saw Baird return, meaning she could fall back into line and do nothing but stare directly ahead.

"Right, line up in front of me, bunk order." He barked.

They were marched amid shouts and instructions out of the barracks and back up the hill to the main complex. Wyn felt her pulse quicken as she saw the Warehouse looming in front of her, distracting her from her first attempt to march in time with the others. Was she finally going to get to see inside? She couldn't help but feel the disappointment when they were led down the side instead of straight in. There was an outbuilding, inside of which was a lecture hall where they were seated in order.

Baird stood to one side of the door and Reece stood on the other. She could feel Carter tense up beside her once again, and the recognition on his face was clear – Training Officer Reece was definitely his brother and Carter was not expecting him to be here. The Training Officers were passing quiet comments, laughing as they both scanned the cadets in front of them, clearly amused by the standard of intakes. Wyn had to fight not to screw up her face when their eyes rested on her. Their scrutiny was another test she would have to pass to pull this off and she couldn't show any signs of weakness, but she knew that the anxiety was reading on her face no matter how hard she tried to relax it.

Baird and Reece suddenly snapped to attention and saluted as a tall broad man walked in. General Baudin. Wyn recognised him from his visits to the Collection and various community events and services. She had never liked the man. He had thinning grey hair and stood straight and rigid, his face fixed in a stern scowl. His expression and voice never displayed any emotion, and she remembered him scolding her on numerous occasions as a child, even if it was just for sitting in the kitchen with a colouring book. He had never approved of the Collection taking her in and made it very clear that he thought that The Retreat was no place for a child. She was certainly grateful that she had avoided him since she was old enough to, so he was unlikely to recognise her now. There was no one who could be worse to discover her identity than this powerful man who had always hated her.

Now he was stood in the middle of the lecture theatre behind a podium, his steely eyes analysing the cadets before him.

"Good afternoon cadets. I, as I'm sure you are aware, am General Baudin. I run this base and will be overseeing your training whilst you are here. Training Officers Baird and Reece will be your direct supervisors and you will have numerous instructors. These are made up of experienced soldiers and officers who have the specialist skills needed to get you through your basic training. As far as you are concerned, they are all officers and you will treat all of them with equal respect, as you will with all other soldiers you encounter. As cadets you are inferior to all soldiers on this base, so you will show everyone due respect or reap the consequences. They are all your superiors and you will remember that and treat them as such. You will refer to them by the title they are introduced to you as, or as 'Sir'. You will refer to me only as 'General'. You are now cadets in The Southern Company in National Service. You are no longer boys—you are men and you will act like it. If you are not up to standard then you will be removed from service and face the shame of returning home. Your Training Officers will now give you an introduction into how your training will work, and I will be meeting with you again in one week for updates on your progress."

All the time he spoke the room was deadly silent and the tension in the air was clear. The Training Officers stood tall, shoulders back with their hands clasped behind their backs, unmoving except for the glances they kept shooting the cadets, gauging the reactions. Once he had finished, the General nodded at the Training Officers and strode out as swiftly as he had come in. Baird was now behind the podium, smirking at them, whilst Reece leant nonchalantly against the wall.

"So, that was the General. He'll stop in unannounced from time to time, so keep an eye out. Other than that, we are in charge." Baird's tone was dripping with arrogance. "Training is split between theory and practical, but tomorrow you'll get a tour, and the next week will just be selection tests to make sure you're up to the job – mathematical and verbal reasoning, fitness, logic tests, general knowledge. There are extra tests introduced for this intake and the results calculated will determine your future here. No pressure." He chuckled to himself. Beside him, Wyn noticed Reece frowning. "Now we are going to go to the mess—you'll fully understand why it's called that when you see the food—then you get an hour and a half in the common room. After that, it's lights out. Big day tomorrow."

Baird was still smirking cockily as he began to lead them out. Wyn following behind Carter, but the line was paused when Reece stepped in and stood in front of Carter, whispering.

"Mate, I'm sorry, I couldn't let you know I'd be here. I couldn't even tell mum. There are loads of top-secret changes going on. This Special Forces stuff is coming in and they kept me and Dean back when our platoon shipped out—we don't even know why they chose us. You're going to have to treat me like you treat any of the other Officers, and I'll try and catch some time for us when no one's around."

Reece was glancing around, making sure no one had caught him talking to his brother, but only Wyn had been able to hear, and only because she had stopped so close behind Carter that she had nearly run into him. He shot her a look that demanded her silence and she nodded slightly, the sooner she could make some allies the better. Reassured, Reece placed his hand briefly on Carter's shoulder and stood back, letting the line move forward. In front of her she could see Carter shaking his head slightly, his shoulders rigid with tension.

The mess was full of other officers and soldiers, but the chatter and laughter in the air made her start to relax for the first time since she'd walked through the gates.

"Okay, guys, these are your two tables. You will make sure to sit here as the ranks do not mix, but you don't have to stick to your order. Grab a tray over there, get your grub served up and enjoy. You get used to the taste, eventually." Reece gestured around the room as he spoke before walking off and getting a tray himself.

There was a pause as the cadets all looked at each other, waiting for someone to make the first move. Breaking the awkwardness Dorian moved towards the kitchen line and the others fell into place behind him. Wyn ended up at the back of the line. On offer were burgers, baked potato, and extremely over-steamed vegetables. She supposed that it wasn't that bad, but compared to Sister Cariad's cooking it sat on the plate like three-day-old leftovers. She forced down as much of it as she could – hopefully Reece was right and she'd get used to it.

Through dinner and on into the common room attached to the barracks, the cadets were starting to get to know each other, joking and laughing and asking questions. Wyn held back, trying to sit and listen and get to know them, learn about what were considered acceptable and normal answers so that she could use them when it came to her. There was talk of sport and hobbies, technology, and then they got onto girls. Wyn cringed as they competed over who'd done what and how many girls they'd had; she wasn't used to this sort of talk. Out of her friends, Isabella and Kiara were the most experienced but their conversations were mostly about the emotions and soppy stuff – they were definitely not this graphic. Wyn had only ever kissed one guy, from the year above, a few times at birthday parties and it hadn't been much to write home about. She'd never really wanted to do it, he had definitely not been her type, but it had stopped the girls going on at her to get a boyfriend. But whilst listening and watching the animated competition, she couldn't help notice that Carter was also staying quiet—maybe Mister Cocky didn't have the luck with the ladies that he boasted about after all. The thought gave her a small shot of satisfaction. Before long it was lights out and Wyn couldn't say she wasn't pleased about how strictly it was enforced. She'd never felt quite so drained and it was a relief to crawl into her bunk; being a guy was exhausting.

Despite the fact she had been struggling to keep her eyes open by the end of the evening in the common room, once she was under the scratchy blanket she couldn't bring herself to close them. She didn't know if it was the noise of the breathing and coughing and eventual snoring, or the tightness of the binding which she hadn't taken off, but she knew that she missed her bed and the warmth of her room, with the reassurance of the Sisters' gentle footsteps as they walked down to midnight prayer. It felt like hours before her eyes finally fell shut, and the sleep that eventually came was restless. She had survived day one.

Chapter 11

That Saturday morning, they were woken as the sun came up. This was how it was apparently; lie-ins were not an option as a cadet. They dressed quickly, straightened their bunks, and lined up before being led to breakfast which was thick, gloopy porridge without so much as a sprinkle of sugar. Wyn's mouth felt claggy and dry just looking at it. Once their bowls had been scraped clean it was the time Wyn had been waiting for: the tour.

"Okay cadets, in order please. There will be operational staff in most of the locations you will see today – remain silent unless spoken to and allow these men to do their jobs. There are areas you may never visit again during your training, as they are irrelevant to your rank. Now pay attention and let's get moving."

Reece finished his instruction and led them out of the barracks and towards the building by the front gate that they had been gathered in the day before. He paused outside, allowing them to catch up.

"This is the A Block. The rooms are used as waiting rooms and meeting rooms for external guests, unless they are of a higher status, in which case we have alternative rooms. There are three meeting rooms in total, and the break-out room in which you waited yesterday. You won't have much reason to go into these meeting rooms day-to-day, but you will have fortnightly reviews which may take place here on occasion." Reece's voice sounded clipped and controlled, he was uncomfortable doing this and it was definitely not his choice to be leading their introduction.

He continued the tour around the camp but didn't feel any more relaxed, rushing his words to get it over with quicker. After A-Block was the main complex—the training annexe where the lecture hall and drill yard were located, as well as a large expanse of empty land that lay behind them—then onto B-Block, which was a building full of offices and slightly tidier meeting rooms. Beyond that, they could see the residential complex that contained the barracks and apartments of those who lived on camp full-time, but as they had their own barracks, the tour didn't extend there. Then there were a few more out-buildings before finally it was the moment Wyn had been waiting for since she was old enough to go outside and play on her own: The Warehouse.

They walked up to the front and Wyn took it in. The dark grey corrugated iron looked more ominous and worn close up, with massive doors that were nearly the full height of it. In these doors were a couple of smaller, normal-sized doors, which was where they were being led. She had built this up so much for so long, that she had created multiple different ideas of what to expect; some sort of magical new world full of excitement perhaps. She knew that was a childish notion, but what else could somewhere so mysterious hold?

The doors opened and she held her breath, closing her eyes as she stepped over the threshold. When she opened them she gasped; they were stood on a platform that ran around the full edge of the warehouse. The man-made ravine it surrounded went deep underground and its floor was covered in vehicles and machinery. In the middle stood a proud, half-finished structure unlike anything Wyn had seen before. It was definitely made for war—some sort of all-terrain vehicle crossed with a weapon that was sat on caterpillar tracks; it also had spider legs coming out of the main tank-like unit and an array of weaponry adorning it. She couldn't even begin to imagine just how much damage it could do, or what all the other weapons were, but she couldn't wait to find out.

"Okay, so, this is the warehouse. If referring to it with higher ranks then remember that it is 'The August Centre' and not 'Necropolis', or else you will face instant disciplinary action. This is the hub of progress in this base; all the machinery, weapons, vehicles, and top secrets come out of this warehouse. Most of it you will never know anything about. This half of the warehouse is for the big stuff and is the main workshop; at the end of this platform, there is a door that leads into corridors and rooms on the other side of the warehouse. That is where the smaller-scale and top-secret stuff are housed. You can only access a limited number of floors without special access privileges, and I don't expect you'll be getting them any time soon. It might look like a normal warehouse from the outside but it goes a couple of floors underground, so there is always a lot going on and a lot of people here. All of the weapons, gadgets, and anything you can think of are created here by our Tactical Development team. This is made up of genius scientists and experienced field officers—some of you may one day be lucky enough to work with them, but don't hold your breath." Baird had taken over the tour for this part, knowing it was the most interesting area, and was clearly enjoying holding an audience.

Wyn paused for a moment before she was ready to take it all in, the magnitude of the building was overwhelming. She knew a lot of people in the city that had worked here doing basic labour or paperwork, though they were forbidden from discussing any specific job roles or what was actually going on, and now she understood why. Getting to see inside had always been her goal since she was a child, she had dreamt of what it was hiding and what the troops did once they signed up. Technically, this building was the main reason she had started on this whole insane plan. Even though her end goal had grown exponentially, she couldn't help but feel a swell of pride at just making it into the warehouse. It was like pressing a reset button on her motivation and she owed it to her childhood imagination to keep going.

They were shown the main corridor in the second half of the warehouse but weren't allowed into any of the rooms and were then led to the mess room for lunch, after which they were herded back down to the barracks. The final thing to be pointed out on the tour was a building that stood right next to the barracks: the gym. This was where most of the cadets headed when they were released for a few hours of free time.

Taking the first steps into the gym was daunting. She had her routine, she knew what she was doing, but showing off her relative weakness was a risk. She couldn't match the muscle of most of the cadets, and she knew from the amount of times she'd been teased by Snapper that she made girly squeaks and curled up the left side of her lip when she lifted. But if she didn't maintain and build her strength then she'd be caught out in no time. Game face on.

She held back and made sure she was the last one in, then paused in the door to scope out what was going on. Some of the equipment she recognised, but most of it was alien to her. She eyed up where each of the others had gone first. Her plan was to go on equipment that was as far away from the others as possible so they couldn't watch her form too closely, but when most of them headed for the free weights, she started to realise she couldn't hide from them forever; half of her routine used free weights. She wandered around examining the rest of the stations; all sorts of weight machines that were completely new to her, but they had names on them and diagrams to illustrate how to use them, so she thought she might as well try one. She figured they'd work the same muscle groups, or at least close enough. After the shoulder press and the leg press, she looked up and realised people were watching her.

"What you doing, Rigg? Too much of a wimp to come work out with the big boys?" Carter mocked. As she scanned the room, Wyn realised she was the only one not in the weights area. "Don't reckon you can keep up?"

Anger flared up inside of her. If it was anyone else but Carter she would've taken it, but he wound her up so much just by breathing that she couldn't control it. She got off the leg press and stalked over to him, in her fury she lost her swagger and could feel the feminine swing of her hips creeping back in, but her focus was elsewhere. She marched straight over and stood square in front of him.

"Maybe I just don't want to show anyone else up, or maybe it's the fact I'd rather be anywhere but near someone as arrogant as you!"

"Prove it." Carter gestured to the bar behind him, where he had been deadlifting minutes before. "Lift that and we'll call it quits."

Wyn stared at the weights, it was way higher than she'd lifted before, but she couldn't admit defeat now. Not to Carter. Not in front of everyone. She walked past him, feeling every eye on her, and planted her feet in front of the bar. Bending over, she gripped the bar—so far so good. She was comfortable with her technique by now, she knew what to do. She prepared herself, took a deep breath and lifted. It barely made it off the floor before it came crashing back down and she heard most of the room erupt into laughter, Carter guffawing behind her. She looked up, sheepish and defeated. A few of the weaker guys were looking at her with sympathy but most of them looked like wolves circling their prey.

"Yeah, I didn't think so!" Carter sniggered, and with that he turned and strode out of the room, the rest of them following him. A few glanced back to watch her as she put her head in her hands, trying not to let the tears that were blurring in her eyes spill out. How had she been stupid enough to let her feelings about Carter nearly catch her out? What if they had figured her out?

By the time she could bring herself to leave the gym and traipse across to the barracks, most of the guys were in the showers or lounging around on their bunks half-naked. She stopped dead in the doorway; she had never seen this much naked flesh in her life, especially not male flesh! She walked over to her bunk with her eyes down, avoiding looking directly at anyone; she didn't know the rules, was it weird for men to look at other men? She guessed it must be so the floor was definitely the safest place to train her eyes.

She made it to her bunk without incident and sat on the edge, putting her head in her hands and running her fingers through the stubbly remnants of her hair, the texture was therapeutic to touch and she could feel the intensity of her heart rate begin to slow. She felt calm enough to look up through her hands and realised she was facing Dorian's bunk directly. He was lying back, propped up on one elbow, shouting across the dorm to a big burly guy sat on the other side. Wyn forgot her new rule of not looking as she stared at the body opposite her; with a towel round his waist and his skin still glistening from the shower, she couldn't take her eyes off his torso. The only way she could describe him was sculpted. Marty, Snapper, and the other muscles at her gym were all just bulk, but she could have happily watched Dorian for ages. She snapped herself out of it when she realised what she was doing—the last thing she wanted was any more attention for being unmanly. She looked up nervously, expecting to see eyes boring into her, but she was safe, no one had noticed.

She busied herself with tidying up her bed and making it as perfect as possible, just to avoid the rows of men changing around her. Hopefully no one would notice that she'd avoided the showers. They were communal, which was something neither Wyn nor Mrs Clay had thought about, and she knew she couldn't risk going in when others were around. She was going to have to bide her time, think of the ideal moment to sneak away and get the shower block to herself. Until then, she was going to have to hope that they didn't care about her lack of hygiene and that it just added to her manly persona. The idea of not being able to wash made her shiver and her toes curl.

Sitting on her bunk and avoiding a direct view of any more of the naked bodies she'd accidentally seen too much of, Wyn listened to the conversations flying around the room. It all seemed so natural, everyone fitting into their order. The quiet, academic guys who were on the periphery, finding their feet, and the confident, loud personalities—like Carter and Dorian—who were quickly becoming the centre of the group. Wyn couldn't help wondering where she was going to fit, or if she ever would; she needed to find her role in the group soon or else they were sure to figure her out. The pressure to keep her secret was becoming overwhelming and it was only day two. She had never expected it to be so intense, and didn't realise she would have to think about it every second. She couldn't relax for a moment for fear of letting the façade slip. Three months was feeling like a long time.

Soon it was time for dinner in the mess, and then a few hours in the common room before lights out. Sundays were reserved for private study, but they hadn't been given any work yet, so it was just treated as a free day. They were allowed to walk down to the Collectioners' Retreat for Sunday Service and it pained Wyn not to go. She couldn't risk seeing the Brothers and Sisters and getting found out, but she didn't remember a single Sunday without having gone to Service, and even though she'd never fully engaged in the religious side she missed it more than she could have imagined. But by the end of Sunday, she felt like she was starting to at least fit in somewhere. She'd approached Andrew and Hugh, two of the quietest and weediest guys in the group, and they'd started talking. She didn't have to put on such a macho pretence with them and being able to talk about authors and music was the most comfortable conversation that had come up since she'd arrived. It was a relief just to talk about something normal and get out of the thoughts that span around in her head.

That night, she fell asleep thinking about her favourite book instead of what they might do if they caught her out, which was what had dominated her thoughts for the last two nights.

Chapter 12

Monday morning marked the start of the selection tests. First they were led to a classroom next to the lecture theatre in the training annexe. It was set out just like the exams they'd sat at school—rows of individual desks with papers set out neatly—and they were sat down in their order before Reece took to the front of the room.

"This morning is mathematical and verbal reasoning. Each paper is two hours and there will be a twenty-minute break between them. Please complete the personal details at the top of the page, we will begin in a moment."

As Wyn waited for the exam to start she was surprised she wasn't feeling nervous, but instead had an odd sort of excitement. She had always been academic, the Collection valued knowledge and education and it had been instilled in her from the moment she had lived with them; completing these tests was like falling back into a place where she was confident and comfortable. She knew there was still pressure for her to do well, and it would be humiliating for her to fail her mission on something that she knew she was good at, but she had far more chance of getting this right than anything else.

On both tests she was the first to finish, so she sat doodling on the scrap paper and looking carelessly around the room. The tests had some questions that had made her think but, all-in-all, she was pretty confident that she'd passed. Her seat was in the back row and as she looked around it filled her with a smug sense of accomplishment to see that some of them were clearly struggling; she almost laughed out loud when she noticed that Carter and Dorian both looked as though they were reading another language.

They were sent to the mess for lunch—some sort of mince and

potato concoction—and on returning to the classroom, were sat down to another test. This time it was a multiple-choice personality test. When setting it up, Baird commented that it was new for this intake and Wyn wondered if it had anything to do with the Special Forces stuff that everyone seemed so clueless about. She didn't know how to play this one, whether she should play up to the male persona she was creating? But she didn't know how a man would answer these questions, so she figured she had no choice but to answer them how she normally would. After all, surely it would look even more suspicious if her answers didn't even match up with each other? She would just have to hope that whatever she came out as wouldn't give her away. They were let off for the day once the test was done.

The next day was fitness and physical, so they were given time to get in the gym and prepare. Wyn kept out of the others' way and went about her normal gym routine, but she couldn't help but watch Dorian out of the corner of her eye. She knew this was dangerous; she shouldn't start liking someone here. It was impossible anyway, they all thought she was a guy, and even worse it was just another thing that could give her away. But even though she was telling herself not to be, she was always acutely aware of where he was in the room and she couldn't help but glance at him every time he was in her eyeline. She'd never really liked anyone much before, why choose now to start? She shook her head, silently chastising herself, but no matter how many times she told herself not to, she couldn't help but feel a foolishly illogical disappointment when he was never looking back her way.

She avoided the showers again, but as she sat there, trying hard not to watch the way the muscles in Dorian's back moved as he got things out of his drawers, she had to admit to herself that she couldn't get away without showering much longer. There was only so long she could avoid washing without someone saying something, only so long before they would ask questions, so she was going to have to work out how to do it without people around. She would also have to come up with a reason why she wasn't going in with everyone else. More than anything, she just wanted to be able to take the binder off, just ten minutes—even if she couldn't swap to the clean one. Just thinking about it made her fidget and try to surreptitiously wriggle it into a more comfortable position. It was tight and uncomfortable, and wearing it for three nights had shifted it round so it tucked and bunched where it shouldn't. As her awareness of the binding became more unbearable, she reached her hand up the back of her top and tried to unfold the edges, but stopped suddenly when she noticed a guy on the other side of the dorm watching her as she twisted and grimaced. She wasn't supposed to be drawing any unwanted attention, especially not for something that would definitely blow her cover.

Throughout dinner and during the few hours in the common room, Wyn couldn't help but keep glancing at the guy who'd seen her—Andrew had said his name was Rowan, they'd been to school together—petrified that he was catching on, but to her relief he didn't pay her any more attention. She was also trying to come up with a plan to get into the showers, and the more she thought about how it would feel to stand under the stream of water, the more desperate she became for an excuse. Andrew and Hugh had to snap her attention back into the present multiple times and were starting to question if she was okay. Wyn passed it off as nerves for the fitness tests.

"We've seen you in the gym, Terrell, you're definitely fitter than both of us. You'll do fine." Hugh reassured, admitting his concerns at his own abilities. They talked about it for the rest of the evening, trying to anticipate what they might be made to do, and it did calm nerves that Wyn hadn't even realised she had. Compared to both of them she was in much better shape, so at least she wasn't going to be the worst and give herself away that way.

Lights out came but Wyn had worked out a way into the showers and lay in the darkness staring at the ceiling. She had to keep herself awake, so she counted all of the ceiling panels in the room and listened to the noises around her. There was someone who kept coughing and she had never realised before that there were so many different sounds people could make snoring; on one side of her Dorian sounded like he was grunting, whilst on the other, Carter snuffled like a hedgehog - if it had been anyone else, she'd have thought it was cute. Adding it in with the cacophony of a roomful of men's noises and it was like listening to some weird sleep symphony, and she wondered how she'd been managing to sleep through it at all. She could feel her eyes growing heavier now, but she was determined to stay awake and wait until the right time. Eventually, all the stirring and shifting in the bunks had stopped. She didn't know how long it had taken but she couldn't wait any longer and decided to risk it; clambering out of her bunk as quietly as possible and grabbing the change of clothes and a towel that she had left on the top of her drawers, she tiptoed out of the dorm and into the shower block.

She crept across the cold tiles, even though she was sure no one was in there, and placed herself under the communal showers, wishing there was at least a curtain that she could pull across them. She was going to have to be on high alert in case anyone came in as there was definitely nowhere to hide. Unwinding the binding was such a physical relief that Wyn felt as though her tension was melting away; she visibly sighed as the pressure was alleviated and she rolled her shoulders, feeling the freedom of her torso as she stretched out her body. After piling her clothes and binding carefully to one side, just within reach in case she needed to cover up quick, she turned on the water. Even though the water was barely lukewarm, the feeling of it cascading down her back and running down her legs was like going out into the sun and feeling the direct warmth on your skin after a harsh winter. She had never appreciated before just how good being clean felt. But she couldn't be in there long—she knew it was too much of a risk. And as soon as she had rinsed off the army-issue soap, she shut off the water and gathered up her stuff. It hadn't taken long; having no hair halved the time compared to the showers she'd have taken before. She did the binding up tight, looked at herself in the mirror with a faint smile on her face, and took a deep breath; no one had come in and it would be easy to repeat every few days. As long as she could avoid having to discuss her washing habits with any of the other cadets then that was another problem overcome… Maybe she was going to get away with all of this after all.

Wyn woke up feeling refreshed for the fitness portion of selection, and she felt like the stress that had been building up had been cleansed slightly by the shower. This was the most important thing for Wyn to pass so far—if she could keep up with the guys then they wouldn't look at her twice. And if she didn't, it wasn't just about being found out; if she couldn't hack it then she wouldn't be taken through to training anyway and it would all have been for nothing. She got into her kit and headed to the mess for breakfast ahead of the others. She didn't want to listen to the over-breakfast speculation about what would come up, her trepidation was growing of its own accord and it definitely didn't need any of their help.

They lined up on the drill yard with Reece and Baird stood in front of them, and Wyn noticed the General watching off to one side. First of all, they had to run a timed circuit, and then they were taken straight off the track and were faced with different weighted mannequins to lift and carry. Finally, they were made to do sit-ups and press-ups. Wyn was relieved that she managed to surpass not just Andrew and Hugh but, on the weights and body-weight exercises, she even beat a couple of the other guys. They were definitely stronger than her but clearly had no idea what they were doing, and learning proper technique from Snapper had made up for what she lacked in strength. She made a mental note to work on her running, bringing her time down would be a good distraction once they got into training.

The cadets were given an hour and a half for lunch and told to make sure they took the time to sit down and reset because the afternoon would be spent doing the obstacles. Baird warned that they would have to get used to completing an obstacle course, and quickly, because it would be a regular part of the training schedule. It was a way for them to be familiarised with the tactical movement they would use in combat, and the obstacles would be tweaked and adjusted constantly over their training programme, so they'd never see the same course twice. They were led past the training annexe and onto the land that they had been shown on the tour; this was where the bulk of physical training was carried out and it was now set up with thirteen different obstacles. Stood by each was a different officer with a clipboard, Wyn recognised some from the sign-up and the mess room and the thought of being watched by all of these new eyes was daunting—even more people to convince and each new scrutiny was a new risk of getting caught. Eyeing up the obstacles, she looked around them in order—walls to scale, things to crawl through, what looked like an expanse of water. Wyn felt a lump jump into her throat, she didn't know how to swim…

"Okay, men. You are going to go one-by-one, this is timed and you will be scored and timed on each individual obstacle. The officers at each station will be making observations on anything that you struggle with or are unable to complete, and this will be recorded. Once you have completed the course you will remain at the finish line to await further instruction. Line up in order and we will begin shortly. Any questions?" Baird revelled in giving orders;

his eyes glinted, feeding off of the power.

Wyn raised her hand sheepishly—so much for not drawing any negative attention.

"Yes, Rigg?"

"I notice that there is an obstacle that looks like water..." She nodded in the direction of the oversized paddling pool. "What do we do if we are unable to swim?"

Baird looked at Reece and smirked; Reece visibly restrained from rolling his eyes at his colleague's response and took a step forward.

"Swimming is not an essential skill at this point and is something that could be addressed during training if necessary. As such, skip this obstacle and a time penalty—using the longest time out of the other cadets plus ten seconds—will be added to your overall time to account for this. Is there anyone else who will be unable to complete this obstacle?"

Three other guys put their hands up. Reece made a note of their names and then directed the cadets to the start line, where they stood in order. There was a nervous energy as everyone geared themselves up to be sent off one after the other. Watching the cadets who were before her made Wyn doubt her abilities even more; people who were bigger and stronger than her were struggling to pull themselves through certain obstacles and making others look ridiculously easy, both of which made her feel increasingly uncertain.

Carter was sent off and Wyn couldn't help but smile when he got himself tangled up in netting and lost precious time. He was red-faced and swearing when he eventually freed himself and sprinted off to the next obstacle. Far too quickly, he had completed the course and it was Wyn's turn. She readied herself at the start line, getting into a comfortable position to start off into a sprint. She was given the command and was off. First, a six-foot wall to scale, then onto the climbing net; as she went round the course she realised that the obstacles the larger cadets had failed on were the ones she found easiest, her small stature and stealthy movements working to her advantage. Other than missing the swimming and taking a few attempts to get over the scaling wall, she was pleased with how she'd done. By no means was she front of the pack, but she hadn't done anything to suggest she was completely incapable, and hopefully that was enough to get her through the selection process.

Once the last person had completed the course—Hugh, who had

come trailing in, breathing heavily and absolutely devastated that he had been unable to get through the last two obstacles—they were lined back up and given a debrief.

"Okay, cadets. You'll be pleased to know that you are done for today. You won't find your results out until the end of the week when they will be given with the rest of the exam results, but most of you did alright." Baird's eyes rested on Hugh as he said it, making it clear that he was not included in the 'most'. "Go and wash up, and you are free for the rest of the evening to do as you wish."

Baird and Reece walked off once they had dismissed the cadets, and left them all standing in the sludgy grass in a daze. Wyn looked down at herself and realised how much mud she was covered in, she looked up and realised that they all looked the same. It was funny how, when they were doing the course, she hadn't even noticed how thick and boggy the grass was turning, but now that she had and was stood still, she was starting to shiver. Looking around, most of the cadets were having the same realisation and they all hurried back to the barracks in one tight group, just longing for the warmth and to collapse in a heap.

Some of the men jumped straight into the shower, but Wyn was pleased to find that once she had peeled off the stiffening kit it was only her extremities that needed to be washed. Even her hair was easy to rinse in the sink, and no one batted an eyelid that she didn't shower fully. Once she'd dressed in a fresh top layer of clothes— over the shorts and t-shirt she kept on to keep her modesty—she dug out something as comfy as possible from the minimal selection she'd brought in, then went into the common room and found a seat. Hugh and Andrew shortly came in to join her and as they approached, the shame in Hugh's face was clear.

"We don't even know what time they wanted from us. Plus, if you ace all the other stuff then maybe they won't even care how you did on the course." Andrew was reassuring him as they walked over.

They sat down opposite her and Wyn looked over sympathetically.

"No point worrying, is there. We won't find out the score until Friday anyway, and you can't change it now." Wyn added, knowing all too well how true it was. She'd had to remind herself of that at least a few times a day since she'd arrived. Whenever she did something that she was scared would trip her up, the mantra would run through her head: she couldn't change something she'd already done so she just had to get on, deal with it, and change how she did it next time. What use was worrying about it? This thought process helped, even if only for a few minutes.

The next few days continued in a similar manner: exams in the morning and afternoon, and then the evenings were spent in the common room picking apart every answer they'd given. By Thursday, the segregation within the group had practically disappeared and they would sit around in one big group to over-analyse. From this it was clear that what some of them had in brawn, they severely lacked in brains. Wyn, Andrew and Hugh were by far the most academic of the group and they were surprised to learn that this made them suddenly more accepted by the rest of the cadets – the fact that they could offer advice and tuition made them powerful allies in theory lessons for the guys that knew they were going to struggle.

All of the cadets were desperate for Friday to come and to get the results, just to alleviate the nervous tension that was growing ever thicker in the air. On Friday morning they all went to breakfast early, before any of the officers, and then sat around in the Common Room waiting to be collected. The normally flowing conversation was stilted; none of them knew how this worked and it made the room uneasy. Everyone knew of 'a friend of a friend' or 'so-and-so's cousin' who had been kicked out based on their selection tests and then had to face the shame of returning to the city as a failure. If that happened, then they would only be given one more chance to enlist before they were struck off completely and considered to have let their country down—and that's if they even did another intake. No-one wanted that fate and by the time Reece was ordering them to line up, the fear of failure was palpable.

Sitting in the lecture theatre, they watched General Baudin take slow, deliberate steps to the lectern, enjoying drawing this out as much as possible just to watch the cadets squirm. He scanned each of their faces before he started to talk, building the tension and unease, savouring the power, and his supercilious nature was only making Wyn hate him more.

"Well done men, you have completed your first week in the Southern Company. You have reached the end of your selection tests and nearly all of you have survived them."

Dorian flinched beside her; in front of her, Marcus gasped.

Nearly all … that meant somebody was being kicked out. A sinking feeling settled into her stomach and she felt physically sick—she knew it was going to be her. This whole idea had been stupid from the start and now she might as well throw her hands up and admit to who she was – her future was ruined either way. She had started to believe she had done enough but clearly, she hadn't. She clenched her fists, waiting for the numbers to be called. General Baudin was continuing.

"We have compiled the results from each test, and from this worked out where each of your strengths and weaknesses lie. These results will be used to tailor aspects of your training so that we can develop and optimise your use in combat. For those of you without enough redeeming strengths, and who did not even reach all the minimum standards, you will be removed from the process. We have not had to remove anyone in the past four intakes, but today we will be removing two of you. This is utterly disappointing and a dishonour to your country. You might get the chance to re-enlist but you will be expected to build your skills prior to coming back and should you fail again, there are no more chances. You will receive a full debrief before you leave to advise you on what areas to work on. Now, let's remove those individuals before we continue."

General Baudin shuffled the papers in front of him, pulling out two sheets and looking up at the forty eyes staring at him intently, not a single one without fear.

"Firstly, Number 3421 – Bowen."

Wyn had to keep herself from shouting out—it was Hugh. Half the room relaxed slightly. This was expected, he had clearly been the weakest candidate physically and it gave a slight grain of hope to the majority of the cadets that maybe it was just the weaklings that were going. Hugh dragged his feet over to the door and stood in front of it looking devastated, but he didn't look surprised.

"Secondly, Number 3429 – Jessip."

This time the whole room gasped. It was Marcus … but how? He had been in the thick of it, one of the most popular, one of the strongest, he definitely wasn't the least intelligent; how was it Marcus? He made his way over to stand beside Hugh, his shoulders hunched and his feet dragging. When he turned around, he was staring unblinking at the floor, and Wyn was sure he was trying not to cry.

"Training Officer Reece, please remove the boys and take them into the classroom. I will be in to debrief them shortly." General Baudin directed. The cadets watched them leave, saddened but consumed with the relief that they'd made it through. The whole situation made Wyn's skin crawl with discomfort. "The rest of you, your results will be given to you in individual debriefs by Training Officer's Reece and Baird. You will wait in here to be called by them. Once released, you will be sent to the Common Room. When all of the debriefings are completed, you will be brought back here and I will address you further."

General Baudin left the lecture theatre, his steps echoing around the silent room which was still stunned from the shock departures. It took the officers a few minutes of whispering in the corner before they centred themselves and called the first cadet, leading him out for a debrief. The rest of them looked around at each other before the comments about Hugh and Marcus started being thrown around.

"You went to school with Marcus, didn't you Carter?" Dorian was talking across Wyn. She had to bite her tongue not to answer and say she did too; for a moment she'd forgotten she wasn't supposed to have known him before.

"Yeah, he was one of my best mates. Can't believe he's gone. I didn't realise he'd done that badly..." Wyn could hear a tone of insincerity in his voice that she couldn't quite work out. Maybe they hadn't been that close after all.

"Yeah, he didn't look like he'd have a problem... That Hugh, on the other hand... He was wet from the start – knew he didn't have it in him. Fair play to that Andrew though, I'm impressed he made it!" Dorian nodded towards Andrew, who was sat on the front row. He wasn't talking to anyone and looked devastated at the loss of his friend.

They started to chat about what they reckoned their results would show, speculating what their weaknesses were. They included Wyn but she kept her answers short—she didn't want to give too much away and besides, she really wasn't sure how she'd done. She enjoyed talking to them though, it felt good to be included and it gave her another chance to watch Dorian more closely, watching his lips move as he spoke and his eyes glint when he laughed. The more she looked, the more she realised how attractive he was.

One by one the cadets were taken out, and soon there were only five of them left. Carter was up next, and he was clearly nervous as his number was called and he followed his brother out of the room.

Wyn and Dorian continued to talk, they'd been discussing sport but she was pretty clueless. She repeated bits from conversations she remembered Snapper and the muscles having at the gym, and it seemed to keep her involved enough to satisfy him. Other than that, she could just sit back and watch him talk. He was animated and inviting, and watching him made her think about how nice it would be to kiss him. She regularly had to bring herself back to reality and wipe the soft, soppy smile that she could tell was appearing on her face. Why choose now to fall for a guy? And why did it have to be someone so utterly inappropriate?

Soon the door was opening and Baird was calling her number. She walked behind him to one of the classrooms down the hallway and took a seat when he gestured to do so. Reece was sat across the table, shuffling papers around, and Baird was looking at her with an arrogant smile.

"So, Terrell Rigg. Let's have a look at how you did this week. What's the verdict Training Officer Reece?" His voice dripped with a cocky malice. He was not a pleasant man, Wyn had worked that much out, nor was he an attractive one. He was in his early twenties with pale, spotty skin and white-blonde hair, his nose slightly crooked with a scar running across his cheek and his teeth stained slightly yellow. Worst of all, he was clearly cut from the same cloth as the General, and that was enough to make Wyn dislike the very sight of him.

"Well, you came top in the logic and reasoning tests and were middle to high on all of the other written exams. In terms of your overall average you were placed within the top three of the class, so you will be given opportunities to further develop these skills in a tactical capacity during training. We provide personal development sessions and we will make sure an officer is available to you during some of these. Standing out at this point means we can give you specialised training to further enhance your skills instead of just getting you up to a passable level."

Wyn smiled at Reece broadly, unable to contain the pride at her results. She had definitely not expected feedback that positive and she released a breath she didn't even realise that she'd been holding. She had shown herself to be valuable in at least some areas. If she focussed on them and made herself worth something then that would definitely help her make an impact on her reveal, just like Mrs Clay wanted.

"But…" Baird smirked at her, watching her face drop as she awaited the negative. "Your fitness tests were not to the same standard. You were distinctly weaker than a lot of the other cadets and not up to the same cardio fitness, but luckily for you, not below the minimum of the range. We will require you to train further on both of those aspects to get you in amongst the rest of the pack—and the majority of this will have to be done in your own time. If you can't keep up, then you won't be able to keep on top of the training provided and will have to be removed. You did redeem yourself slightly during the obstacle course – eight of the officers running the obstacles commented that what you lacked in strength you made up for in stealth, which is something that could prove valuable in certain circumstances. Keep that in mind when you enter scenarios and we will see if we can make use of it."

Baird finished and eyed Wyn's response. He revelled in delivering bad news, but she was determined not to show him that she was concerned. She smiled politely at him and nodded.

"I can put in the required effort; would you be able to advise me on what level I need to reach?"

"Here… these are the guidelines…" Reece passed a sheet of paper over the table to her that listed the times and weights that cadets were required to reach, and an overview of all the specific obstacles and the different variations of them that they might face. "Keep them. You can go to the Common Room now and we will be along to collect you all shortly."

Reece gave her a small, respectful nod as she stood up to leave whilst Baird just watched her leave with total contempt. But Wyn left the room with her head held high. It hadn't been all good news, but it hadn't been horrendous, and they were things she could definitely work on. She was now more determined than ever to improve and be the best in the class, just to wipe the look off of Baird's smug face.

Back in the Common Room, everyone locked eyes on her as soon as Wyn walked in, questioning her on her feedback before she had even made it halfway in. She gave them the bare basics, stating that she needed to work on her running times but had done pretty well in the written exams, especially logic. Before she had entered the room she had gathered herself together and decided what she would and wouldn't say, but even though she had initially decided against it, she ended up nonchalantly dropping in that she was in the top three for overall theory scores. She could tell from the looks being shot around the room that this surprised them and she smiled to herself; maybe showing them that she was genuine competition wasn't such a bad thing. It was time to try and get a bit of respect; she figured she'd need it to survive the next eleven weeks.

As conversation continued, and Dorian and the others returned one by one from the last few debriefs, she gathered that some people had struggled a lot more than others and their abilities were definitely varied. Carter, she was surprised to see, had come fairly high in the academic stuff – she'd never considered him to be that clever. Dorian was sitting in the middle of the pack but had come top for mathematical reasoning. Andrew was top three on his test scores but had been bottom in the fitness. She was starting to piece together a map in her mind of all the cadets and where they sat overall; she needed to work out who was best to befriend in order to use their skills to her advantage and make sure she was a force to be reckoned with.

The room jumped and spun round as the door creaked open revealing Baird, stood silhouetted, his broad frame filling the doorway.

"Line up cadets. The General is ready to speak to you."

They filed back into the lecture theatre where General Baudin was waiting for them. He started speaking before they had all completely sat down.

"Okay, men. You have had your results so I hope that you now know what you need to be working on. There are three afternoons a week scheduled for your personal development, and you will be informed if this will be done in groups with an officer, one-to-one with an officer, or independently. You also have the weekends and evenings which we expect you to use, and the library—located down the corridor as I'm sure you are aware—is open twenty-four hours so make the most of that resource. If you are not seen to be improving in all aspects, but particularly those we have advised you on, then you will be reviewed by the officers and myself and may be removed from the training programme. You will only be given one warning to accelerate your progress, so take it seriously. You are now free for the rest of today. On Saturdays and Sundays, we hold sports tournaments for which you can create teams, and there are other activities. Some of these can directly benefit your training whilst others are just a bit of fun and good for morale – details are on the noticeboard in your Common Room. It is advised that you get involved in the lifestyle on base in order to maintain morale and feel a part of a team, so please do come along."

General Baudin barely took a breath as he spoke to them and his voice maintained an unenthused monotone. Even when trying to inspire recreational activities he managed to make it sound boring and like hard work. He left swiftly without excusing himself and the training officers took back control of the room, releasing them for the weekend.

Chapter 13

The atmosphere had changed completely over the weekend. The cadets examined the noticeboard and set up different teams to enter the tournaments, but Wyn had no interest in embarrassing herself trying to play a sport she had no idea about, so she looked at what else they could do. Saturday afternoon there was an archery session with one of the officers, and she convinced Andrew to go along with her.

She couldn't believe how much fun she found the archery, and the thrill of learning a new, exciting discipline gave her a release of endorphins that lifted her spirits and her self-esteem. Just handling a weapon, albeit primitive compared to the stuff they'd had a glimpse of in the warehouse, gave her a shot of excitement – this is what she'd dreamt about since she was a child. With each go she imagined herself out in the middle of enemy territory, shooting to protect the honour of a nation and becoming a hero in the process. Andrew was excelling with a bow, what he lacked in physical power and strength he made up for in hand-eye coordination and Wyn was pleased to see it. She hoped it would spill over when they got onto weapons training, and that Andrew could come into his own; she couldn't admit to him how concerned she was that she might soon lose one of her few friends in here if he didn't start to show improvement. She couldn't help but get attached to people and she wanted to help him succeed, even if it was distracting her from her main focus. However, she was slightly concerned about her own weaponry skills. She'd always been clumsy and badly coordinated and despite her enthusiasm, by the end of the two hours, she was only just managing to hit the target. However, Officer Crest who ran the session told them that he did it every Saturday, and they were welcome to join him again.

"We'll get you hitting the bullseye lad, just stick with it…" Officer Crest cajoled. He was an older, stocky man, with a round face and glasses. He seemed like a genuinely pleasant and helpful guy and Wyn warmed to him immediately; he reminded her of a slightly larger Brother Aster, which gave her a strange feeling of comfort mixed with homesickness.

Sunday there were other activities but Wyn decided to spend the day in the gym. It was nice to take advantage of it being quiet – most of the others were still involved in the recreational stuff and the cadet's gym was separate from the main one used by the rest of the base. It gave her a chance to practice the free weights that she had tried to avoid when it was busy. Normally, she was worried that her stance and form would be too feminine and give her away, but this way, with only Andrew and another guy she didn't really know, she couldn't be so easily judged. From the guidelines Reece had given her she planned to work methodically through the levels: build up to the next weight, get comfortable with that and then keep getting heavier. She was only just hitting the lowest acceptable requirements; she had a long way to go if she was ever going to impress.

Monday morning was the start of their official training programme. They had been told to get to the lecture theatre for 0900 hours and were all surprised when the man stood at the front was someone they had never seen before: tall and thin, his face was weathered and Wyn noticed that, as he leant forward on the lectern, the hands that rested on top looked like they were made of leather from years of combat and hard graft. This man was no stranger to the military.

"Good morning cadets, I am Major Hardy. I will be taking a portion of your theory classes, initially in the history of the military. These sessions will be the same for the first three weeks, then you will change subjects. The rest of your timetable will be consistent across the next ten weeks. You will be with me this morning, and then this afternoon you will be taken out to run drills and begin training on different equipment. Now, you will find paper and pens in front of you, it is advisable to take notes as you will be tested on the information given. And we are ready to begin…"

Major Hardy launched into an overview of the history of the

forces. Wyn recognised some of it from school history lessons, however, she quickly realised just how much had been left out of their education. Halfway through the first morning and already she knew about wars and weapons that were kept out of mainstream knowledge, but she still noticed a distinct lack of information on the motivations behind the conflict. The first session was just a timeline, and the Major finished off by giving them an outline of the upcoming sessions, identifying that they were going to be given an informative breakdown of everything. There was also going to be special mention of the individuals of note that had displayed bravery or initiative, and the people that had revolutionised and changed how the army did things. Wyn made a mental note to pay attention to this bit, hoping that in the future her name would be up there.

Wyn was finding the whole thing fascinating and was scribbling furiously. Glancing side to side, she noticed a stark contrast between her notes and those of Dorian and Carter – hers were delicate cursive and diagrams, but the boys' looked like spider-scrawled bullet points with rough sketches. She tried to cover the page with her arm as she wrote so that they wouldn't notice, and contemplated just writing the bare minimum, but she knew that having the information would be too important when it came to exams and she was just going to have to try and stop them from seeing her dainty, feminine script.

The session lasted three hours and they were then given an hour for lunch. After that, they were led back out to the field, where the obstacle course had been set back up with the relevant officers back at each station. The cadets were sent to obstacles individually, with the exception of a few who were doubled up—Wyn noticed that these were the stronger, more physical guys who clearly hadn't struggled as much and didn't need so much individual instruction – Dorian and Carter were among them—and they all spent the afternoon facing each of the obstacles again. The officers would make them complete the obstacle, critique them and advise them, making them go again and again until they were doing it consistently, or until their time was up and they were moved on to the next one. By the end of it, they were all exhausted and covered in mud, and acutely aware of where they struggled. There were definite weak points that Wyn would have to address, and back in the Common Room it became apparent that no one had been good at everything.

It was a fairly subdued evening, barely anyone made it into the gym, dinner was fairly quiet, and people showered and got into bed as early as possible. Wyn couldn't work out if it was the physical tiredness from the repetitive obstacles or the mental exhaustion from their first lesson, with information being thrown at them harder than they'd ever experienced before. Whatever it was, she was struggling to keep her eyes open, so she risked sneaking out to the showers far earlier than she felt safe, and, feeling refreshed and free of the caked-on mud, she fell asleep before her head even sank back into the pillow.

Tuesday morning was a tactical session. They were given overviews of different tactics and formations that had been successful through the years, and how that influenced what was used in the modern forces. And the afternoon was the first personal development afternoon of the week. They were called into groups and sent off with different officers, with each group tackling different subjects that the cadets needed to improve on. Wyn, along with Andrew and a slightly overweight guy called Sam, was put through her paces on the relay that had made up the first portion of the initial fitness tests. Between the sprinting and weight carries they were doing sit-ups and push-ups and other bodyweight exercises. By the end of the session none of them could do more than walk from one end to the other, dragging whatever equipment they had behind them, and being yelled at to pick the pace up each time they did. But hopefully the benefits would outweigh the tears that Wyn was trying to hold back as she felt close to collapsing.

The week continued in the same pattern: two sessions a day, with different officers from all across the base. Wednesday morning was sciences and maths – the academic people had a chance to shine and Wyn revelled in the chance to learn aspects of biology, physics and chemistry in more depth than she'd ever done at school. Wednesday afternoon was one-to-ones in enhancing the skill sets they showed most promise in, and they worked with her on her logistics and academic abilities. She was told that her skills could be useful as a tactical adviser or in weapons development, and there was no doubt to her that this was a good sign; if they already had positions in mind that she could fit then she was one step closer to proving herself and ensuring she made it through the process. Thursday was a general skills day; map reading and first aid, survival skills, anything that they might use in the field. Friday morning was more physical

training—either self-directed or with one of the personal trainers—
and the afternoon was more personal development. They were
supposed to take control of their training and build on their weak
points independently, but Wyn watched most of the cadets sneak
back up to the Common Room, avoiding the officers as they tried to
get out of doing any extra work. For Wyn, it was time to start
working on the new goals she had set herself during the week; even
though the morning session had been exhausting, she set herself up
on the track to work on her times. Muddy and tired, she finished the
afternoon with a two-second improvement and extra motivation to
crush the guidelines.

The first week of training had passed as a blur of pain, stress and
exhaustion. The days when she was so close to crying and giving up
were made worse by the fact that she couldn't show it in front of the
rest of the cadets. In those moments, the loneliness of the whole
situation struck her. The only thing she wanted was someone to put
their arms around her and tell her she could do this, but instead, she
could only hug herself under the scratchy blankets at night. Despite
this, interspersed with the difficulties, there were times that she'd
swelled with pride and believed wholeheartedly that she could really
achieve this. She had no doubt that she was going to be pushed to the
edge, but her determination was now more solid than ever. She was
in this for the long haul.

Chapter 14

Training continued and as it continued, it got harder. Each week new officers got involved, and with every aspect mastered, they were given more information to retain and pushed even further past their physical limits. By the end of the second week, another cadet had left, this time of their own accord because they simply couldn't take being shouted at and put down each time they struggled. As guilty as she felt for feeling it, it gave Wyn a sense of smugness and relief to know that no matter what happened now, she hadn't lost face first. At least she hadn't disgraced herself the most. If she was stronger than just one person then maybe she could be strong enough to surpass the rest of them – and that would definitely help her case when she finally got to expose who she was. She needed all the evidence she could in order to avoid the potential retribution.

Even though the training got harder, it seemed that it only brought the cadets closer. Wyn and Andrew were being welcomed in with open arms as the rest of the group continued to realise just how useful they could be when it came to academics and, one-to-one, Dorian would chat to her easily as they got ready for morning line-up. His innate ability to charm gave Wyn a strange tightness in her stomach and made her smile a little bit too much. She really needed to watch that, it was getting a bit out of hand, and she knew from years of watching Kiara that this meant she was one step away from being completely besotted. And with that would come the girly giggle. It was in lectures where she noticed it most. His body was so close to hers that she was always conscious of where he was. Was his body angled slightly towards hers? Wasn't that a sign that he must like her? What if he turned around one day and confessed his love for her and they passionately embraced and...? She had to catch hold of the fantasies that she was creating and remind herself that she was a man now, he wasn't going to like her, but the feelings and the girly excitement came back each time. She chastised herself, but couldn't help but enjoy the daydreams. It was as close to being a girl again as she could get.

By the end of week three, she had successfully started bringing her track time down. She'd started concentrating on her breathing after Oscar, another cadet, had suggested it might help, and she was surprised to see how much of a difference it made. After the first week she had realised that she couldn't survive doing it on a Friday after the physical session, so she got up early on Saturday and Sunday morning and headed out to do a few circuits before most of the base had even ventured past the mess room.

Her Friday afternoons had been replaced with helping some of the other cadets with their studies. Although most of them still tried to get away with a few extra hours of freedom, everyone was acutely aware of their downfalls and time was moving quicker than they'd expected. Wyn liked to help them, going through the lectures from the week and clearing bits up, and it worked as a bit of extra revision to refresh her own memory. Plus, it felt like she was lying to the Collection slightly less – she really was teaching. The added bonus was that it wasn't a one-way deal, they'd trade back ideas and advice, like Oscar on running, or offer out the food stashes brought from home. Wyn had missed decent chocolate.

Most enjoyable for Wyn was the fact that Dorian had asked for help. He liked throwing the tactical plans back and forth and running through them so that they made more sense to him, and she was more than happy to be half of that debate. The only downside was that he and Carter had linked up and she couldn't sit with Dorian without Carter being there. She could have sworn that he was getting cockier, his ego swelling with the top dog status the two of them had gained. She noticed it most when Andrew was helping some of the cadets with their mathematical reasoning; there were a few of them that Carter would snap at to give him some space if they dared to sit too close. The arrogance astounded her and Wyn scoffed under her breath at how pathetic he was each time.

Unfortunately, despite the comradery having seemingly increased, there was still unease in the barracks. Things had started going missing out of people's bunks. It started off just being food and then it went on to being toiletries as well. No one was sure who it was, but Dorian had mentioned to her during their morning chat that he had heard it was Gardiner. He was a quiet guy with a very large stature who kept himself to himself most of the time, and Wyn wasn't sure she'd ever had a full conversation with him, so it sort of made sense that they wouldn't trust him. But in the Common Room she had overheard someone say that they had told Carter about something a few days ago, and now it had gone missing... and Carter seemed far more plausible to Wyn. She made a mental note to watch him even closer and figure it out.

Week four of training meant moving on from Military History. The next subject was Weaponry. Officer Crest was the lead, which made Wyn feel more confident already; they had continued to do archery each weekend so she felt like she was already one step ahead of the others. Monday was theory and all of the cadets were enthralled by the technology and power being presented to them. The complexity and variety along with the different mechanics and engineering were fascinating, even if the level of detail was daunting. From weaponry like bows, swords and daggers, shotguns and rifles, machine guns, lasers and the newest technology on the market, it was an endless stream of exciting tools and gadgets to study.

Friday morning's physical session was taken over by a practical weapons session. The first exercise was taking certain weapons apart and putting them back together, to prove that they had understood the content of the theory session, and then they were let loose on the target range. They were only being taught how to handle the standard technology, they wouldn't be allowed near anything more advanced until they were experienced in the field, but Officer Crest brought a few pieces out of development to demonstrate to them when he knew the General wasn't around. All of the cadets were in their element; this was the sort of stuff that had made them want to sign-up in the first place. Wyn was most pleased to see that her archery sessions were definitely paying off as she hit the target nearly every time, but the same could not be said for everyone—the hand-eye coordination of the group certainly needed work.

The end of week five of training signified being halfway through. The week of selection tests felt like a lifetime ago and Wyn could barely remember what it was like to be able to freely be a girl. The self-awareness she had started with had settled, but she was never relaxed and never forgot, her improved sense of ease just meant that she didn't need to check over her shoulder every five minutes. She'd learnt lots of tricks that made it easier. Changing had started off being a problem and she'd had to hide in a toilet cubicle, but if she always wore a vest then no one saw the binding even if she changed in the dorm. The next thing she'd learnt was to pack pretty convincingly; in fact, she was quite proud of how good she'd gotten at it even if it was an odd skill to have. And the strict rules helped her out as they were regularly given haircuts, so she didn't have to worry about her hair growing out too much. The only thing that still filled her with trepidation was showering. She limited herself to three times a week, less if she could get away with it, and she was starting to feel a bit too used to the grimy membrane that covered her skin.

Mondays were the best showers, after the obstacle course, when they were all caked in thick sludge. She'd brush off what she could once it had dried and get into her bunk as quickly as possible so that no one would comment on the obvious film of dirt still covering her, but when she finally got to wash it off, it was like getting rid of an extra skin and in those few moments, she felt like the stress and pressure were coming off along with the mud. She knew that the beginning of week six would feel no different. The realisation that they had been away from home for so long and the relief of having made it that far was a common emotion running in the air of the cadets; not that any of them could possibly admit to having feelings. But whether they said it aloud or not it was clear that the homesickness was rife, and Wyn had not escaped it; she missed Sister Cariad's cooking, Brother Aster's pep talks and most of all, she missed Sister Astrid, the closest thing she had ever known to a mother. Knowing she was halfway towards breaking their hearts with her deceit was weighing heavy on her. The guilt was overwhelming and brought a lump of panic into her throat whenever she thought about the moment she would have to face them.

She always tried to avoid creeping out to the shower block before about midnight, just to ensure that everyone was asleep, but today she hadn't been able to wait. Leaning against the sinks in the shower block, she looked at herself in the mirror and let the relief course through her as she finally let her guard down. It was the only time she could ever start to relax, not realising how tense she kept her muscles until they started to release. Every inch of her ached with exhaustion. She could feel her eyes closing as she stared at her reflection but shook her head slightly to bring herself back to the present and, taking a step back, she began to unbutton her bed shirt ready to take off the binding.

"I thought you'd be in here."

Wyn jumped, and gathered her shirt closed across her chest, she'd only undone the bottom of the binding so prayed she could keep it covered as she spun around. Carter was stood meekly in the doorway, watching her.

"Carter, what are you... What do you want?" She snapped; her composure was lost as she tried to keep both her modesty and her secret intact.

"I wanted to speak to you, and I've seen you sneak out in the middle of the night before. I've been waiting for days for you to do it again." He took a few steps before her. He looked nervous and sheepish and Wyn was surprised to see his strong, cocky façade missing.

"You what? Speak to me about what?"

"Well, I know who you really are ... and it's such a relief ... you don't have to hide it anymore..." He took a few more steps towards her.

"What? How? I've done everything I could to fit in. How did you know?" Panic coursed through Wyn, nausea rising through her—she'd tried so hard, what had she possibly missed?

"I've seen the way you look at Dorian and watch the boys... Hopefully you look at me like that too... You have been looking my way more recently ... and you've got a gentle side that you can't help but let slip out. You're such an amazing person even though you try to act tough. The way you help everyone with their studies ... and I just, it's such a relief not to be alone anymore. We don't have to tell anyone, we can keep it a secret. But to just have half a relationship with you would make this place worthwhile."

"What do you mean, Carter? How are you not alone anymore, we've never been friends! Why would I ever be with you?"

Carter's face dropped and she could see the hurt flash across his expression as he dropped his eyes to the floor. She was taken aback, since when did he care about her?

"Carter, we've been in school together as long as I can remember and we have never once got along... I don't understand how you think that's changed just by being here!"

Carter's head snapped back up, his brow furrowed and he looked at her in confusion.

"School? What? I never met you before sign-up. I've never even met anyone called Terrell before! I didn't even know it was a name!"

"But you said you know who I am? That you know I'm not really Terrell?"

"You aren't?" Carter stumbled further back from her, his expression a jumble of fear, confusion and panic. "Who the hell are you?!"

Wyn stared at him; she didn't understand what was happening. He seemed so baffled, but he said he knew who she was? She ran her hand through the stubble on her head and looked at him; her eyes pleading him to make this all make sense. There was no escaping this situation now, her secret was out.

"Carter, it's me. It's Wyn."

His eyes widened in recognition. He reached out to catch the wall as he stared her up and down. The horrified confusion was replaced by pure shock, his mouth hanging open as if he was on the verge of saying something but he felt too sick to get the words out.

"Wait, who did you think I was?"

Carter clearly wanted to run, but instead he gave in to the heaviness that was taking over his body and slid down the wall to sit on the bathroom floor. Wyn took a few steps forward and knelt in front of him. She needed answers and she needed to make sure that Carter wouldn't talk. If he'd worked out that she was a girl, even if he hadn't got her exact identity, then surely others were onto her too. If she'd blown her cover then her life was pretty much over.

"I didn't think you were anyone else... I thought you were still Terrell... I just... I just, you were different; you were softer and kinder..." He paused and took a deep breath as though he was about to spit out something disgusting. "I thought you were gay." He whispered the words as if it hurt to say them, staring at the tiles on the floor to avoid her gaze.

Wyn felt the world freeze around her as all the pieces fell into place.

"Wait, does this mean... Carter ... are *you* gay? But, what about all the talk about girls? What about Kiara?"

His head was hung, trying to avoid the question, but she could make out the subtle nodding as a tear rolled down his cheek. He was holding his breath to try and stop the sobs that were rising and he screwed his eyes shut. Wyn looked at him as he shrunk against the wall; she'd never seen him look so human, not a shadow of the arrogant chauvinist that she'd come to hate. Her heart softened and she tentatively reached out a hand and placed it on his arm. He opened his eyes and looked at her with the sadness and shame reading clearly on his face.

"Hey, come on. Breathe, talk to me. Why all the secrets? You were the biggest flirt and womanizer at school? How could you do that to Kiara ... and to all the others? You're gay, so what, nobody cares about that stuff anymore, it doesn't make you any less or anything!" He'd always been the most confident and popular guy she knew; how could he go from that to this quivering wreck curled up on a bathroom floor?

"I ... it's ... I couldn't tell anyone." His chest heaved as he tried to keep his composure and get the words out. "No-one at school was gay..."

"Yes they were, Alex and Jameson in the year above were. I'm sure there were others; we just didn't have a big class." Wyn tried to reassure him before he continued.

"But my dad ... he hates them. He works with a gay man and he's always talking about that 'queer', and how they shouldn't be allowed in society. What if he talked about me like that? What if he disowned me? My brothers would never speak to me again. So, I had to pretend. I've tried so hard to be the top dog. Then no-one will work it out... It's so lonely. I'm just living a constant lie, and I can't bear the thought of kissing a girl when I don't mean it, so then I just have to be a dick and hurt them whenever it gets too far. How I treat people because of it every single day makes me hate myself and what I am even more..." Each word had become more laboured and muffled by the held back emotion until he couldn't control it any longer, and the tears began to fall.

Wyn could feel the core of anger and frustration she'd always held for him melting. He was so lost and she knew now better than ever what it felt like to have to live a lie; she couldn't even imagine the pain and exhaustion of doing it for years. As her feelings towards him softened completely, she reached her arms out and pulled him towards her, letting him sob silently onto her shoulder.

As the snuffling subsided and his body stopped shaking, Carter pulled away from her; his eyes were red and puffy and his cheeks red and glistening from the tears. He looked up at her and smiled meekly.

"I don't get it. You hate me. And … wait…" His eyes widened as he remembered where he was and how she didn't fit. He sat upright, knocking her away from him, his face was serious and his eyebrows furrowed in confusion. "What are you even doing here?"

The abrupt change of attention on to her took Wyn by surprise as she tried to gather together her story in as few words as possible. She hadn't planned for this, she had no back-up or decoy stories. She was just going to have to tell him the truth.

"I… well… I've always wanted to see what was inside. I've always watched the troops going in and out. And Mrs Clay found out that I've always wished to be a part of it. And she's been trying to prove that women should be allowed back in the forces, and back into all the jobs that they used to have before the government got corrupt. So, we had a plan: I prove myself to be good enough to be a soldier and then, when we pass out, I reveal who I am and show them that there is no reason that they can't accept women. Especially when they're so short on people left to sign-up. I just… I wanted an adventure and some excitement, and living in the Collection wasn't it… And Mrs Clay made it sound so important. Like I could change the world…"

As the words tumbled out she could hear how insane she sounded, and the look on Carter's face reflected that straight back at her. She reached forwards and grabbed his hands, clutching them to her.

"You can't tell anyone, Carter. Who knows what they would do to me… People go missing or end up dead. Please." She begged as she squeezed his hands, pure desperation resonating in her voice.

Carter wriggled his hands out of her grip, took a deep breath and locked her gaze.

"You don't tell anyone my secret, I don't tell anyone yours. Deal?"

He held out his hand and she shook it, nodding at him vigorously and silently pleading with him not to betray her. She couldn't easily get rid of the years of mistrust and detestation she'd held, and putting something so massive in his hands made her feel sick, but they both had something to lose so she figured she should be safe … for now at least.

Carter smiled nervously at her and swiftly left the bathroom. In the silence he left behind Wyn tried to work out what had just happened, but the bizarre encounter was still buzzing through her mind, so to distract herself she stripped off as quickly as she could and jumped in the shower. She took a little longer than she would normally risk, allowing the warm water to wash all over her and draw the tension out of her muscles. She couldn't tell if she was relieved to have someone know, that she could maybe even have a confidant to ease the burden, or petrified that she'd lost control and was now more vulnerable than ever. But she knew that it changed things. She closed her eyes, angled her face towards the torrent of water, and savoured her last few moments lost in the therapeutic consistency before traipsing out, doing her binding back up, throwing her clothes back on and sneaking to her bunk. Closing her eyes she felt the familiar choke of anxiety rise into her throat. What was she going to do now?

Chapter 15

The reality of the previous night's revelation hit her the moment she woke up. She'd had a restless night with dreams of being stood in the middle of the yard, guns tracked on her from every direction and the bodies of the Collection lining the path that led to the gates in front of her. She woke up in a cold sweat and felt sick to her stomach; she really could be the reason that their lives would be destroyed and having to trust someone with her secret just made the possibility even greater. She was in too deep to back out but she had so much to lose, and now she had to put her faith in someone that, until last night, she'd loathed for as long as she could remember.

Carter was clearly feeling the same trepidation from their encounter. He was lying on his side watching her as soon as she woke up. His forehead was furrowed and his lips tight, the worry on his face making him look like an eight-year-old waiting for a telling off. Wyn raised her eyebrows at him, reflecting the concern right back at him. He squeezed his eyes shut and took a deep breath. The mutual relief was palpable but, throughout the day, they couldn't help but keep sending each other quick, pleading glances, just to check they weren't suddenly being betrayed. This trusting Carter thing wasn't going to happen easily.

The week passed without any cause for concern as they both grew more comfortable with each other and found they were even voluntarily sitting and chatting in the Common Room. Wyn couldn't help but feel protective over him now, the vulnerability she'd seen in him was something she hadn't even realised he could feel. Maybe he wasn't so bad after all. And he was actually pretty funny and kind of sweet when he wasn't trying to put on a pretence; it made her feel slightly ashamed that, after all those years of being the first to vilify him, it turned out that she might have been wrong. They only talked about what had happened once, and that was when Wyn had caught up with him as he walked back from the mess with the sole purpose of telling him that he needed to tell his brother. He'd looked at her like a deer in headlights, but nodded slowly; now that he'd said it out loud, even he knew it was time he started confronting who he was. She'd also taken the opportunity to ask how he hadn't recognised her despite the fact he'd been in the same class as her every day for years. He scoffed as he agreed how strange it seemed but that, with the shaved head and being completely out of context, she was the last person he'd expected to see so it had just never crossed his mind to put the two together. She was pleased with this response, and it had protected her well enough so far.

Andrew was wary of the new-found friendship, scared both of losing Wyn but also of them being double-crossed. He kept asking Wyn why she was suddenly talking to Carter, reminding her of the rumours about the theft and the distasteful womanizing they'd heard him boast about. But after they sat together a few times in the mess and helped him with his mathematical reasoning skills, he was starting to warm to Carter. And having a little unit was comforting – safety in numbers.

Training wasn't going too badly for any of them either. Wyn finally hit her goal times on the track; she could officially meet the minimum standard for fitness across the board and was still acing anything tactical. All the time they'd spent doing archery had made Andrew top of the class in weaponry, and Wyn could tell the rest of the cadets were jealous that the least macho guy out of everyone was the best at the most masculine thing they could imagine doing. And Carter, with the extra coaching he was getting from Andrew, was finally getting the hang of all the theory.

Wyn was pleased to find that she was even enjoying some of the more practical training, like the survival skills sessions that they had on Thursday. Split into groups of four, each with an officer, they had to complete a full navigation across the moors that spread out beyond the base, accurately obtaining water, food and fuel. They then had to pitch an army-issue tent single-handedly and start a fire, emulating setting up their own camp as they would whilst completing a tour of duty. Wyn's group was by far the least practically-abled, made up of the most academic cadets, and was being led by Training Officer Reece. Over the weeks it had been clearly established that he was far more intelligent and more human than Baird, which had been part of the reason Wyn had encouraged Carter to tell him his secret, but as she worked closer with them, she realised that he also had a great deal of empathy and was a natural teacher. Despite the group not being very practically skilled, he successfully broke down and explained the processes, giving them handy hints and tips that ensured they were successful in achieving their camp. It was a completely draining day, both physically and mentally, but the group ended it confident with their new skill set. Wyn even gave up her evening to practice and master all the different types of knots.

It was permanent chaos; the hours were gruelling, they were being worked harder every day and constantly expected to put more hours in. Each fortnightly review highlighted more things to work on and more personal goals, and the pressure put on them was ever-growing. Evenings and weekends were more training and more practice, no one dared stop or slow down – they'd been threatened every time the General came to watch that no one was safe. One wrong move and they were gone.

Week seven was just as gruelling, and was full of rumours around the mess that things had gotten worse in the field and that they might be called out earlier than expected. It did appear that a few of the regular faces around the base were no longer there as much to train them, so there was certainly reason to believe it, and by the Tuesday of week eight, they were all anticipating something exciting. The afternoon session was starting early and they were all summoned to the lecture theatre instead of individual tuitions. Even though they had been pre-warned that there was an important announcement, not one of the cadets was pleased to see General Baudin stood behind the podium; he eyed them all as they took to their seats, his face never breaking the static scorn that he radiated. Wyn glanced down and noticed that there was an empty seat in front of her. Oscar hadn't come back from lunch and she felt instantly sympathetic for the wrath he was surely going to receive.

"Afternoon. Thank you for bothering to return from the mess room early." He stared at the empty chair as he said it. "This week is an important week for us. As you know, we are now opening up a connection with Special Forces. There is no guarantee that any of you will be selected, or that any of you will be remotely good enough to be considered, as only the true elite will be eligible. This is the potential to gain some of the most prestigious operational positions, after those like myself of course. I expect at least some of you to be good enough or else you will be the most disappointing intakes we have ever had, and we will need to reconsider letting you remain in the Company at all. As such, you should start to look even closer at your weaknesses and get your acts together if you want to survive. Friday afternoon the Head of Special Forces will be coming for an introduction and to inform you of the process they will be taking over the coming weeks; be aware that this was not a planned part of your training so there will be changes to your training programme." The General looked uncomfortable with this thought and Wyn rolled her eyes. Of course he didn't like the lack of control he'd have, especially not around something so important.

The door to the lecture theatre creaked open and Oscar crept in, tiptoeing across the floor despite it being very clear he had nowhere to hide. His face was flushed and he was struggling to conceal the fear as he glanced at the General's overbearing eyes. He wasn't fooling anyone.

"Thank you for deciding to join us; it is simply an honour to be in your presence. What is your name, cadet?" General Baudin's tone was colder than usual, and his gaze pierced through Oscar accusingly. He stopped in his tracks, metres from getting to his seat.

"Um, it's Dartington. Oscar Dartington..." He stuttered as he spoke, staring at the floor and shuffling his feet.

"Well, Dartington, consider this a warning. We will be keeping a closer eye on you." He turned to Reece and Baird. "I'd like a daily report on Dartington's progress – including any indiscretions. Make sure he is behaving with the utmost respect, or else he will need to be dealt with accordingly. I will leave it to you to fill him in on the information he couldn't be bothered to attend for." Wyn could almost detect a hint of enjoyment in Baudin's voice that echoed the joy that was apparent whenever Baird reproached someone, although the General was definitely better practiced at hiding his pleasure.

General Baudin left the cadets without another word and, as Oscar slunk into his seat, the room was silent. Special Forces were coming. They all needed to up their game and the General's threat to Oscar was a reminder of just how disposable they all were.

"Alright, we better get on track. As we have you all gathered we will be doing an additional group lecture. Today we will be looking at the basic communication methods in the field, including the technology we set up in camp to keep a connection with home and therefore receive information for tactics and formations. It's extremely important to know how to use it, and use the radio technology to keep in touch with each other when you're moving around camp, so that you always know where you're expected to be and what you're expected to do. So, let's begin."

Baird launched into a discussion on the basic technology they would use even though it was clear that everyone was still thinking about the information they had just received. If tension had been high before, it was even higher now. Special Forces was the unknown—no matter how strenuous it had been they had all fallen into their routine, and the idea of someone coming in and breaking that was nerve-wracking.

By Friday morning it was all anyone could talk about, speculation was rife: what the Head of Special Forces would be like, what would he be looking for, how many people would they take? The cachet of a role was clear, and the competition for a spot was beginning to unfold. Wyn tried not to listen as they made it sound more and more exciting, it was too much of a risk to be out in the open and under scrutiny, and it was unlikely she'd ever be good enough anyway.

Before they knew it, they were sat in the lecture theatre on Friday afternoon awaiting the arrival of the Head of Special Forces, Special Agent Maddox. General Baudin stood at the lectern looking uneasy. Wyn knew this person was important but clearly they had far greater status than she'd realised—she'd never seen anyone able to make the General look so jittery and awkward. There was a new childish excitement hanging in the air; Special Forces was such an enigma and the chance to be let into their secrets was sending waves through the cadets. Even all of the prior speculation couldn't have predicted the intensity of their curiosity. They sat in anticipatory silence as they waited for their guest to arrive.

It wasn't long before they could hear the melodic footsteps of a group of officers and special agents approaching. As they grew closer, people started shooting looks around the room, questioning each other – were they hearing it too? Amongst the heavy sounds they associated with standard-issue boots was a 'clip-clop', and the closer the noise got, the sharper the clip-clopping became. The questioning looks turned to confusion as it became more and more incontestable – they were definitely the sound of high heels... Was there a woman in the Special Forces team?

It was as if the whole room held their breath when the door was pushed open. In filed five men in full uniform, badges emblazoned their shoulders and chest and the air of authority was clear. In the midst of them was the owner of the noisy walk that every cadet was waiting for. It was so incongruous to see a woman walk in: a mixture of feminine glamour and military order, her pressed uniformed shirt tucked into a tight black pencil skirt, her black court shoes the culprit of the giveaway clip-clopping. She had a flame-red asymmetric bob that faded to a yellow blonde as it got longer, like a fire burning around her immaculately made-up face. Wyn wondered if her personality matched her fiery appearance.

Wyn sighed as she looked at her. She guessed this woman must just be a secretary, there to do the jobs the men didn't want to do. She had never heard of any women being in the military in any sort of capacity, not even in admin, but if there were some then surely getting in by that route would have been easier, and maybe she could have worked on it once she was in. It explained why the General was so uncomfortable; he must hate women even more than they realised to not even want them performing entry-level jobs. Even Mrs Clay had underestimated how much of a problem they were facing trying to change opinions.

General Baudin took a step forward and grimaced slightly. "May I introduce to you the Head of Special Forces, S.A. Maddox." He gestured towards the woman.

The gasp in the room was audible; she was Head of Special Forces? How was that even possible? There weren't supposed to be women in the forces, especially not as the heads of anything! It didn't make any sense!

All eyes were fixed on her as she walked over to the podium with very deliberate, authoritative steps. The cadets were waiting with bated breath to see what she had to say. Reece and Baird were stood to one side staring in shock, whilst the General looked like he was ready to bolt out of the room. S.A. Maddox looked so out of place but stood in front of them with an easy confidence. It might be incongruous to all of them to have a woman around, but she was clearly comfortable holding power over a room full of men.

"Good morning cadets, Training Officers, General." She nodded at each group in turn, and then her eyes slowly scanned the cadets.

She paused as she looked at Wyn and as they locked eyes, her face twitched, but only slightly. Wyn had to fight the panic down; maybe a woman's eyes could work her out. But she'd made it this far, she couldn't fail now, and she frowned in what she hoped was a manly way before swiftly breaking eye contact.

"I am the current Head of Special Forces and have been so for the last twelve years. As we are facing more difficult and more complex opposition, we are requiring new recruits; not just for the numbers but new blood to freshen and motivate the team. We are working our ways around the bases to find the best, and we are hoping some of you will be just that! Following the tests you did in the initial stages of your training, we will be giving you further exams over the next few weeks so we can watch your training. This will allow us to find the candidates that would be best suited to Special Forces and who will give us the greatest advantage over our enemies. Things are not easy and it means the pressure is high for all of us. The specialised training and the situations you will face will far surpass anything you've ever done before. Not everyone makes it through the initial stages, but I'm sure some gems among you will make it all the way!"

She spoke with such passion that the cadets were hanging onto every word, but what they were really hoping for was an insight into all the secrets and mystery that enshrouded Special Forces. They were out of luck, she was choosing her words carefully so as not to give too much away, making it clear that things were on a strictly need to know basis. Wyn hadn't given Special Forces much thought before—her priority was staying under the radar and not drawing attention to herself—but seeing S.A. Maddox made things different. If a woman could defeat the odds and break all the rules to get to such a prestigious rank then surely that was the place that Wyn could have the most impact when she revealed herself. Maybe working with this woman would give her more validity when she proved her worth, and the fact that they had already accepted a female could get her listened to even more. Maybe she could even have an ally against the chauvinistic boundaries. Wyn could feel her focus shifting. She was no longer interested in fading into the background and keeping away from any attention, her sights were set much higher: she was going to make it into Special Forces!

Chapter 16

All of the cadets threw themselves deeper into extra preparation that weekend. Nobody really felt comfortable competing in the weekly tournaments or social sports, and preferred working on their fitness in the gym or their theoretical study. Weeks nine and ten would be a normal timetable but they had already been warned that week eleven would be interspersed with exams and tests specifically set up by Special Forces, and without any idea what they were after it was panic stations for everyone.

The cadets weren't alone in feeling the amped-up pressure and tension; the whole base was in frenzy. All of the officers were pushing themselves into the limelight to try and attract the attention of the Special Agents: the Tactical Development team conveniently started to test new weaponry on the training fields, the mechanics were providing random tours of the vehicles they were working on and repairing, even the older officers were trying to sit with the special agents in the mess and tell stories about their experiences in the field. Wyn found it almost comical to watch but equally unsettling, as she knew that she had nothing she could safely reveal that would set herself apart. Were Special Forces worth the possibility of condemning herself?

Week nine was constant scrutiny. Even in lectures where they were just listening and making notes, there was an S.A. sat at the front, watching them all and writing everything down. Wyn's mind wandered off the subject matter at hand and drifted to what the S.A. could possibly be recording; was it how much attention they paid, how studious they looked, or some deeply psychological reading of their body language and reactions? The more she thought about it, the more she carefully navigated every movement, ensuring she kept her posture strong, made a note of everything said, and nodded along in all the right places. She had put so much effort into trying to come across the way she thought they might want her to, she completely missed half of the theory and had to sit with Andrew in the Common Room each evening so that he could explain to her the bits of her notes that had become spider-scribbled nonsense.

Wyn was pleased to need Andrew's help, even if she found it embarrassing to admit to falling behind. It wasn't quite as lonely as it once had been as she had Carter now, but Andrew's involvement in the wider group made her uneasy. He spent a lot of the time with Dorian and a couple of his sidekicks, and there was a small knot of jealousy that lay in her stomach whenever she thought about how it could have been her getting close to Dorian until Andrew had taken that away from her. Even from a distance she couldn't help but feel all girly at his cocky demeanour as he commanded the attention of the group. How was it that the very thing that she had detested in Carter she was starting to find attractive in Dorian, and why did these feelings have to start at all? It had been nothing but frustrating since day one; not to mention inconvenient.

Alongside Andrew, Wyn had continued to help the other cadets in the academic subjects that they struggled with, and she was pleased that the tutoring had given her more chance to get to know Carter; not the idiot she'd spent so long avoiding but the person who had finally opened up to her. And, whilst they were going through some chemical equations in a break between lectures, Wyn took her chance to bring up one of the few things she couldn't shake, the thing that had been playing round in her head and that she was desperate to prove wrong: was Carter really behind the thefts?

"Look, Carter…" She pushed the textbooks aside and stuttered as she spoke, keeping her tone hushed as she feared being overheard. "All the stealing that was going on, in the bunks… Dorian said, well, he thought it was Gardiner first off, but then everyone was saying it was you … and I just, I need to know. I need to know if I really can trust you … with everything…"

Carter's face visibly dropped and the hurt that ravaged his expression made her feel like she'd just kicked a puppy. He stared at the table a moment before raising his head and locking his pleading eyes with hers.

"How can you think that? I get that you didn't like the person I was at school, but that was a front, you know why I was like that… And even then, I never did anything like that! I never would! And don't even get me started on Dorian…" Anger was creeping into his voice. "He's to blame for all of it. He told me not to say anything, and I wanted to keep him on my side, so I didn't. But he's stealing it. He's using Gardiner – tells him what he wants and then Gardiner gets it for him. I've seen what he's like. He threatens and he bullies and … and now he is blaming everyone else and getting away with it! He's vile… And you need to stop him getting his claws any further into Andrew before he starts using him as well…"

Wyn hushed him as the volume of his voice raised with all of the frustration built up behind it. She glanced across the room to where Andrew was sat with Dorian, Gardiner and another cadet. They weren't studying, just chatting, and Wyn feared that Carter may be right. With the way Dorian behaved it did make sense. How could she have been such an idiot to fall for someone who was so cocky and full of himself? He reflected back at her all of the traits she'd always despised; she'd known it from the start but hadn't listened to her intuition and she'd just let herself get sucked into his charm and handsome appearance, using a potential romance with him as a fantasy distraction from the macho world she now inhabited. And even now, believing all that Carter had just said, she couldn't help but get distracted from her frustration by the way his arm muscles moved as he reached for his glass.

She looked at Carter and nodded, silently reassuring him that she believed him before she pulled the textbook back in front of them and carried on as if the conversation had never happened. After dinner she headed out to the track to work on her time and clear her head; she needed to figure out a way to protect Andrew before he got manipulated.

Chapter 17

Time on the track and re-visiting that week's lesson on the different types of grenades and ambush tactics took up most of her Sunday, which meant Monday morning came all too quickly and with it her least favourite part of the week: obstacles. She felt a bit brighter about it after lunch, which had been a jacket potato with chilli left over from the night before—she always enjoyed it when it was something that reminded her a bit more of home—but the feelings of dread returned the moment they walked back to the barracks to get changed. Reece was stood to one side, watching them all as they passed out through the doorway ready to head towards the field. Once Wyn had crossed the threshold and was on the path he, cleared his throat.

"Cadet Rigg, please step aside. Everyone else, you may continue to the course."

He didn't normally sound this official and there was an odd undertone that Wyn couldn't put her finger on. She looked up at him with quizzical concern; what had she done? Surely if she'd made some sort of mistake it would be Baird staying to reprimand her, no one was blind to the fact he revelled in being authoritarian. She couldn't think of any reason why Reece would need to talk to her, and her mind was desperately running back through the last few days in case there were any indiscretions that she had managed to miss. He took a step back, ushering her to follow him so that they were concealed between the barracks and the adjacent block. Her concern grew.

"Okay, um … well … Carter told me what you did for him. I can't believe he's been keeping this a secret for so long. It doesn't make him any less of my brother so I don't know why he was so worried about it. And, Wyn, I just wanted to say thank you..." He looked nervous as he started to talk and his words quickly faded away as he saw the horror that had spread across Wyn's face.

"What? He told you? He told you who I am? What are you going to do? Are you going to tell them? What are they going to do to me?"

The panic was setting in and she couldn't control the rambling questions that were spilling out. She'd been an idiot. She should have known she couldn't trust Carter. He was still a snake in the grass just like she'd always thought; her life was over.   Her breathing was quick and shallow and she could feel a lump in her throat; she felt physically sick. She could feel herself shaking but didn't know what to do next or how to escape this moment without making it worse. Staring at the floor, she couldn't even bring herself to look at the man who might be about to destroy her future.

Reece looked at her with unease and, without thinking, reached forward and grabbed hold of her hands to stop her shaking.

"Wyn, breathe, please, calm down. I'm not going to tell anyone. You've been there for my brother even though I know how much hard work he can be. There is no way I won't help you out – it's the only way I can say thank you. That's what I was going to talk to you about, I have the report for your last obstacle course – I can tell you what you need to do." He was squeezing her hands as he pleaded with her, his grip strong despite his clammy, rough palms. As his eyes locked with hers she started to believe that he was genuine in what he said; she'd never seen him treat anyone with anything less than complete decency and her intuition was telling her that maybe she really could trust him. His eyes were deep mahogany like his brothers, and by concentrating on his intense stare she slowly managed to regulate her breathing.

"Really? You'll really help me?" She questioned, though she could hear the cracks that still echoed through her voice. "I'm still going to kill him," she added under her breath.

Reece laughed softly and nodded at her before he realised that he still had a tight grip on her hands. He dropped them suddenly and smiled at her gingerly.

"Of course I will, I even remember you from school – you were always in Carter's class and everyone was always fascinated by the girl from the Collection. You were always so different... I mean, it wasn't a bad thing... Look, I told Dean, I mean, Training Officer Baird, that we had some housekeeping to go over at the request of the General—that you needed to straighten your bunk up a bit—so they are expecting you to be a few minutes late for the session. Shall we sit down and I can go through it with you quickly?" He gestured back towards the barracks and the common room, and Wyn nodded gratefully. She followed him back into the block and sat next to him at one of the round wooden tables.

"Okay, let me find the report from last week..." Reece fumbled around in his pockets trying to locate the paper he had brought with him. Wyn watched him carefully as her mind went over what had just happened.

"Wait, Training Officer Reece, before you do that, I just wanted to check... You really are okay with Carter, aren't you? With him being gay?" Even with the sense of betrayal that she now felt, she couldn't help but want to protect him, even against his own brother.

"Wyn, please call me Cole—when it's just us of course... Training Officer Reece sounds so ... official. Of course I am; he's my baby brother. Our older brother and my dad find it hard to understand—something to do with an uncle that I don't really remember—but it's never bothered me. When I was a new recruit there were a couple of guys, including an officer, who were openly gay, and it doesn't change who they are. Thinking about it, I don't know what happened to them in the end, haven't seen them in a long time, but, anyway, I think even Dad and Caleb would be able to see past it eventually. It'd definitely take a while but they'd always love him regardless, even if they didn't agree. Anyway, we don't have much time. Here's your obstacle feedback."

Wyn admired the way he spoke, it was just a stream of contemplative consciousness, his voice unwavering, and she was relieved to have one less person to protect Carter against. Having lived by the Collection's values for so long, she felt instantly connected to Cole's words. She couldn't help but smile at how accepting the man in front of her was and how he took it on board without a second thought. It was as it was and he was okay with that. Wrapped up in her thoughts of how much she admired his openness, and caught up again at the depth of colour in his eyes, she barely noticed that she wasn't paying attention to what Cole was talking about until he snapped her back to attention.

"Wyn? So, what do you reckon, which obstacle will be the

hardest to work on...? Wyn?"

"Sorry, what? I... umm..." She looked at the sheet he'd placed in her hands; her scores weren't terrible but they definitely needed to be better to impress S.A. Maddox. "Well, the water obstacles I struggle with most. I think I'm getting to grips with most of the rest of it..."

"Right, yeah, your scores aren't too bad. You need a bit of work on the wall, you just need a bit more force behind you when you start. You start off too slow and don't have the power to propel yourself up, that's why you struggle to reach the top sometimes. Go at it with a bit more confidence."

He glanced down the list, leaning closer to her as he adjusted his angle so he could see the paper a bit easier. Wyn was acutely aware of the warmth coming off his body as his shoulder grazed hers.

"You ace all of the fiddly stuff. Going through the nets and negotiating small spaces everyone is really impressed with. Your size and agility make you perfect for it – and I reckon that's the sort of stuff that Special Forces are going to want. But you're right; the water obstacles are what let you down. It doesn't help that you can't swim."

Wyn looked down, embarrassed. There were three water obstacles – one was to swim underneath a series of obstructions, another was a distance swim across a manmade lake, and the third was an ice bath to wade through. That one wasn't so bad, but the other two she had pretty much had to miss out every time. She'd given doggy paddling a go once but she had ended up splashing about in a panic, choking on a cascade of water in the process and embarrassing herself even more, which was attention she certainly didn't need. They had said from the beginning that it wasn't a vital skill and it wouldn't stop her making it through as long as she really upped her game on the other obstacles, but she was sure Special Forces would look at it differently. She needed to impress. Cole saw the change in her expression and smiled sympathetically. He screwed his face up briefly and then looked at her determinedly.

"You know what, sneak out after lights out and I'll teach you to swim properly. I'll meet you by the lake at eleven and we'll sort this out. Just be careful, you can't get caught or else both of our lives are over, and you'll have to cope on a few hours less sleep for a day, but it'll be worth it to impress Special Forces!" He paused, caught off guard by his own offer, and the seriousness of what could happen to them was heavy in his eyes; Wyn knew how much he was risking by offering to help her, and gratitude mounted inside her. "Now, we've got to get to the course. Don't forget what I said about the wall."

He smiled at her softly before getting up from the table, running his hand nonchalantly through his hair as if trying to reset to the serious, impersonal training officer he had been before their conversation. Wyn followed him, grabbing her feedback report off of the table and dashing into her bunk to stash it in her drawer as they passed the dorm, pleased at the concept of finally getting a chance to complete the whole course.

They walked up to the course with a massive gap between them and didn't say a word, trying too hard to make it look like a normal training officer and cadet interaction. But out of the corner of her eye Wyn couldn't help but watch him and his strong, confident strides. She smiled to herself; maybe Carter really had done her a favour after all. Cole could be her ticket into Special Forces.

By the time they got there, the briefing was complete and the rest of the cadets were already lined up ready to start on the obstacles. Cole sent Wyn straight to the back, shooting her a subtle half-smile as their eyes met, before straightening up and turning to Baird who was policing the front of the line. One by one they completed the course, were called back to order and sent again. They completed the circuit three times each and Wyn couldn't help but feel a swell of pride at how much of a difference she had made on the wall with Cole's advice in the back of her mind; there was no way that this course report wouldn't be an improvement!

Chapter 18

That evening their time in the mess and common room passed quicker than usual and it was lights out before Wyn knew it. She lay in the darkness staring at the ceiling, counting the ticks of the clock as she waited in trepidation for her swimming lesson. The slivers of moonlight that came through the windows and cast shadows around the room shed just enough light on the clock for her to work out when to get back up and, at 22:55, she crept through the dorm door towards the shower block where she had stashed a pair of old shorts and a t-shirt. She slipped into them and, as silently as she could manage, tiptoed back down the barracks corridor, out of the heavy swinging door—guiding it shut as gently as possible behind her—and headed down towards the lake.

As she neared the water's edge Wyn started to panic. She couldn't see Cole and the mistrust she felt towards his brother rose once again towards him; had he stitched her up, was he not going to show? She stared intently at the water, mentally running through all the options she had if he didn't turn up and had betrayed her secret instead, until she heard heavy boot steps walking down behind her. She could feel herself holding her breath involuntarily, subconsciously trying to make herself invisible just in case it wasn't Reece. And she could not will herself to turn around, putting off the moment she found out for sure for as long as possible.

"Come on then miss, let's get you in the water, you'll be as comfortable as a fish in no time."

It was Cole, thank goodness. She wasn't used to this jokey demeanour when he was in officer mode and his encouraging tone put Wyn at ease, her tension was broken and she could feel herself physically relax. She turned towards him and smiled slightly as she watched the moonlight highlighting the strength of his chiselled jawline. There was something about the mystery of the moonlit shadows that highlighted a handsome bone structure in a way she hadn't really noticed before, but she supposed it made sense – he was Carter's brother and she'd spent hours listening to Kiara and the girls outlining just how attractive *he* was, so there were obviously good genes at play.

"Umm… Okay…" Wyn stammered. She didn't know why she sounded surprised. Yes, she was apprehensive about the swimming but she knew she would have to get in the water. But doing so, with the attention of someone who was very much her superior solely focused on her, was far more daunting than she'd anticipated. She slipped her shoes off and dipped her toe into the edge of the lake, gasping at how cold the water was.

Cole could sense the nerves radiating from her and kicked off his own boots before striding down the bank of the lake until it lapped against his knees. He shot her a reassuring smile and raised his eyebrows, signalling her to follow his lead. She swallowed, squeezing her eyes shut as she pushed down her anxiety and stalked in after him. After the initial shock of the temperature, she started to adjust; if nothing else then the cold might stave off the inevitable tiredness that would set in shortly. She looked at Cole intently, waiting for her first instruction.

"Okay Wyn, let's see what you've got." He gestured to her to demonstrate how far her skills in the water went. Wyn splashed down and attempted to doggy paddle but barely made it a metre before she panicked at how difficult it was to keep her mouth and nose clear, and she stood back up abruptly. Her embarrassment meant she could barely look at him long enough to gauge his reaction to her failed attempt.

"Come on Wyn, you can do this. Just put your head under the water and get used to how it feels. You need to try and get used to the water if you're ever going to be a strong swimmer."

"I can't! I'll drown!" She couldn't keep the childish whine of fear out of her voice.

"You won't; for a start, I won't let you, and secondly, your body won't let you—well, not easily." Cole went quiet, thinking about where was best to start. "Tell you what, there's something my dad used to do with me and my brothers to show us that our heads would always float." He stepped towards her and cupped his hands under the water. "Make your face touch my hands, but without forcing your head down – it has to sort of just drift down."

Wyn looked at him in horror, but she knew that, with all that Cole was risking to help her, she couldn't keep behaving like a petulant child. She had to get over herself and start to put in the work. She lowered herself into the water and attempted to do as instructed. She was frustrated to find, despite trying more than once, that she couldn't. She'd failed at the first hurdle and she huffed, brushing the water from her eyes as she regained her balance. She was moments away from stamping her feet in a toddler's tantrum— she couldn't do anything right! She threw her hands into the water in anger, splashing herself and Cole in the process.

"I can't! It isn't working…"

"Exactly, your head is pretty buoyant so it will never be that far from the surface of the water even if your face is underneath, so you don't need to worry about not being able to get back up for air. Unless you are intentionally trying to swim deeper, but we don't need to worry about that bit just yet, let's get you happy with the basics first."

Cole was a natural teacher; empathetic and encouraging, and he quickly tried to introduce her to the basics that would hopefully get her swimming. He helped Wyn lie in the water and see that she could float, despite her horror at having to take her feet off the bottom. He made her hold onto his arms for support whilst she started to practice kicking her legs, and he showed her the different arm movements that made up the different strokes.

Two hours later and Wyn was exhausted. She was relieved when she noticed Cole trying to stifle a yawn and hoped that the lesson would soon be over, despite the fact she still hadn't actually successfully swum anywhere. She just didn't know how much longer she could cope without falling asleep in the water and her desperation to sleep far outweighed any urgency to master the skill. Seeing the weariness that was evident as Wyn struggled to regain her balance, Cole decided it was time to quit whilst they were ahead.

"Okay. I think we've done pretty well. You seem more confident with the water and you've got to grips with a lot of the basic movements, now all we need to do is put them together and get you moving. So how about the same time tomorrow and we'll get that together. After that, you'll be in a position to start practicing in your free time and you can do it for PD sessions too?" He continued as he noticed the questioning look he was being shot. "People always start working on new things once they've got to grips with all their other challenges, so it won't seem that strange... Plus, everyone will be getting more on top of things for Special Forces so you won't be the only one."

Wyn crawled back into bed, having changed back into her bed shirt and towel-dried her hair—another convenience of the boyish buzz cut she was now used to—but she was sure that she smelt like the lake. The murky water scent lingered in her nostrils as she fell into a deep sleep that gave her dreams of underwater caverns with banished sea witches; a world where she was the hero who swam into the depths to rescue the prince. She awoke to the early reaches of sunlight cascading between the blinds and was disappointed that she hadn't managed to reach the prince in time for morning. Even in her dreamland she couldn't complete her tasks; what hope did she have in the real world?

She was drained after what felt like half a night's worth of sleep and it had given her a new-found pessimism at the world, despite the progress she had made in the water with Cole. Even the Tuesday morning tactical session, which was normally one of her favourites of the week, didn't hold the same allure as it usually did and the squiggles on the paper in front of her barely resembled real letters. But at least for once her notes looked closer to those around her.

"What's up with you, Rigg? You're as pale as anything today. And you've barely touched your lunch." Oscar queried as they were sat in the mess at lunch.

Wyn looked down at the slop of grey lamb stew in front of her. Just the sight of it turned her stomach. There were two cooks on base: Mary, who cooked proper, homemade food with love, and Agnes, whose method was batch cook something that would give her leftovers to use for lunch the next day. Wyn wasn't sure the woman even knew what seasoning was. This was definitely a dish courtesy of Agnes. She was eternally grateful for Mrs Clay's insistence that she brought extra supplement bars with her; she'd saved them for the days she couldn't face the mess food so that at least she was still getting some sort of nourishment. On seeing her expression when she eyed up the plate, Oscar continued.

"I'll have it if you don't want it?"

Wyn grimaced and pushed the tray over to him, she was more than happy to get rid of it.

"I'm just really tired. I don't know if I'm coming down with something maybe…" Wyn flapped. There was no pretending to be fine today, there was nothing she could do to cover the dark circles sat underneath her eyes and her lack of concentration had led to more than one exasperated call back to the real-world during conversations. She just hoped she could brush it off and get through the afternoon. How she was going to survive her next swimming lesson she really wasn't sure.

Being week ten, they were now trusted to pretty much guide their own personal development session based on the feedback in their fortnightly reviews, so she had been planning on finding a quiet corner of the common room with a notepad and pretending to study whilst using up as little energy as possible. But as she left to walk across the yard from the mess, Officer Crest was also coming out and called her name. Wyn stopped and spun round. If it had been any other officer she'd have been in a panic, but there was always something comforting about Crest.

"You look rough today cadet, and I heard what you said to Dartington. I'm down to oversee PD this afternoon so, tell you what, sneak back to the dorm and crash for a few hours. I won't tell, and I can still put you on the sign-in sheet so no one will pick up on it. Better you sleep off whatever you're coming down with now—you need to be on top form for Special Forces next week." He shot her a friendly wink and chuckled at himself before turning back towards the mess. Wyn let out a deep breath and smiled to herself.

After an extra few hours' sleep, Wyn felt almost human again and had revived rigour to crack the whole 'swimming after dark' thing. When she joined the rest of the cadets at the dining table she was shot a few knowing looks, but no one said anything. She'd started to think back through other mysterious recoveries and temporary disappearances during personal development, and suddenly they all made sense. Her afternoon nap had reset her spirits and she wasn't even disheartened when yet another ladleful of lamb stew landed on her tray, although she really couldn't understand how Agnes had made it last for a third meal – it was impressive laziness if nothing else.

Worn down by days of non-stop study and practice, the cadets all decided they needed something a bit more light-hearted for the few hours before lights out and, to everyone's surprise, Andrew brought out some playing cards he'd smuggled in. Wyn was proud of her friend as she knew he'd been scared of admitting this contraband to the rest of them; he just hadn't had the confidence to have all eyes on him. But the impressed expressions around the common room combined with the swell of pride and well-needed arrogance as Andrew puffed his chest out that little showed that he'd had nothing to worry about. No-one had expected goody-two-shoes Andrew to have snuck anything in; he was certainly not perceived to be a natural rule breaker and in doing so, he had earned himself a small nugget of respect. The card tournament that ensued was just what everyone had needed, and the laughter and friendly banter thrown around the room gave Wyn a warm glow; this was the comradery she'd always imagined when she'd watched the troops marching together, and she was finally a part of it.

After lights out, Wyn had no problem staying awake for her late-night swimming lesson. The evening had left her in a good mood which gave her reinvigorated motivation, and it wasn't long before she was creeping back down to the edge of the lake.

Cole was waiting for her in the same spot they had met the night before and greeted her with a nod and a slightly apprehensive smile. He instructed her to get straight into the water, as they had a lot to cover and he couldn't risk them sneaking out for a third night. He followed her in and immediately waded away from the edge until the murky water was hiding his shoulders.

"Okay, out here today. You can't hide in the shallows forever." He watched as Wyn tentatively inched across the bed of the lake. "You're nearly there, keep going," Cole encouraged, but there was an intensity to his voice she hadn't heard before. He sounded serious and lacked his usual softness, Wyn wondered if someone had noticed him missing the night before or if she'd done something wrong. The thought hung heavily on her, she didn't want to upset the most genuine person she'd met since signing up.

As she neared Cole, Wyn was having to stand on tiptoes to keep her head above the water and she could feel the panic set in. She hadn't properly swum at all yet, so what was she doing out where she could so easily drown?

"Okay, one more step out, and then I want you to tread water. It's good to be able to do it anyway, but once you've done that, you can easily be out in the deep water. Then you've just got to piece together everything we've done." The look on Wyn's face made it clear that she had no idea what he was talking about. "Okay, move your arms forward and backwards under the water, and circle your legs under the water. Then you'll keep your head out of the water and keep yourself floating upright. Ready? Step towards me and then go."

Wyn did as she was told but the panic coursed through her as she realised she could no longer touch the bottom. After just a few seconds of keeping herself upright, drifting further into the middle of the lake, she was consumed with just how dark and endless it seemed below her and, looking around for the comforting sight of safety, she gasped as she realised how far away from the bank she now was. The sudden intake of breath brought with it a mouthful of water; she spluttered and as she tried to keep herself afloat whilst trying not to choke, fear completely overcame her. She felt the darkness setting in as she was consumed with terror. She writhed around and sent waves across the lake, before reaching out to Cole, who had been hovering nearby in case she needed help, and clasped her arms around his neck. She pulled herself into him and buried her head into his shoulder, trying desperately to regulate her breathing. Cole brought one arm across her back to support her, and used the other to push through the water and get back to somewhere he could comfortably stand. He could feel how much she was shaking and, with two feet now firmly back on the lakebed, he used both hands to gently prise her away from his shoulder so he could look down at her. Wyn released her grip, realising she had been clawing her nails into his back, and rested her arms on his shoulders as she tried to feel secure stood on the soil that felt like it was melting away underfoot; she looked back up at him with terror-stricken eyes.

"Sorry, Wyn, maybe that wasn't such a good idea. I shouldn't have made you do it. I'm sorry... I just wanted to help." Cole's whole demeanour was deflated and he immediately broke eye contact with her. Wyn felt a rush of emotion towards this man who had gone out of his way to help her, and she was overcome with disappointment in herself for having let him down.

"No, Cole, I'm sorry... I shouldn't have panicked... I..." Cole still wouldn't hold her gaze and, desperate to reassure him and make him realise that he'd done nothing but be wonderful, Wyn reached one hand up and pulled his face down to meet hers. As she did, she brushed her lips against his. Cole stepped back, shocked, and looked at her with wide, questioning eyes.

"I think it's time we stopped. You can always try again in your free time or something. I'm… We…" Cole stopped mid-sentence, unsure of what he was planning on saying next and, without another word, strode out of the water and back towards the dim lights of the residential complex. Wyn stood in the lake on her own, completely baffled and taken aback by her own impulsivity. What had she been thinking? Even though he knew the truth, she was still a boy to Cole—of course he was going to freak out. A solitary tear ran down her face as she stared after him and, with a tiny, almost inaudible splash, it dripped into the lake.

Chapter 19

Sleep did little to diminish Wyn's embarrassment about the night before. She didn't know if she was more embarrassed for having done something so out of character in the first place, or about the horrified rejection she had faced in response to it. Equally, she was angry at herself, frustrated that she allowed her emotions to take over and had let him get under her skin. She was dreading having to face Cole, and was hoping that whatever one-to-ones they ended up with during their afternoon session, Cole was in no way involved with hers. However, not knowing what he was thinking was sending her imagination into overdrive. As she splashed cold water over her face to wash off the shaving foam she used as a pretence every morning, she steadied her breath and stared herself down in the mirror. Only the two of them knew about her humiliation, so she couldn't show anyone else that something was up. If anyone found out that she'd tried to kiss an officer, then her secret would most certainly be out.

As they traipsed out of the barracks to breakfast, Andrew matched his pace to Wyn's.

"Are you alright Terrell, you still don't seem normal? If you are coming down with something then maybe you should go to the health centre after breakfast."

Wyn smiled appreciatively at Andrew's concern and shook her head.

"I'm fine, just not sleeping right. I guess I'm just nervous about what Special Forces are going to make us do next week."

Andrew seemed content with this answer and began to express his own concerns over Special Forces. He was certainly not at the top of his game physically, although he could at least hit the minimum requirements across the board now, and although his intellect far surpassed any other cadet it would only be any use if he had the confidence to show it. They started chatting about what they were going to focus on over the rest of their PD sessions and during their free time. And over breakfast, some of the other cadets joined in the discussion.

"I'd like to practice swimming, so I can complete the obstacle course." Wyn threw into the conversation, pleased she'd had a chance to bring it up so it wouldn't seem quite so out of the blue if she did get a chance to try it again. That was one thing she was now determined to do – put Cole's teaching to good use. If nothing else, she wanted to show him that he hadn't done anything wrong by helping her.

"Ooh, that's a good idea! If they let you use the lake, I might come and give it a go too." It was Rowan; Wyn remembered he was one of the cadets who also admitted to being unable to swim on their first obstacle course. Now someone else wanted to do it, she really had to follow through.

Once in the lecture theatre ready for their morning session, Wyn had to face up to seeing Cole, who was stood in his usual spot at the front of the room watching the cadets as they filed in. The moment he saw her he looked at the floor and, despite trying to catch his eye for the rest of the morning, silently pleading with him to give her a look that would show everything was okay, Wyn didn't get another opportunity to communicate with him.

By lunchtime, she was feeling even more frustrated and mortified by the lack of reassurance. She ate as quickly as possible so that she could wordlessly disappear back to the barracks and once she got there, she sat in the eerily peaceful silence of the dorm room for as long as she could before she was due back. She just needed the time to clear her head, which was incessantly spinning; the whole Cole thing had made her feel emotional and vulnerable, and that had given all the emotions she'd been trying to ignore an opportunity to come bubbling up to the surface—fear of being caught, concern she wasn't going to be good enough and, more than anything, a desperate sense of homesickness. She'd kept it buried for so long and tried not to think about the Collection, but having someone be caring towards her and then losing them just made her want to curl up in Sister Cariad's arms like she had done as a child. She rubbed her eyes as if to brush the thoughts away, then put back on the emotionless mask that Terrell showed the world, and headed back down the corridor.

"Wyn! Wait up!"

Wyn jumped, taken aback by Carter, who was tucked into the doorway of the shower block. She spun towards him and scanned the rest of the corridor to check no one else was around.

"Carter? What are you doing? Why would you use my real name? And why did you tell Cole… You promised you wouldn't, how could you?" She spat the words out at him in anger. She had intentionally been trying to avoid him, she didn't even want to look at him; all she saw reflected back was betrayal. Carter looked at her sheepishly.

"I'm sorry, I really am, but Cole will be fine, he won't say anything. That's what I wanted to talk to you about—what did he do to you?"

Wyn looked at him, puzzled. Had Cole told him about the kiss and Carter got confused?

"What do you mean, he didn't do anything, what has he said?" She tried to keep the edge of panic out of her voice.

"Well, he said he upset you. He was being really quiet, so I asked what was wrong. He said that he'd tried to help you to say thank you for helping me, but that he got it wrong and upset you, and…" He trailed off, not really knowing anymore to the story and struggling to work out how best to question an already prickly Wyn.

"He didn't do anything, he was being brilliant. I misread the situation and I…" Wyn stopped herself, suddenly remembering her anger towards Carter, and becoming overcome with annoyance at herself for nearly telling him what happened. She didn't need to relive the humiliation, especially not for Carter's sake. She shook her head at herself and tried to take control of the situation. "Look, it doesn't matter. It's fine, we're fine, tell your brother that. Now just drop it; you are in no place to be questioning me after how you risked my entire future. You forget about this and I'll give you a second chance, just don't betray my trust again!" She spat the words at him before finishing abruptly and sternly. Before Carter could get a chance to respond, she turned her back and stalked away, leaving him baffled in the doorway.

Wyn felt a bit better for her outburst and knew that deep down she had forgiven Carter, she just didn't want him to know that yet. But she was still concerned by just how much she had affected Cole. She really needed to speak to him even though she didn't want to face up to it; she couldn't bear the thought of him ruminating on it. She didn't get an opportunity to catch him alone for the rest of the day, nor did she on Thursday, when they spent the day doing group skills work. It seemed to her that Cole had intentionally put himself at the head of the other group and left Baird to be with hers. He had smiled at her across the room, and it gave her a warm, butterfly feeling as well as a shot of comfort, but it still wasn't enough to get rid of the tension.

Friday morning, they gathered at the entrance to the gym as normal for their physical training session. They had been doing circuits the week before and everyone expected there to be more of the same. However, they were surprised when Garth, one of the personal trainers, stood in front of them and commanded attention.

"We've had a suggestion today that we start to look at the specific physical skills you need to work on, see if we can apply any new techniques that'll help you in things like the obstacle course. We've identified that some of you need to work on your track skills – like how best to get off the mark, breathing techniques, and all that stuff. A couple of you need to work on your flexibility for all the fiddly stuff, so you're going to be doing a yoga session and learning some new stretches. Then we've got the couple of you that need to learn to swim." Wyn's head shot up from where she'd been watching a spider spinning a web across the corner of a window frame. "Thank you to Training Officer Reece for the suggestion of the session." He nodded in Cole's direction and then divided them up in accordance to who needed to learn which skill, directing them towards the relevant trainers.

Wyn's eyes flew over to Cole, who was watching her with a small apprehensive smile and concerned eyes. She locked his gaze and smiled, trying desperately to reassure him that he'd done the right thing and convey her thanks through her eyes, but she wasn't sure that the message had been fully received. Once they'd been dismissed to go to their relevant training, she walked slightly out of her way so that she could slow her pace as she walked by him. As she passed a tiny bit too far into his personal space, he quietly whispered:

"I hope that's okay? I thought this way at least no one will think it's strange when you suddenly know how to swim…"

Wyn nodded at him. The instant relief in his eyes overwhelmed her and she got the urge to give him a hug; she walked off as quickly as possible so she didn't let her impulses overcome her once more.

The session went surprisingly well from there. It was Garth that took the swimming session and, thanks to her night-time lessons, Wyn felt a bit more natural and comfortable being in the water. Cole's instructions were at the back of her mind and she was pleased to see that, alongside Garth's teaching technique, she could piece the basics together a lot quicker than Rowan and the others. After three hours in the water, Wyn had just about managed to clumsily swim an entire length of the lake and couldn't help but beam at herself as Garth called out his praise in amidst a few pointers. Of the four of them, three had made the full length of the lake, and Wyn was pleased to note that she had been the first.

"Well done guys, you all made progress." Garth addressed the group. "I've spoken to Major Hardy and he's agreed that you can have access to the lake during personal development sessions and in your free time if you want to continue to build on this skill; you might not be up to the underwater obstacle yet but I think you should all be able to tackle the other two with a bit more confidence."

They were dismissed for a well-earned lunch, and Wyn left the lake physically exhausted but with a strong sense of achievement. This was the kind of step she really needed to be taking if she was going to impress Special Forces.

Chapter 20

As she was focusing on her swimming, the weekend flew by and she slept better than she had in weeks thanks to the physical exhaustion. Before they knew it, Monday morning had arrived and with it the week that had caused so much intrigue and fear: Special Forces week. The first session on a Monday was normally a lecture but today they were greeted by General Baudin as they assumed their usual seats in the lecture theatre. Whilst waiting to be addressed, Wyn watched him and thought to herself that he looked even more miserable and serious than normal—she hadn't realised that was even possible. He waited for the last of them to be seated before he threw his authoritarian bark across the room.

"As you know, this week we will have specialised input by Special Forces, and this will mean a disruption to your normal timetable. This morning you will be doing an initial examination, the results of which will separate you into tiers for later in the week. You will complete obstacles as usual, but these will be timed and submitted; from tomorrow, all theory sessions and your personal development slots will be exams instead. Thursday's skills sessions will be interspersed with individual interviews with each of you. I do not need to stress again how important this is for your future within the services and for the reputation of our base. Don't screw this up." He eyeballed the cadets, his steely glare perfectly echoing the contempt he showed for them in his voice. This was all about what it meant for his position and esteem, and they didn't matter to him at all; they were simply useful bugs he would happily squish into the ground if they didn't get him what he wanted.

As the General finished dictating to the cadets, Baird opened the lecture theatre door, escorting one of the special agents into the room. He was an extremely tall man with thinning, jet black hair and dark, hooded eyes. Wyn had noted throughout the previous weeks that he seldom spoke, even to the other agents when they sat around in the mess. There was an air of mystery and danger to him, and he looked like he could do somebody serious harm if he wanted to. As he adjusted the papers in his hand, Wyn wondered if he had ever killed anyone; those lean, pointy fingers certainly looked deadly. When he looked up and finally addressed the room, Wyn was surprised at the tone of his voice, which was far too high and lyrical to match his gothic-seeming appearance. But despite how he sounded, his intense black eyes still remained both mesmerising and terrifyingly mysterious as he spoke.

"Okay, cadets. I am Special Agent Finnell and I am here to administer your first test of the week. This will cover a range of basics – a few logic puzzles and basic academia to get you going, and the bulk of it is a personality test. We do this to see who has the demeanour and characteristics required of a special agent. Don't try to second guess your answers – we can tell if they don't match up and we aren't always looking for what you think." Looking like a daddy longlegs with his lanky appendages, he took two long strides across the room and handed the pile of papers to the cadet at the end. "Please pass these along and do not begin until instructed."

S.A. Finnell waited for the rustling of paper to cease before telling them to fill out the personal credentials on the front of the test whilst he wrote the start and finish time on the whiteboard at the front of the room.

"And begin…"

The front covers were all flapped open in unison and seventeen pairs of eyes nervously scanned the first page. Wyn groaned inwardly; she hated these types of logic questions, common sense had never been her forte. She muddled through and onto the academic questions, which weren't so bad—maths, science, basic linguistics—and she breezed through them with little cause for concern. She paused once she had completed the second section to regain her composure, then turned the page to start the most important part of the test, the bit they all knew that Special Forces were most interested in: personality.

The questions covered such a wide variety of things and bounced between things that made perfect sense to others that seemed completely pointless and irrelevant. Some of them, like identifying your favourite academic subject or rating yourself out of ten for concentration, she could answer honestly as she didn't reckon there was too much gender difference, but others made her think a little more. Empathy, tolerance, aggression… there were so many traits that were gender-stereotyped and she didn't know if it was better to answer like she thought a man would, so that they wouldn't catch on before she had completed her training, or answer honestly as if her answers were completely incongruous for both men and women… She decided to go with her true answers. If she made it into Special Forces, then hopefully it wouldn't be too long until she'd be revealing herself and returning to being female anyway, and she didn't want to keep up the masculine pretence any longer than she had to by lying on a test.

After two and a half hours, their time was up and their exam was over. They were released to the common room and the second they burst through the door, they began interrogating each other on how they had found it.

"What did you put for the biology question about natural selection?"

"Why do you reckon they want to know about our eating and sleeping habits?"

"What's my sense of altruism got to do with Special Forces, I don't get how that fits with fighting people?"

Everyone was confused about something and baffled by how the questions all fit together. It was clear that no one had tried to answer tactically because no one had any idea how they were expected to answer. Wyn felt instantly better about answering truthfully, nobody else thought they'd made any sense either.

Mary's infamous tomato, pesto and goat's cheese tart at lunchtime set them up for the afternoon obstacle course, and there was a familiar sense of unease in the air. It was like the first timed course all over again except this time, the people timing them were a variety of special agents, which was far more daunting than their everyday officers. Wyn found watching them fascinating; S.A. Finnell was by no means the strangest of them, and not a single agent was the type of cookie-cutter one she'd seen in movies. She'd never seen such a mismatched group of people. Greeting her group at the first of the obstacles was S.A. Pinder, who was bald but had a bushy auburn beard; it had been so long since she'd seen someone with whiskers that she found it hard not to stare. Every spare inch of his skin from the neck down was covered in tattoos. Alongside him was S.A. Barb who was a short, rotund man that looked like he could barely run ten metres—it would probably be easier to roll him. He had a deep chortle that fit perfectly with his round face as he made inappropriate jokes to the cadets. Wyn was disappointed that, despite looking around at the groups being arranged, S.A. Maddox was nowhere to be seen.

The course went smoother than Wyn thought; despite being petrified as she came up to the water obstacles, she was surprised by just how well she managed them. Her new-found confidence in the water made the ice bath easy; she swam the length of the lake and, seeing as Special Forces were watching, she knew she had to at least try swimming underwater. As she swam through, she screwed her eyes shut, which meant she banged her head on the obstructions a few times and came up trying her hardest not to splutter and flap, desperately trying to hide the panic that she was starting to feel, but she was pleased when she made it the full length of the obstacle. And since Cole's advice, getting over the scaling wall was a breeze.

At the end of the session, Wyn was happy with her performance. Her time was by no means the best but, without the penalties on the water obstacles, it still showed an improvement if they compared it to her previous weeks and she could always be confident that Andrew would be slower. Despite all the practice, his physicality had not improved vastly and she could see that he was not as confident in his own performance as the rest of them.

"What's up, Andrew?" She matched her pace to his as they dragged themselves back up the hills to the showers.

"It's that stupid net. I just get tangled every time, and I could tell the special agent was laughing at me." He shook his head, frustrated, and pursed his lips. "What does it matter, they won't want me anyway, it's fine."

"We don't know what they're looking for, Andrew. Besides, you know you're the best at all the clever stuff, so that's probably what they want. No point worrying now, we won't know until after all the tests and everything."

"It's fine Terrell, forget it." They'd made it as far as the dorms and Andrew shot her an insincere smile and walked off into the shower block.

Tuesday followed suit and was spent under the intense and

constant scrutiny of Special Forces. Their morning theory session was replaced with an exam on the topics they had covered—Military History, Tactical Development and Weaponry, Tactical Theories, People of Note. Wyn was in her element; she had found these subjects fascinating in the first place, so had reread them at her leisure as much through interest as necessity, and that meant she easily regurgitated the information in line with the questions asked. She even sort of enjoyed completing the test, although she was the first to join in the moaning and groaning once they left the lecture theatre – she couldn't make herself the misfit now by admitting to actually liking an exam. But at least it meant she had left it confident that she had done enough to pass, whatever the pass mark may have been.

The afternoon Personal Development session was replaced with a practical tactics test which was unlike anything the cadets had done before, and it filled them all with boyish excitement as soon as they saw the set-up they would have to face. They were led in groups into a room that had projected images of buildings and signs on the walls, as if they were stood in the middle of a street. They were instructed to put on a headset and live out the scenario, talking together to decide the best plan of action to get to a group of hostages hidden in one of the buildings. The special agents read out a rough description of where the hostages were, using the road and shop names and any key markers that were in the virtual reality projected all around them, but once inside the relevant locations, they would be on their own to work it out. The special agent made it clear that in the real world—unless they had informers on the inside—aside from the basic brief they got at the start of a mission, they would normally be going in completely blind to what they were facing. The headsets added extra characters on top of the virtual environment, and they could see projected figures representing each other that reflected where they were stood in real-time. A special agent, off to one side, carried an electronic pad and explained that if they decided to make any tactical moves—even something as simple as ducking down— they were to say it aloud and do it in real life, and he would reflect this into the projection for the other cadets to see visually. And, most importantly, the enemy was anyone in red.

It was like the violent, exciting war games they'd heard about in school, which people used to play in their own homes before Lint took over the military and banned them. She was full of nervous butterflies at getting a go at pretending to be a real agent. They passed the first obstacle easily—a pair of enemy soldiers patrolling with menacing guns—by ducking into a greengrocer's doorway and behind the produce so that the enemy walked on by without a second glance. They crept down the street to the marker that represented the building that contained the hostages, and that was where the real challenges began. They made their way through the windy corridors but as their instructions of where to go once inside the building were limited, they made more than one false turn. With her in the group was Oscar, Rowan, and a cadet named Angus Tarshan. He was a broad, stocky guy who Wyn had always thought was fairly attractive but who was, unfortunately, not overly intelligent. And as such, as they made their way along one of the windy corridors, he was the first cadet to fall victim to a booby-trap, Wyn spun round as she heard him cry out and saw his virtual reality counterpart hanging by his feet from a rope rigged up to the ceiling. They tried to cut him down but as Oscar reached out to do so, two figures in red rounded the corner and, with cries of support from the figure dangling from the roof, they made the quick decision to run back down the corridor and away from the enemy. From that moment, Wyn was on high alert, spotting more than one trap along the way. Before too long, they found the hostages and the exercise was over.

They talked through the scenario as the four of them walked back to the Common Room, feeling completely drained despite the lack of physical activity. Wyn was surprised when Oscar, Rowan and Angus all commented on how bossy she had been during the training exercise.

"Seriously, Rigg. I don't think I've ever seen you take control. It was like we flicked a switch and sent in a pro ... you were fully in the zone." Angus sounded impressed.

"Yeah, I don't think we'd have actually made it to the end without you. Some of what we suggested was pretty stupid, thinking about it..." It was obvious that it pained Oscar to admit it, but he shot Rowan a look that made them both laugh. Wyn chuckled along as they analysed their every move. They weren't wrong; suggesting they climb out a fifth-floor window had been pretty stupid.

Two days into Special Forces week and all of the cadets were exhausted. The endless exams and feeling the need to constantly be on top form was taking it out of them, and Tuesday evening was surprisingly quiet in the Common Room, with most of them in bed before lights out. Wyn decided sleep was far more important than sneaking out for a shower, and it wasn't like she'd done that much running around even if the stress of virtual reality had got her extremely sweaty.

They awoke Wednesday morning to yet another exam – this time to determine their intelligence. It was full of maths, science, and logic puzzles which Wyn spent the morning second-guessing. They broke for lunch and were told that, after the Agnes special of leftover fish pie, they were to head to the lecture theatre as normal, to find out who their individual and group sessions would be with. After all the exams, everyone was relieved by the idea of some sort of normal routine, but this was short-lived when they walked in to see S.A. Maddox and S.A. Pinder stood at the front of the room amongst the officers. The change in the cadets' demeanour was immediate; this was the first time they'd seen S.A. Maddox since her initial introduction and they were all still fascinated by her. She seemed to have a spell over them and suddenly backs were straighter and expressions more serious. Everyone was the picture of professionalism and utmost respect. Wyn tried to stifle a laugh as she saw just how much Rowan had tried to improve his posture—arching his back so much that he reminded her of a banana—but as she looked up, she realised that both of the special agents were watching her amusement and she instantly tried to regain composure, silently chastising herself for drawing more unnecessary attention.

They took their seats and waited to be told what the afternoon had in store. They all scanned the superiors stood at the front and were hopeful that they were free of tests, as there was a lack of test papers in sight. One of the special agents was carrying a clicker and the projector was on, so it looked like they were having a lecture after all. Officer Crest took a step forward and cleared his throat.

"Cadets Dartington, Cobbler and Tarshan, you are with me, the rest of you will remain here for direct input from Special Forces."

Panicked looks were sent between them as they watched the three named individuals pick their way out of the rows. They all looked both confused and petrified; what had they done, why were they being separated? Wyn had a sinking feeling that this meant they definitely hadn't made the cut for Special Forces and her heart broke for them, but she retained the tiny glimmer of hope that this meant that she was still in the running.

Once Officer Crest and the cadets had left the room, S.A.

Maddox took centre stage.

"Thank you for your attendance this afternoon. The cadets we have removed have, unfortunately, not answered or performed to the requirements of Special Forces and are no longer being considered as potential recruits." There was a palpable concern but equally an increase in excited energy in the room, which the special agent was quick to squash. "Don't think that this means you are in, or safe. We still have concerns for what we have seen so far in some of you, and the next few days will still be make or break. This afternoon, most certainly, will separate the 'men from the boys' as they say. We will be giving you information, and showing you images, that are strictly top secret. Even once you leave the base and return to your families in the future, you cannot tell anyone what you have seen—you can't even tell the other cadets." She gestured to where they had just exited the room. "Any sign that you have spread this knowledge will mean instant imprisonment for both yourselves and those found to be spreading it on your behalf, so don't underestimate the seriousness of the infraction. Officers, you may now wait outside" Her tone was serious and commanding, and it was abundantly clear that she was not messing around. She nodded at the remaining officers, who swiftly left the room at her instruction. The excitement in the room was replaced with slight apprehension, but their interests had definitely been piqued.

S.A. Pinder took over centre stage.

"You are probably aware that the war we are fighting was started a long time ago, but I am sure that you are far less familiar with who we are at war with." He paused for dramatic effect. "Before it began, life was very different. Men and women were seen as equals, the world was liberal and people could do what they wanted, be who they wanted, and even travel the world should they wish. People even modified their bodies and changed gender if they felt more at ease that way." Wyn couldn't help but dart her eyes around the room at that point, just in case someone had worked her out and associated this comment with her, but thankfully no one was looking her way. "But society was getting greedier and expected the world – what they wanted, when they wanted. It was getting out of hand and turning people increasingly selfish. The Government, which Chief Lint was pretty high up in by then, felt threatened as people were willing to do anything to get what they wanted, and so they tried to put more control and restrictions in place to discourage the behaviour. We were not the only country with this concern and, alongside other world leaders, we gathered to create a new plan. Countries were separated into areas, each centred round a military base and disregarding the old names and set-ups to ensure increased security. Alongside this, each area had a new governing board and stricter rules regarding entering and leaving the designated location. We returned to the gender divide from previous centuries to maintain control over who got what jobs and what knowledge, thus making it harder for people to infiltrate and influence. It is this restructuring that we refer to as 'The Breakdown': society was broken down to the basics in order to rebalance and reset. The military took control over all important industry and dealings, to ensure it was under constant scrutiny and could not be corrupted. The Central Government remains, which is where Special Forces are based."

S.A. Pinder paused to allow the cadets to absorb this information. He watched them closely as they all took in how their society was structured as it was, before he continued with the information that they were really desperate to hear.

"The people who had caused this new system to be created through their behaviour found this new system too oppressive. So, they started to protest, led by a few key individuals, mainly people who had previously been wealthy and, even though they still had a good lifestyle, were angry that they could no longer travel, spend their money or socialise freely as they had before. A lot of them had been removed from their professions as they had been considered unnecessary, so had lost their higher incomes. As they became increasingly frustrated they created a group that aimed to fight back, take control, and run the country in line with the lifestyles they wanted. They called themselves The Hegemonists. It started with a small group of them, but they began to attract a cult following. They promised their followers a world where they could have what they wanted, whenever they wanted, with a hundred slaves each should they wish, and they tried to take any opportunity to lead and control. You can imagine that this cult did not attract the pleasant, kind-natured members of society but the narcissists and villains. This was when it became a problem; they would stop at nothing, using violence to influence religions, political parties and to grow international support. But, with the societal restrictions we have, they were not making the progress they wanted and they fled overseas, overthrowing a city and taking it as their base, using its inhabitants as the start of their army. That's when they declared war."

The cadets' minds boggled. There was a whole world prior to theirs that they had never known existed; a world of freedom and travel and equality that no one ever spoke about. How did one group of people cause so much trouble that they could destroy all of that? The special agent went quiet then, allowing the brief history to sink in, and both he and S.A. Maddox carefully watched the cadets to see how they responded.

"This is where we come to the present time and the challenges we now face." S.A. Pinder continued once it was clear the cadets were back in the present moment and listening intently. "The Hegemonists have a large following now and, with it, came a lot of intelligence—some of it voluntarily and some of it forced. They've been known to threaten entire families in order to coerce extraordinarily bright minds to join their cause, and these people have been developing weaponry for them unlike anything we had imagined before... And they have also been developing genetic engineering." He adjusted the gadget in his hand and clicked, throwing a picture up onto the projection. "Things like this..."

An audible, shocked gasp rumbled around the lecture theatre. In front of them was an image of something that appeared to be half man, half animal; with the torso and head of a man, long, cat-like claws, and legs that looked like they'd been taken from a kangaroo. The thing that struck Wyn most was the eyes, which were solid black and emotionless without a shred of humanity shining through.

"This was the result of a fairly early genetic experiment, created when The Hegemonists wanted a soldier who could easily work on the ground and get into enemy camps; they can attack in two ways: using the claws, and with their extra-strong red kangaroo legs, which have the strength to crush bone or tear you open with a double kick. The longer they've been doing it, the more adventurous and downright grotesque the genetic engineering has become, as you will see in the next slides..."

S.A. Pinder and S.A. Maddox watched the cadets carefully as they flicked through the slides, analysing each and every reaction. Every slide showed an experiment more complicated and developed than the last. Wyn stared at them in horror, questioning what sort of monsters it took to create these creatures. The majority of them clearly had some sort of human part, and that made her feel stomach-churningly sick. She certainly wasn't the only one and, when she glanced along the row beside her, she couldn't help but notice that Rowan had gone a very unattractive shade of green. But the next slide took everyone by surprise—particularly Jason in the row in front of her, who let out a girly scream and slid off his seat into a crumpled puddle on the ground. They stared upon an image of row after row of mutilated human bodies, many with their eyes still open and completely lifeless.

"This is what those barbarians sacrifice in order to make their experiments. Innocent people, often who have volunteered to help their cause and don't know that they will become a living ingredient and that this is the fate that awaits them. Other times, the victims will be people they have captured and mercilessly utilised for their own purposes. But this is just the start and until we defeat them, we have no idea how many more unsuspecting lives will have to be lost."

The room was silent as the cadets tried to take in the horrors that they had just learnt of. Barely any of them had ever seen a dead body before, even in a photograph, and these images had been burnt into their brains. This was the ultimate test. None of them could show any weakness because if this was the reality they would have to face, then it would, no doubt, be essential they could cope. But, although they wouldn't have admitted it out loud, each of them was tempted to show just a little bit of weakness so that they would fail at Special Forces and never have to see those monstrosities again.

"You will appreciate that this is top secret. You cannot breathe a word to anyone, including the others on base and the cadets we removed previously. You cannot even discuss this amongst yourselves upon leaving this room. And be aware that this is little more than scratching the surface, there is a lot more to learn should you be successfully recruited for Special Forces. This evening, in your Common Room, there will also be a box. If, after seeing these images, you do not want to be considered for Special Forces, then you can place your name in there and no one will know if you withdrew or if you didn't meet the criteria. But please appreciate what giving up such an opportunity would mean for your future."

S.A. Pinder rounded up the session to the shell-shocked cadets as S.A. Maddox leaned through the doorframe and gestured for Officer Jeffries and Garth to come in and scoop Jason off the floor and out to

The August Medical Centre.

The atmosphere in the Common Room that evening remained tense. No one could get the images they'd seen out of their minds, and the cadets who had been removed were on edge, completely clueless as to where the icy cloud over the room had come from. The box sat in the centre of the table like a beacon, taunting the cadets with the opportunity to never have to face those horrors again. However, without even being discussed, everyone knew that putting your name in would be a sign of weakness and your reputation would never recover. Conversation was limp and lacklustre, and everyone was fidgety; a few people headed to the gym to burn off the apprehensive energy and others tried to lose themselves in study or books, just for a way to distract themselves from the nervous buzz that was rife. Initially, nobody went near the box in case people assumed they'd put their name in and judged them. As the evening went on though, people were finding more and more reasons to wander around the room just so they could walk past it and surreptitiously see if there were any pieces of paper inside. By lights out, there was no sign of anyone having withdrawn their name from Special Forces recruitment.

The fidgeting continued throughout the night, and Wyn could tell from the grunts and rustling sheets that no one had fully settled. It took her hours to get to sleep herself as she ran through all her options in her mind. Was she strong enough to face the reality of bodies and death and whatever other creations they would have to face? What would happen if she got into the field and then couldn't cope, surely that would completely destroy everything she was trying to achieve? But she was so close, she couldn't give up now. Throughout the night Wyn noticed cadets disappearing from the dorm and wondered if they were just heading to the toilets or if they would wake up to find people's names in the box. She clearly wasn't the only one to have noticed and as soon as the first cadet started to get up in the morning, they all unashamedly flocked around the box and peered in. There were three pieces of paper sat on the bottom; all folded multiple times to ensure no one could see who it was. As S.A. Finnell swooped into the room and swept the box up in one movement the cadets all eyeballed each other, looking for any hint of who had submitted their name in the middle of the night. Who was looking more sheepish than the others, who couldn't make eye contact, who seemed embarrassed? Carter was looking at the ground and Toby was shifting his weight from foot to foot, so Wyn already had them pinned as two of the three, but the nerves about the interviews that they were scheduled to have was yet another thing putting everyone on edge, so she had no way to know for sure what it was that was making them antsy. In reality, they probably wouldn't know who had withdrawn until Special Forces announced who they were recruiting, and that was only if the rest of them were selected.

After the box was gone, they had nowhere else to direct their attention so everybody set about getting ready for the day and heading to the mess for breakfast. Thursday had been set aside for interviews and, as they ate, Officer Crest came round with a timetable to let them know when each of them would be; everyone was still on the list, except the three that had been removed from the lecture theatre the day before, and Jason who still hadn't returned from the medical centre, so they had no way of working out who had withdrawn themselves. The timeslots were alphabetical so Wyn was dismayed when she was near the end of the day, meaning she had all day to overthink and work herself up about it. They could use the rest of the day for personal development and right after breakfast, Wyn headed into the gym; there was nothing like a good workout to clear her head and prepare her for what she would face that afternoon. After completing one of her old workouts from Snapper—which always made her feel better because it was like bringing with her a slice of home—she sat down with all her notes and refreshed her knowledge. She was determined to be prepared for whatever questions they threw at her.

When Carter emerged from his own interview, he looked pale and uncomfortable and, despite the strict instructions not to divulge any information on the questions asked, he sat next to Wyn at the table in the Common Room. He glanced around to ensure no one was nearby and started to whisper, his voice flustered as he tried to get the words out quickly. There was a twenty-minute gap between interviews and they were both very conscious that she would be up next.

"They asked everything. My background, how I did at school, why I signed up, what I've found most interesting in my training and what I've not liked, why I want to be in the Special Forces … everything. I have never felt so interrogated. You'll do much better than me, you're much better at talking to people."

Wyn's mind went into instant crisis. Her background—that was the bit she still wasn't sure how to answer. No matter how much she'd thought about it in case it came up, she still didn't have a clear story; so far, she had managed to avoid the subject, but there was no escaping it if they asked directly in the interview. She could be honest about school and all that stuff, but she was the only child to have ever grown up in the Old Collection and that would give her real identity away instantly. The Collection was all she knew, so how could she pretend to have a standard childhood when she wasn't entirely sure what one was? She appreciated his heads up as she faced up to the lies she was inevitably going to have to tell, and resolved herself to using what she knew about Kiara's childhood, planning to answer the questions as vaguely as possible. Between the flashes of panic about her own interview she also realised that, with the questions he had been asked, it meant that Carter must not have withdrawn his name from the recruitment. Maybe he wasn't as much of a coward as she'd come to believe, and the idea of having an ally if they did make it through was comforting.

Wyn thanked Carter for the information and then scurried out of the room and across the yard, taking a seat outside the meeting room for her allotted time.

"Cadet Rigg, Terrell Rigg."

S.A. Barb stood at the doorway, watching her intently as she walked towards him, and gestured for her to take a seat on one side of the table as he walked around and took a seat on the other, alongside S.A. Maddox. The intensity of their gazes as they watched her made her feel as though they could see her soul. She had never felt more vulnerable than at that moment, but she was even more confused and petrified when S.A. Maddox finally spoke, breaking the tension in the air.

"Agent," she turned to S.A. Barb, "I have left an important file in the office in A-Block, would you please go and collect it for me and I will begin the interview."

The agent looked completely baffled; this was clearly unusual behaviour and entirely unexpected, but he did as his superior instructed and swiftly left the room. The door clicked behind him and Wyn and S.A. Maddox were alone.

"So, who are you?"

"Umm... Rigg, Terrell Rigg." Wyn stammered.

"Tell me the truth, who are you?" S.A. Maddox had a tone that was both accusatory and encouraging at the same time. "I know that you are not 'Terrell' because I know that you are not a boy. Don't get me wrong, you've done a very good job at hiding it—to the layman you're a run of the mill cadet—but I was you once; I was the girl in a world of men and trying to fit in. I could immediately tell there was something different about you, that you didn't quite belong. And then when I heard you talking to Cadet Reece the other day, it all made sense. What was it he called you... Wyn?"

Wyn's face dropped, horrified. She had told Carter not to use her real name, but he had assured her that nobody was around. Her life was over.

"Yes, I... What's going to happen? What are you going to do to me?"

S.A. Maddox smiled at Wyn softly, her eyes full of empathy.

"Nothing is going to happen to you. Like I said – I was you once. I got to where I am through a lot of pain and knockbacks, and not without my fair share of lies. I was fortunate, I had a head start thanks to a previous relationship opening the doors, but I admire the fact that you have created your own opportunity. And so, I will keep your secret and will try to think of ways to help you get through this process. Women need to take the world back."

"Really, you mean it? You won't tell anyone?"

"I won't. Though I can only do so much. When S.A. Barb returns we must continue this interview as normal, with you as Terrell, and you'll have to continue as you have been and keep doing your best because there is nothing I can do to ensure you make it successfully through the training programme, but just know that you have my support."

As the door handle started to move and the door clicked open, both Wyn and S.A. Maddox straightened up and fell back into roll.

"Agent, we have just got onto discussing Terrell's school life, would you like to take the next portion of questions?"

Wyn breathed a sigh of relief; in order to cover up the time spent on their conversation, it looked like she would get away without having to make up a childhood after all. She directed her attention towards S.A. Barb and continued the interview with a boosted confidence and renewed vigour to achieve her goal.

The questions passed with little concern – she could use most of her real school life, she was always academic and so she focussed on that; there was no reason to lie about anything since she started her training; she signed-up to "make a difference to society" and because she "wanted the opportunity to develop a well-respected and successful career." None of which was a lie, she just left out exactly what difference it was she was planning to make. Wyn left the interview feeling happy that she'd answered well enough to cover her tracks but also, hopefully, given the sort of answers that might have been what they wanted. Fingers crossed she'd done enough.

Thursday came to an end and Friday was an expansion of their usual physical session – filled with drills and physical tests which Wyn was fairly pleased with. She was by no means the best in the group but over the weeks she had made her way comfortably to the middle of the pack. Her times in the shuttle runs and dummy drags, along with the weights she could now lift, reflected this. She'd pushed herself to her limits to improve and every time she proved that to herself, she got a sharp flash of pride in her chest. She ended the week on a high; overall, she was happy with her performance in front of Special Forces and, above all, she was completely in awe of and inspired by her new supporter.

Chapter 21

With the end of Special Forces week came the end of week eleven, which meant only one week left until the end of their training programme and until they knew if they had made it into The Southern Company or not. That meant that, before the end of Friday's session, they had to input the names and addresses of the two people they wanted to invite to graduation. Wyn had been dreading this moment as it meant she would really have to start thinking about what she was planning to do at graduation, and as she dropped Mrs Clay's name and address into the box it was heart-breaking that she didn't have a second person to invite. She had considered sending an invite to one of the Brothers or Sisters but receiving it would just confuse them, and she couldn't risk them working her out so close to the end. If she was found out even a few days too early it could ruin everything she had been working towards. She knew Brother Dane often attended graduation anyway so she might still have a member of the Collection with her for it but, equally, having to watch someone she cared about inevitably getting hurt by her deception when she revealed herself would be devastating. Just thinking about it, stood in the doorway to the gym, brought a lump into her throat and she could feel the tears prickling in her eyes. She rushed back to the barracks and the safety of her bunk before anybody could see the first one fall.

The cadets weren't entirely sure what their final week would involve, they only knew that it was no longer a normal timetable and their basic training was now over. Speculation was rife all weekend and filled every spare moment of conversation but equally, they all wanted a distraction. Everyone else was using the weekend as a chance to try and relax after the stress of the tests and exams of the past week, spending a lot of time in the gym and joining the rest of the base in the weekly sports tournaments, but Wyn held back. She had to plan what she was going to do if she made it to graduation; what she was going to say when she revealed who she was and how she was going to make the biggest impact. Thinking about it was all-consuming, so she removed herself from the others and she sat in the corner of the library making draft after draft of her reveal speech. She found books from world leaders and tried to study their most famous speeches for ideas and tips, but she was unhappy with everything she wrote and could feel herself growing more lost with each sheet of paper she crumpled up. The only moment of slight relief came when she rid herself of a tiny bit of anger as she ripped each one into tiny pieces—she couldn't let anyone find the evidence.

Lost in her shreds of paper, Wyn suddenly noticed the tell-tale clip-clopping of S.A. Maddox as she strutted across the library and took a seat opposite her at the table.

"Afternoon cadet. Are you not joining in the sports tournaments this week? What are you up to in the library all by yourself?"

Wyn looked up at her and, noting the reference to being alone, she glanced around and realised that she was the only person in the library. She was sure there had been a few people in here when she arrived, but she had been so engrossed with trying to work out what to do that she had been completely oblivious to everyone leaving.

"Just preparation for the end of our training programme, Agent. It's a lot to take in." Wyn tried to be as vague as possible; she might know her secret but equally, Wyn didn't know how far to trust or how much to tell S.A. Maddox.

"I've looked all over for you since I realised you weren't involved with the social activities and this has worked out quite well – we can talk properly about what it is that you are planning on doing, how you are planning on really making your mark as a woman in the military. So… Wyn, that's an unusual name?"

"Yeah, it's short for Terrwyn, I'm not really sure where it came from."

"And my name is Enya, so when it's just us, you can call me that."

Recognition overcame Wyn and she looked at S.A. Maddox in disbelief. Enya—that was the name of Mrs Clay's friend who had disappeared. Could they be the same person? S.A. Maddox noticed her shock.

"What's wrong, you look confused?"

"Umm… How I got here… I mean, back home I had help from my teacher, Lydia Clay, who encouraged me to sign-up and she helped me make it happen. She had a best friend called Enya who was taken when she stood up to the city. I was doing this to continue that fight. Was that you?"

It was S.A. Maddox who looked shocked now and a lump rose in her throat. She hadn't heard that name in years, but it was one of the few people from her old life that she missed and thought about often. She knew it would renew her homesickness to return to the city she grew up in, even if she didn't venture out of the base, but she had changed so much in the years since she had left that she had not expected to face being recognised. So many feelings came rushing to the surface.

"Lydia? Really? Is she okay? Is she happy? I… I've never forgiven myself for not being able to tell her I was okay and that I was doing well. She must have thought the worst." S.A. Maddox closed her eyes as she said it.

"She's okay, she's a teacher now and I guess she must like it except for the drivel she has to teach. She's married, but she's angry at the government and how women have so few rights left. And I think she's angrier because she thought they'd locked you up or tortured you or something worse; she spent years planning how to continue fighting for women, and then I came along. She's coming to the graduation."

Wyn watched S.A. Maddox as she spoke. It was clear that this poised and well-groomed woman was desperately trying to hold it together and not allow her emotions to overwhelm her. Was this how it would feel for Wyn once she had to face her deceit and the pain that she might cause the Collection because of it? But at least they never thought she was dead.

"So, what are you planning on doing next? Are you staying undercover or…?" S.A. Maddox brushed the conversation away and turned the attention back to Wyn, regaining her composure in the process.

"Well, the plan was to reveal who I really am during graduation. Then they can't deny that women can make it in the military because I'll have made it through the training programme. Plus, I'm not completely bottom of the pack, so I've proven women can keep up... It's what I've been trying to do today, work out what exactly I should say, but I don't know where to start." Wyn looked down at the paper surrounding her and, seeing S.A. Maddox peering across, slid the most recent attempt across the table so that she could see it. She scanned the muddle of words in front of her and pursed her lips.

"Hmm, well you need to work out what it is you want to say first, before you try and turn it into a speech. What is it that you want to say to people?"

Wyn hadn't thought about it like that; she was so concerned about making the best impact and people taking her seriously, she had completely neglected the content. It was a difficult question because there were so many possible answers; she had to really decide what her message was and what was most important.

They talked it through for a while, but were both acutely aware that they couldn't be caught together whispering in a corner, so the conversation was stilted. They both flinched at each noise in the corridor and spun themselves around at every potential opening of the door. Before long, they drew the conversation to a close and S.A. Maddox swiftly left, wishing Wyn luck with her speech.

Wyn watched S.A. Maddox leave the library, lost in thought as she contemplated all of the unanswered questions. She desperately wanted to know what had happened and how Enya had gone from just a rebellious woman in society to head of Special Forces, and how nobody seemed to know that it was her. But she was also envious that she had made it so far and achieved the sorts of things that Wyn had spent the past few months dreaming of; she couldn't shake the feeling that it really put the pressure on to equal, if not surpass, the success of S.A. Maddox. Wyn looked down at the list they had created and set her mind to turning it into a speech that would be abundant with impact and passion—at least having something to say would mean step one was complete.

She sat in the library for a few hours longer, until she was struggling to keep her eyes open and found the words blurred together and danced across the paper in front of her. At least she was looking at some semblance of a finished piece now though. She was brought back to reality by the sound of the door swinging open and heavy boots coming towards her. She looked up, alarmed, and saw that it was Cole. It was the first time they had been alone since the kiss and Wyn didn't have any idea what to say. Cole came to a stop at the edge of the table and smiled down at her nervously.

"Wyn, hi, I... You were missing and you weren't in the gym, so I guessed you might be here... I just needed to talk to you. I'm so sorry, I was an idiot and I just got scared... I didn't mean to annoy or upset you or anything, it's just, nobody's ever done that before..." He trailed off, embarrassed both by his words and at his incompetence in getting them out.

"Nobody's ever what? Tried to kiss you?" Wyn tried hard not to break Cole's gaze. There was something about his vulnerability which made the small shreds of resentment she'd held on to melt away, and the depth of his eyes was helping her make that small bit of their reconnection.

"Well, yes... I didn't have a girlfriend at school and then there haven't been any girls here. And I do like you... I just didn't want to screw it up. But then I did anyway."

Cole broke eye contact with her as he screwed his eyes shut in his own self-annoyance. Wyn could tell by his sincerity that he knew he'd dealt with the situation badly and that he had been silently punishing himself ever since. She figured that he'd suffered enough and she pushed the chair out from behind her and swiftly stood up, taking a small step towards him and squeezing his closest hand. She was fully prepared to try the kiss again and was beginning to lean in towards him but, just as her lips came close to touching his, the library door creaked open and they jumped apart and spun around in unison. They were both visibly relieved to see that it was Carter.

"Woah, what's going on here? Were you two going to kiss? When did this start?" Carter looked a strange combination of confused, horrified and amused, and was completely distracted from the reason he had come to the library to look for them. He had half expected to find them in the same place when he knew they were both missing, but the compromising position was something he had certainly not prepared himself for.

"Carter, what are you doing...? Are you spying on us?" Wyn was immediately defensive in the face of questioning. She was annoyed at herself as, even if it was only Carter, she had still let her guard down somewhere dangerous; it could have been anyone coming into the room, and explaining what was happening would have led to far more complications and questions that she just couldn't justify so close to the end.

"What? No, why would I do that? You really were going to kiss, weren't you?" He smirked as Wyn's clear panic answered his question, before he shook his head and brought himself back to the reason he was there. "But anyway, we've all been called to the lecture theatre by Baudin. Something's going on!" His eagerness and animation reminded Wyn of an excitable puppy—he was clearly expecting something big.

Carter turned on his heels and exited the library as quickly as he'd entered, with long bounds and twice the normal walking speed as his anticipation for what was coming heightened. Wyn and Cole set into a half jog to catch up with him. Just before they reached Carter's side, Cole reached out and grabbed Wyn's hand quickly; holding it just long enough to make her heart jump and a small smile creep onto her face. She couldn't deny how much she liked him any longer, and there was something about their almost-relationship being a secret which was just intensifying her feelings. By the time they'd made it to the lecture theatre, Wyn had managed to get her head back in the game, ready to face whatever was coming next.

General Baudin was stood behind the lectern, glowering at each cadet that entered. Wyn felt a small knot of fear when she realised that they were the last, but they took their usual positions without any comments passed, and the General had started addressing the room the moment the door had shut behind them.

"Cadets, Officers. You will be wondering why I have called you here out of schedule, especially on a weekend and out of training hours. We have received grave news from across the water; we have learnt that a full platoon has been taken out whilst travelling to the frontline and that this attack was particularly brutal. Unfortunately, it is currently believed that no one survived." She could feel Carter stiffen beside her and saw him glance desperately at a worried-looking Cole; their older brother had gone out a few tours before and she knew that they were both fearful for his safety. "We have not yet received the names of the dead. Hand-to-hand combat was involved, which suggests an increase in enemy tactics as they have predominantly relied on weaponry on the front before this. Their increased boldness takes our fight to a new level. As such, the decision has been taken to deploy the current Special Forces team earlier than anticipated; they require their new intakes to begin specialised training immediately to fill the spaces left behind."

There was a tangible change in the room. This meant that some of them must have successfully made it through to Special Forces, but what did this mean for the last week of their training programme? Despite their initial, naïve excitement at the thought of Special Forces, the taster of what horrors it would involve was still sitting heavily with the cadets and no one was sure if the prestige of being selected was worth having to face the reality of it again. For Wyn, the apprehension she was radiating was more to do with how this would affect graduation and her opportunity to reveal herself. They all sat in silence, subconsciously holding their breath in unison as they waited for General Baudin to continue in his emotionless monotone.

"It has been decided that those of you who have been successfully selected, alongside recruits from other bases, will be taken to the Special Forces headquarters this evening to commence your training. The cadets who will be joining Special Forces are… Lewis Brightcoff, Andrew Freemantle." Andrew glanced around in astonishment, Wyn smiled broadly at him, "Percy Gardiner, Carter Reece and Terrell Rigg. Take this as successful completion of your training programme with The Southern Company, the rest of you will be required to complete the programme as intended."

Anxious looks were being shot around the room. Only five of them made it. Those that did were trying to hide how scared they really were at the prospect; those that didn't, were trying not to show how hurt and embarrassed they felt—even those that had voluntarily conceded their places. Wyn was just sat in shock. She'd done it; she'd made it through to Special Forces. Maybe it had been with Enya's help, maybe not, but this changed everything and she could make a much bigger impact now, as long as she did it properly. Caught up in the moment, the cadets couldn't help but make comments and express disbelief at who did and didn't make it. They had completely forgotten about the General, who was still stood at the front of the room watching them all with contempt. He cleared his throat and everyone fell silent.

"Congratulations to the successful intakes. You will have a gruelling journey ahead of you, and you are still representing The Southern Company so I expect nothing but the best and most committed behaviour, or you will have to return and answer to me. Also, Training Officer Reece, you have been selected to accompany the intakes through this process."

Wyn couldn't help but smile at Cole, who was still staring at General Baudin as if he'd suddenly grown horns and a tail. She hadn't even considered the fact that they might have been separated so early, and having another ally with her—especially one that she was starting to really want in her life—took a tiny bit more weight off her shoulders. Cole, Carter and Enya—she already had three people who knew who she was and who were on her side. With their help to work out a new plan to fit with Special Forces, she was confident that she could still work out a way to really make her mark.

"You have half an hour to pack up your belongings, say goodbye to your comrades and meet in front of The August Centre. From there, you will be escorted to your new location." With a defiant grunt, General Baudin had finished his address and dismissed the room, who were all still trying to adjust to the dramatic change of direction their journeys were going to take.

The selected cadets scurried back to the barracks and threw all of their possessions into the canvas bags that they had been given when they first arrived – army order, as were most of their toiletries and clothes now. Each of them only had a few personal belongings to pack and Wyn clutched her notebook from the Brothers and Sisters to her chest briefly before she hid it amongst the army issue clothing. Now, more than ever, she knew she needed to take that small piece of home with her. She had anticipated being able to return to see them in a week, once she had revealed herself, and now she was going to a completely different city with no idea when, or if, she would return.

Swinging the bag up onto her shoulder, she followed the others to the Common Room, where the rest of the cadets were waiting to say goodbye. It was an awkward and stilted affair; a mixture of jealousy and superiority, fear and anticipation. No one who was going knew quite what to say to those who weren't good enough for selection; no one who was staying knew how to say goodbye to people who were one step closer to those monstrosities and potential death. Despite the odd 'Good luck mate!' and 'Say goodbye to my mum for me!' many things were left hanging unsaid in the air when the successful Special Forces recruits left their friends and paced up to The August Centre.

Stood outside in the dark with the cool air whipping around her ears, Wyn stared up at the ominous structure that had started her endeavour. Necropolis had been her goal long before she'd developed more noble motivations and her inner child still felt a small sense of glee as she listened to the familiar buzz of electricity that was feeding the secrets inside, secrets that she had been within touching distance of. But instead, she was heading towards even greater secrets, even more ambitious goals, and hopefully, a chance to change the balance of society. With that thought dancing in her mind Wyn was made to jump by a heavy, black armoured truck trundling towards them. S.A. Barb, who had waited with the successful recruits, ordered them into the back of it. Through the tinted windows, Wyn watched Necropolis slip away into the background as they left it behind.

This was it, Special Forces.

Chapter 22

Special Forces Headquarters was based in the centre of Lordington. It was the busiest city in the country and Wyn had seen many pictures of it during history lessons. Derived from what had been the original capital city before areas had been segmented off, it was still home to the central government and was a world away from what Wyn knew. Her home city of Suthchester was fairly spread out, more like an oversized bustling town, and was separated into the Gild which held the wealth, Millston that was the poorest area, and the rest of the city which contained all other walks of life. On the outskirts, this dissipated into tiny villages that controlled the farmland at the perimeter and, of course, The Southern Company Base which stood proud alongside the civilians. But Lordington was the opposite – skyscrapers the heights of which Wyn couldn't comprehend and no further than a few metres between even the most separated of buildings. As they drove along the narrow streets she couldn't help wondering if the people who lived here had any idea what a garden even was, living like sardines on top of each other in a world made of concrete, steel and glass. The only greenery she had seen was the trees implanted periodically into the pavements, and she had a whole new pang of homesickness for the space and nature that she had never fully appreciated before.

They pulled up in front of what appeared to be one of the largest and most overbearing skyscrapers. Even in the dark of night, Wyn could tell that it was made almost entirely of black-tinted glass that screamed of secrets and drama. As they were ushered out of the truck and towards the sliding double doors, Wyn caught a sight of her reflection and she was taken aback by how rough and unkempt she appeared. The surprises of the day and the two hours of travelling had clearly taken their toll and she was suddenly overcome by weariness; hopefully they would soon be allowed to rest. They obediently followed S.A. Barb into a lift with a wall of buttons, each accompanied by a number alongside a symbol, and watched as he selected '17#'. The lift whirred upwards and before they knew it, they were coming out onto a carpeted corridor with doors that Wyn could only assume led to offices.

S.A. Barb led the six of them down the corridor, almost to the end, before he stopped and directed them through a door on the left. As they entered the room Wyn was taken aback by the sight before her; if she had thought the city overcrowded before, she was severely underestimating its offerings, as the office they had walked into had a full wall of windows and, sat under the night sky, were more twinkling lights of buildings than Wyn could have possibly imagined. They reminded her of a mixture of the stars you could see in complete darkness and iridescent glitter just thrown haphazardly at a pitch-black canvas, and the way they faded in and out in front of her was absolutely mesmerising. Taken aback by the view, and just how many hundreds of buildings the lights must belong to, Wyn had stopped abruptly and felt Carter and Lewis careen into her, breaking her from her reverie. She spun round and apologised in a fluster, before remembering where she was and directing her attention to the solid mahogany desk sat in the centre of the room, and the figure behind it. She was relieved to see that it was S.A. Maddox.

S.A. Maddox watched them all as they entered, smiling to herself at the look on Wyn's face whilst trying to keep her professional and controlled demeanour. Once they were all in a bundle in front of her she pushed herself away from the desk and stood up smoothly, smiling reassuringly as she intentionally scanned the group and maintained a brief moment of eye contact with each of them. Despite it being slightly uncomfortable to hold the intense gaze, they all felt themselves relax, comforted by the maternal edge that she radiated as she allowed her sharp edges to visibly soften; she was clearly well-skilled at manipulating her body language to influence a room. Once they themselves had softened and begun to spread apart, no longer needing safety in numbers, she began to address them.

"Good evening gentlemen and, might I say, congratulations! We have selected individuals from bases all across the country and have taken the highest proportion from yours. You are now standing in the

National Headquarters for Special Forces and this is where things will really change for you; more training, more knowledge, and then you will be fully fledged Special Agents ready to go on missions. S.A. Barb will escort you to your new chambers this evening, and I suggest you get a good night's sleep, as over the next few days we will launch you straight into your specialised upskilling. Any questions?"

"What about our families? They've all been invited to graduation next week and we won't be there. What will they be told?" Lewis, who was shifting his weight from foot to foot in trepidation, glanced at his fellow recruits who echoed back his concerns. He was clearly relieved to have confirmation that this was the right question to ask. They watched as S.A. Maddox's face broke its composure, trying to piece together the best way to answer.

"Your families will attend the graduation as planned and, of course, we cannot hide that you will be missing. There will be an announcement during General Baudin's welcome speech that will identify that a number of cadets showed promise and were selected to undertake further training in order to apply for higher opportunities within the military. They will then be informed, individually, that this training is off base due to its highly sensitive nature and that they are entitled to send you a letter, via army courier." She paused briefly, before deciding to continue on the subject. "If you should choose to, you can provide us with a letter to give to your loved ones at graduation, but it will be read by a senior member of staff to ensure there is nothing compromising in the content. Dependant on how long you serve with Special Forces, you will be allowed one letter home a year."

She knew that the isolation of Special Forces would be an upsetting thought and it would be easier for them to digest overnight, but the reality of how little they were going to have to do with their loved ones was painful to think about. S.A. Maddox could feel her heart break slightly for them and she quickly dismissed them into the corridor where S.A. Barb was waiting, in order to hide any potential emotion. She only allowed emotion to be seen when it served her interests.

Nobody said anything as they were guided back down the corridor, down to the ground floor in the lift, and along a connecting walkway to what was very clearly the residential area. They were all suddenly hyperaware of just how far they were from home and everything they knew and loved, and the vulnerability was overwhelming. The quarters they were allocated were much like the barracks they had back on base, but with crisper lines and more exposed steel. The dormitory led onto a communal area with sofas and tables, and a kitchenette off round one corner; the area was surrounded by doors which S.A. Barb pointed out to be toilets, showers, and more dorms that housed recruits from other bases. He left them all to crawl into their bunks and, despite the exhaustion from a long and unexpected day, the night was full of restless, broken sleep interspersed with apprehensive dreams of what might come next.

They awoke to the harsh realisation that they no longer had a mess room to go to for breakfast and, alongside the recruits who had ventured out of the other dorms, they set about cobbling together what they could in the kitchenette. It was fully stocked with ingredients but it was rare that any of them had needed to be self-sufficient and it was clear that only a few of them knew their way around a kitchen. Wyn knew she had watched Sister Cariad cook enough to know the basics but, with no idea when they would be called to begin their first day in Special Forces, they all agreed that quick and easy was the safest idea. So they ended up with rounds of toast and jam

Before long, all of the Special Forces recruits were summoned to another room with a glass wall overlooking the city, which Wyn was disappointed to note was not nearly so magical in the daylight. In the centre sat a large conference table and the recruits took up three edges of it, facing various special agents on the fourth. To begin, S.A. Maddox ran through the recruits by name and identified which base they had come from – more for the other agents' benefit than for the recruits themselves. Wyn was interested to note that from the five main bases in the country, the split of the recruits was 5:3:3:2:1 and, alongside Cole, one other base had also provided a training officer, making sixteen of them in total. S.A. Maddox began to address them once more.

"So, today you are officially Special Forces recruits. You are no longer cadets or training officers." She nodded at Cole and Toby, who was sat with him, "you have successfully achieved your place in the army and this is the next step in your careers. We are going to take this morning to give you more detail on Special Forces – who we are and what we do. But this will be the truth, not the heroic, watered-down stories you will have heard before. It will include first-hand accounts from some of my colleagues." She gestured to the agents sat either side of her. "Special Forces, for the most part, are a set of highly trained individuals who go on special missions, often kept out of the public domain. These missions will normally be conducted in very small groups, with partners or solo. As we get to know you, we will decide in which format you will work best and make sure you have the specific skill set to do so. S.A. Finnell, who some of you may remember, is one of our solo agents." She looked at S.A. Finnell expectantly, who took his cue and began to talk.

"Well I was, in fact, the longest-serving solo agent in the field, before I decided to go after a role at Headquarters. My speciality was infiltrating enemy camps, and, more specifically, their bases and head offices, in order to obtain intelligence and secrets over what they were planning and what weapons and creations they had at their disposal." S.A. Finnell paused with a smug smile as he looked at the recruits hanging onto his every word. "I remember, one of my earlier missions was to penetrate a base in Eastern Europe in order to find the records kept on a platoon of soldiers who had gone missing. We were sure they had been used in experimentation. I dug for two days in order to tunnel under the barbed wire fencing, whilst ensuring that the tracks could not be seen by the armed guards that paroled the perimeter and, once inside the fence, under cover of darkness, I felt my way along the walls until I found the door I had scouted from the outside. I had to pick the lock, using a combination of sticks I'd filed down to create a point, and once I made it in, I was taken by surprise with a series of intruder alarms that could be triggered by laser beams. Luckily, we have glasses specifically created to identify the lights they emit, so I was able to navigate through them. I made it into the record room and found the information we had been looking for; although we had dreaded finding it, it confirmed that the soldiers had been used to create a new hybrid creature—a mixture of monkey and human—and they were being kept to study and experiment on. The genotypes were close enough that they wanted to see if they could manipulate the desired characteristics from each. I do not dare think about what those poor men must have been going through. We can only pray that they could no longer feel or reason."

S.A. Finnell was clearly enjoying holding an audience, proud of his achievements and the stories he had to tell. It was certainly a story to hold everyone's attention; some of the recruits were drawn in by the idea of the high-tech gadgets, others by the whole dramatic theatre of it, and some were just morbidly fascinated with the experiments and what The Hegemonists were capable of.

It was clear that this story was a test as much as it was for information, with the S.A.'s intently watching the reactions to ensure that the recruits could cope with the reality; this would be the kind of horrors they would have to face and if they were caught, they might even have to endure the same fate. It was important they were mature enough to take it on board and treat the situation with respect. And the stories that followed from other agents really pushed this to the limit. Over the next two hours, the recruits heard stories involving the heads of special agents' in jars, trekking across the desert with only your own urine to obtain any fluids from, and performing emergency open-heart surgery in the middle of an active war zone. But alongside the horror stories used to test their constitution were ones designed to inspire and motivate them to what they might achieve; of rescuing an entire orphanage of tortured children from their abusers, single-handedly taking down someone trying to assassinate a world leader, and obtaining information that stopped what could have potentially been the most lethal nuclear strike in history. By lunchtime, the recruits' minds were spinning with a whirlwind of emotions and the intensity of the knowledge they had been entrusted with.

After the stories were completed—all highlighting just how varied Special Forces was, and the fact they only accepted assignments that held an insane amount of danger—there was a polite knock on the door. As S.A. Maddox called for the owner of the knock to enter, all the recruits were delighted to see a hostess trolley wheeled in. It was stacked with dainty, triangular finger sandwiches, perfectly formed cakes, an array of deli meats, crudités and dips, sausage rolls, and all the other makings of a perfectly exquisite buffet. As the petite blonde in a floral pinafore apron lay the platters out across the table, alongside pots of tea and coffee, Wyn couldn't help but think how incongruous this refined tea party seemed when compared with the rough and ready, unhygienic stories of rationing they'd just heard. The recruits were unsure of the protocol but, on seeing the special agents dive straight for the plates and start piling them up, one by one they got the courage up to follow suit. Chatter round the table slowed as everybody savoured the offerings, which were a world away from the mass-catered, one-pot solutions they had grown accustomed to at base; how could they get so much flavour into such tiny food?

After lunch, they were removed from the meeting room, leaving the carnage of empty platters and crumbs behind them, and walked the full length of the building, up two floors in the lift, and out into a small hallway with an ornately carved door in front of them. It was engraved with the figures of an angel and a devil, with the Special Forces logo held between the two; the beautiful filigree door handle was also impressive. It seemed so out of place in the modern glass of the building, and S.A. Finnell, who had led the group, stood in front of it triumphantly.

"This is the library. You will find books on every subject imaginable, including many first editions that we have managed to rescue and acquire over the years. Through this door you will also find, straight ahead, a museum of artefacts from Special Forces history—the good and the bad. This room is open to you to peruse and utilise as you require; we often find that people use it as a place of sanctuary – a break from the real world and the stress that goes along with it. Please note, people may also use this as an area of prayer if they do not wish to venture to the local places of worship, so be respectful and maintain a strict code of quiet and peacefulness whilst inside."

With a flourish, S.A. Finnell pushed the heavy doors open and Wyn almost took a step back in awe as she took in the beauty of the room before her. She had revelled in the depth of the library on base but it paled by comparison; this room was two stories high, with floor to ceiling books and gold edged bookshelves. It even had a golden ladder on a rail that ran the full perimeter of the room, just like in the libraries in fairy tales, and the desks all had quaint lights on them with beautifully intricate thin shell lampshades that cascaded colours across the floor. But what drew everyone's eyes most of all, completely out of place in the middle of the far wall, was a solid, dark wood door with a solid gold doorknob; this must be the entrance to the museum and, without even discussing it, it was where the recruits all headed immediately.

They were instantly mesmerised from the second they stepped over the threshold. The walls were lined with framed pictures from missions, sketched plans and tactics, and plaques detailing the stories that went along with them. As they ventured further in, these were interspersed with pedestals with artefacts on top: weapons, preserved body parts that made Wyn's stomach turn, and items taken from civilisations and enemies that Special Forces had infiltrated and uncovered. It was fascinating and provided even more inspiration for the recruits. It was really hitting home that they would get to see and do things that no one else would ever get close to, and for Wyn, with her humble background, that was incredible.

They finished their familiarisation with the library and museum to find S.A. Finnell stood back at the library door. He gathered them together at the desks that sat in the centre of the room.

"Whilst we are here, you can take the opportunity to write your letters home and we will collect them up and have them taken by army courier back to your individual bases, where they will be given to your families. If you do not wish to, then you can use the next thirty minutes as a chance to relax and explore further. Paper and pens can be found in the resources area, at the end of this wall" S.A. Finnell gestured to his right. "The letters must fit certain criteria, and we will be reading them to ensure they meet it, as you risk not only your safety but everyone here and everyone at home if you give away information unnecessarily. As such, your letter must not refer to Special Forces by name. However, you can refer to it as a 'highly specialised tactical group'. Also, you must not identify the location of Headquarters. We feel this will allow them to read between the lines and understand the magnitude of your new opportunities, but maintains the elusion to ensure that there is still an element of guesswork required should the letter fall into the wrong hands. You must not repeat any of the specific stories you have heard here today and make no promises for the future. You have half an hour—pop the name of the recipient and which base it will be going to on the front and then I will be collecting up the envelopes."

Wyn scurried along the wall of books and reached for a pen and some paper. Getting there first, she handed some back to the recruits following; it looked like everyone except Andrew and Toby, the second training officer, were planning on writing something home. Carter and Cole sat together at one of the desks to make sure they compared what they were saying, ensuring they made the most out of the opportunity to send two letters to the same family, and Wyn sat opposite them so she wouldn't have to worry as much about hiding what she was writing. It was difficult to know exactly what to say. Wyn decided it had to be a letter to Mrs Clay, because that was the only person she'd invited to graduation. Although she would have loved to be able to send something to the Sisters, it just wouldn't work – she still hadn't revealed herself and couldn't guarantee that it would be S.A. Maddox that would check it, so it would be too much of a risk to write it from herself. It would have to be from Terrell. Could she even mention S.A. Maddox to let Mrs Clay know that she was alright? With only thirty minutes to pen something, Wyn didn't have the time to overthink, so she just started to write and see what came out. After two false starts, she ended up with a letter that she was happy with.

Dear Lydia,

I am very sorry I'm not at graduation to celebrate reaching the end and to talk openly about everything that I have achieved, but I have been selected for a highly specialised tactical group and that means being taken away for more training. I am hoping that, although it will take longer to reach the end, adding that to successfully completing the basic army training programme will mean more respect and impact in the future, when I do get to return home. Unfortunately, we don't know when that will be yet. I'm not sure whether to wait until then or not, so let me know what you think.

Give my love to the Brothers and Sisters, and tell them I am safe and doing well, as I cannot communicate with them directly and would have hoped to have done so by now. Please give them nothing to worry about. Let them know that my career opportunities have developed and I'm being kept on. And, so that you are aware, your long-lost friend is here as well, and is safe and doing everything we have hoped for.
    Love,
    Terrell

It seemed pathetically short once she had signed off the ending but, writing it from Terrell, and with so much she couldn't give away, she didn't know what else would be safe to include. It said all the important bits—that she was in Special Forces, didn't know when to reveal herself, and that Enya was still alive—whilst also reminding Mrs Clay to maintain her cover with the Old Collection as she was growing increasingly worried about what they must be thinking about her not returning home. She would just have to hope that Mrs Clay could read all of those points within the slightly cryptic and non-descript language she had used, and that she would understand from this format to use the same back. Wyn was pretty sure that letters in would be just as scrutinised as letters out, and she couldn't risk Mrs Clay giving her away without warning.

Once their letters were collected up, the recruits were all invited to join some of the S.A.'s for dinner in the agents' own residential quarters, so that they would have the opportunity to start to get to know the recruits a little bit better and let down their guards a bit. It seemed like an appropriate end to a day that had been a surreal mix of information overload and blurred professional boundaries. All of the recruits were taken aback by just how welcomed they were by the special agents; unlike joining the army bases, they were immediately treated like part of a team and even close to equals, although they were never completely unaware of the agents' experiences and status. S.A. Maddox had even commented over dinner that it was important for them all to bond together because, if selected to work together on missions, their lives would quite literally be in each other's hands.

Unlike the scramble of exhaustion of the first night, the recruits now had time to set themselves up properly in the new dormitory and without the regiment of the base, they could choose their own bunk order. Wyn was pleased to end up between Carter and Cole; it was comforting to be flanked by the safety of people who knew her secret and who she was really starting to believe were willing to protect it. It was made that little bit better by Cole who, when the lights went out and he was sure everyone was nestling down ready to sleep, reached across and brushed Wyn's arm with his fingertips. She took his lead, untucking her hand from the covers and reaching out for him, enjoying a moment lost in just being able to hold his hand and forget all the fear and anxiety. But the moment didn't last long, as the second they were brought back to reality by snores from across the room, they both rolled to face opposite directions so that no one could notice the subtle tenderness they were sharing. Despite the secrecy, as she drifted off to sleep completely exhausted by the emotionally charged day, she had a small smile on her face, grateful for the people she had managed to find in her chaos.

Chapter 23

The following morning was an entirely different affair. In stark contrast to the static meeting and gentle exploration of the library the previous day, they were thrown immediately into their first day of specialised training—learning the skills they had heard of the others using the day before. Day one, which was held in a gym that spanned the full floor space of the windowless basement, was hand-to-hand combat.

They had two trainers, both of whom made it very clear that they were martial arts specialists and not special agents so, "Call us Jackson and Cairo." By the similar button noses and almost identical eyes, Wyn would have confidently guessed they were brothers, and it was very apparent that they were passionate about what they did; proudly telling the recruits that they were the only ones trusted to train all Special Forces agents up to the standard required for missions.

"We will teach you a range of hand-to-hand combat based on martial arts including, but not limited to, Krav Maga and Jiu-Jitsu. We will also teach you how to use weapons, and how to improvise weapons in the field. But before we begin, Cairo and I are going to demonstrate to you some of the most effective moves, to give you just a small taste of what is to come."

Jackson and Cairo took to the centre of the mats and respectfully nodded at one another, before launching into a variety of moves, using sparring pads to keep themselves from real injury as they explained just how effective these actions could be.

"First up, the throat punch – do this right and you can crush your opponent's windpipe." Jackson lunged straight for the pad covering

Cairo's Adam's apple.

"Or there's always a fishhook – just be careful of the teeth." Cairo reached round and shoved his fingers into Jackson's mouth before using his grip to twist his head around, manipulating Jackson's position.

"Or you could go for an ax stomp – you can easily crush bone this way." Jackson pushed Cairo to the floor before dropping his body weight through his heel on top of him.

"Or, how about crushing the eyes with an eye gouge?" Cairo aimed two fingers directly at Jackson's eyes; he pulled the sparring pad up to protect his face just in time for Cairo's hand to collide into it.

As soon as they had finished their demonstration both men erupted into laughter, clearly loving what they did, although Wyn was sure it must still have hurt despite them not using full force. Beside her, Wyn could feel the others becoming increasingly full of boyish excitement as the idea of fighting and the impressive technicality of it got their testosterone flowing. Wyn was surprised that she was starting to feel a bit of giddy excitement herself. She was enthralled by the power of it and desperate to prove she could hold her own; she might not have the same strength but she was pretty sure she surpassed most of the other recruits in agility, so hopefully that would work in her favour.

Feeding off the buzz in the room, Jackson and Cairo moved on, got the recruits to warm up and began to teach them the basics, starting with which areas of the opponent's body were most vulnerable and should be targeted, and different ways to manipulate their bodies that they would later develop into actual moves. As they came to a natural break and were released for a short lunch, S.A. Maddox appeared at the doorway.

"Gentleman." She nodded respectfully at Jackson and Cairo. "Please can I borrow Terrell Rigg, it will only take a moment."

"Of course, we were just stopping for ten anyway. Re-join the others once you're done lad and we'll be good to carry on after some chow." Cairo dismissed Wyn who, with concern written all over her face, followed S.A. Maddox out of the gym and into a small alcove across the hallway.

"No need to look so worried; I just wanted to check-in. I didn't know what you would put in your letter to Lydia so I made sure that I got it in my pile to review, just in case, and it was really touch-and-go as to whether I could send it; especially as you mentioned me."

Wyn looked at her with a pained expression. She'd tried so hard to write a letter that wouldn't be specific enough to leave her vulnerable and she'd still got it wrong.

"I'm sorry, I tried really hard not to give anything away, but it's just so hard writing when I can't write as me. I still need help to know when to tell everyone who I am and..."

"You don't need to explain yourself, Wyn. You didn't use names and you didn't mention anything specific enough, so you got away with it in the end. As long as it goes straight into Lydia's hands and no one else reads it along the way then we're fine. And to be honest, it would probably just confuse anyone who didn't know about what you were doing. But it did make me think about when you should reveal yourself and I've had some ideas about that—but here is not the place to explain them properly. I think I've got a way for us to spend some time one-on-one though, away from everyone else, which should become clear soon. So, I just wanted to let you know that you're definitely not on your own here. Now, go join the others."

Wyn watched after S.A. Maddox in a mixture of confusion and intrigue as she clip-clopped away, but this was certainly good news. She just had to have faith that Enya was going to come through for her and that soon they would have a plan. Wyn joined the others, brushing off her 'chat' as concerns about the content of her letter, which wasn't a complete lie. She wolfed down some sandwiches and returned to hand-to-hand combat with an extra spring in her step, thanks to S.A. Maddox.

Over the next few days, Jackson and Cairo explained the differences between strikes, punches, stomps, chokes and kicks, taught the recruits how to counter common attacks, and even explained breathing techniques that would ensure they stayed calm and collected when faced with an opponent. They built up the moves logically and soon everyone was feeling increasingly confident in their ability to fend off an attacker, but ached as they used their bodies in completely new ways.

Once the recruits were considered to be at a consistent level of basic self-defence, they were given a few days break from the exhausting physicality to start on another set of skills considered essential for Special Forces survival in a class entitled Subterfuge.

This involved being back in a lecture theatre and once seated for the first time, the agent who was taking the subject handed out an overview of what they would cover:

- Interrogation – how to carry out an interrogation, how to survive being interrogated without giving away vital intel. Specific focus on how to manipulate a subject when conducting an interrogation and how to deceive the interrogator with false information.
- False identities – how to create and maintain a false identity convincingly.
- Cryptograph – codes and secret languages used within Special Forces and a brief introduction to more widely known codes, such as Morse code.
- Coding – the basics of hacking and recoding a simple computer system.
- Forgery – an introduction to the basic documents that Special Forces can counterfeit and the simple methods for mocking up your own in the field.

Wyn looked at the list and was absolutely enthralled by the specialisms, as well as slightly fearful at the idea of ever needing to use any of them in the real world.

"We call this unit subterfuge because deceit is very much at the centre of keeping yourself alive in the field, particularly when going solo. Being able to convincingly manipulate your environment and your enemies can very much be the difference between life and death." S.A. Crianz began. "But we will just scratch the surface of what you can do with these skills because once you have learnt what methods you can use in one scenario, you will realise you can apply it to many more."

S.A. Crianz scanned his audience and was delighted to find that they were all hanging off his every word. As they got to know the recruits from the other bases, Wyn had confirmed that the lure and prestige of Special Forces was not isolated to The Southern Company, and that the rumours of the intense, thrill-seeking missions were apparent across the board. So far the supporting information and new knowledge was not disappointing this reputation, and there wasn't a single recruit who wasn't getting more and more drawn into the excitement of becoming a real Special Agent.

"First, we are looking at interrogation. We have many different techniques to look at, both looking at how to carry it out and how to survive it. This includes the obvious ones like 'good cop / bad cop', torture, or even using mind-altering drugs, but we also have techniques needing a bit more flair and talent: utilising body language, playing on someone's ego, increasing someone's suggestibility through various methods. It is very likely that, should you be captured at any point, you will need this knowledge and understanding about interrogation and, through personal experience, I can vouch for its importance. In fact, using these skills to keep myself alive when I was pretty sure I was a dead man is why I volunteer to teach this unit."

A ripple of increased respect ran through the recruits, as did the intrigue of what exactly had happened to him. Wyn squinted her eyes to inspect him a little more closely in light of the new information and saw a silver scar running across his jawline and down the left side of his neck; her stomach flipped slightly as she thought about the pain and terror that must have gone with it. With that thought in mind, she reset her focus and listened that little bit closer. The day flew by as they became familiar with different interrogation techniques and even had a go at acting out some scenarios using their new knowledge.

The next day was Friday and, despite the lure and excitement of the new information they were absorbing every day, there was a different feeling in the air. An uneasy tension was following the recruits around as they were all thinking the same thing—today was graduation, today was the day their families found out that they were gone. The homesickness that had been so rife in the base—when they were only minutes away from their homes and loved ones—was multiplied exponentially by the increased distance, and not knowing how people were reacting to the news, and to their letters, was weighing heavy on everyone's minds. It also brought home just how uncertain their futures were, with no idea when, or even if, they would ever return home again. They had no end date for their Special Forces training and any missions could come up spontaneously to take them entirely by surprise; nothing was guaranteed.

By lunchtime, S.A. Crianz knew he was fighting a losing battle. Although they tried it was apparent that the recruits were not as focused as they wanted to be, and he found himself repeating and over-simplifying things just to ensure the information was being taken in. He sent them off for lunch but stood back and pondered if he had the energy to spend the rest of the day going over and over the same things. He decided that he didn't and made contact with the lab technicians in time for the recruits to return.

"Okay lads, it is very clear that none of you are in the right head space for theory today and we are going round in circles and wasting time doing so. Don't worry, I understand, I had to leave my family once too. But I have arranged for you to do a session this afternoon that was actually planned for next week. Take the lift to floor seven and someone will be there to meet you and explain what you are going to do."

The recruits looked at each other completely baffled, but grateful for how well S.A. Crianz could read a room—he was a body language expert after all—they did as instructed. As the lift creaked to a halt and the doors opened, they were all surprised by what was in front of them. In stark contrast to the carpeted hallways and modern fixings they were used to on the other floors, this was crisp white and sterile. A large curved reception desk, displaying a cursive font sign that identified the floor as 'Special Forces Laboratory', took up the space right in front of them. Behind it sat a woman in a clean, pressed white tunic. She greeted them with a warm smile and stood up, rounding the desk so she could place herself in front of them.

"Afternoon boys. So, we've got a bit of a change in your timetable at the request of Special Agent Crianz. I am May, and I am the receptionist here, I will be taking you to Dr. Goodwine for the afternoon. You'll probably be wondering where you are and what we do. We are the Special Forces Laboratory and we cover a wide range of duties. Samples taken from the Medial Centre—whether they are standard blood tests, tests for toxins, or any other medical investigation—come here for analysis. Samples are also brought back from missions – both human samples and samples from the environment so that we can see what we are dealing with; especially unknown substances that could be used as weapons against us. Finally, we analyse known poisons and toxins, develop antidotes against them, and create our own new chemical weapons for use in the field. So, many secrets are held in this lab and today we are going to explain to you some of the ones that might help you survive when you're out there on your own."

Once her introduction was done, accompanied by a patronizing undertone, she led them past the reception desk and along the corridor, passing many different rooms as they went. The recruits were fascinated as the white walls were regularly interrupted by windows looking into different laboratories, all clearly designed for different things. One was full of analysing machines, each with little screens running through information as they scanned the samples; the next had racks of chemicals, test tubes and Bunsen burners; another, which piqued the most interest, was a testing unit with gas-tight suits and masks hanging up just inside the door. About two-thirds of the way down the corridor, they stopped at the next doorway and May held it open for the recruits to enter. Behind a large bench in the centre of the room stood an extremely thin man in a lab coat and goggles, who they could only assume was Dr. Goodwine. He was the perfect picture of a mad professor with his sporadically sprouting grey hair and round glasses perched on his long nose.

"Fresh blood. Nice to meet you all, welcome to the labs. Today I am going to run through some of the most common poisons you may encounter, and some basic antidotes – particularly ones you can make ad hoc in the field." Dr. Goodwine had a chaotically jovial nature and a laugh lingered behind his words. He was most certainly the distraction that the recruits needed. "Grab a lab coat, gloves and goggles from behind the door and come back to join me."

The recruits busied themselves getting ready and returned to line the edges of the bench. Dr. Goodwine had laid out a row of different coloured liquids and pots of different substances and ingredients.

"So, what do you all know about poisons?"

There was silence around the room; education was so limited, especially in the sciences, that no one had any idea where to start.

"Okay then, let's start at the beginning. What is a poison? Basically, anything that can do pretty major damage or kill you if it's ingested, inhaled or even if it's just absorbed through your skin. All of them do it by affecting different cells and processes in your body, and it is important to understand how they cause the damage in order to understand how the antidotes work. Over time you'll learn enough to be able to work out what might be worth trying when you come across something new. There'll be some poisons you've heard of before – things like cyanide, which has been used in gas chambers for years. It binds to the iron in your blood cells, choking them so they can't transfer oxygen around. It's a pretty inhumane way to die. But we have also made antidotes, such as hydroxocobalamin, which is something we use to treat vitamin B12 deficiency. Although there are other poisons, like batrachotoxin, which we find in the skin of certain poison dart frogs, which we don't have any antidotes for yet. That is actually a particularly fascinating poison, one of the most powerful neurotoxins we know of... Since studying them, we found it's actually caused by what they eat, which is annoying because without that food source they can lose their toxicity. Anyway, it impacts the body's ability to transmit electrical signals and can cause paralysis and death. The frogs are called that because people used to hunt them and use the poison in their dart guns, and we know of people still using it as a weapon today, so finding an antidote is an ongoing challenge."

The recruits were staring at him, open-mouthed with horror at the thought of how painful and terrifying it must be to suffer from these substances, but absolutely fascinated nonetheless; home was certainly a million miles from their thoughts now.

"Then we get onto more bespoke poisons. Ones we've found our enemies using and have had to create our antidotes for, as well as ones we've created in retaliation. I try and make things that you could find the components of or at least something very similar, out in the wild or even in kitchen cabinets, so that you can protect yourself when you're on a mission. And this afternoon, you will start to learn those combinations. Grab a pen and paper; you'll want to remember these."

Dr. Goodwine pushed the stationary products into the middle of the table and then picked up a vial of translucent pink liquid.

"This is a poison I affectionately refer to as Pink Lady. We first came across something very similar when we lost an agent on a mission in South America. It's made predominantly from a poisonous berry taken from a native tree, which is then enhanced using some common kitchen cleaning products. They react together and create something even more potent which, once ingested, can cause a fatal heart attack in minutes." He passed around a petri dish containing some of the whole berries and a few leaves from the tree. "It is worth knowing what these look like because then, if you see them when you're on a mission, you can use them to fashion your own poison."

Wyn drew a quick sketch of the berry and the shape of the

leaves, hoping that her rough diagrams would be enough to later identify the right thing, and listed the other chemical names that Dr. Goodwine stated were required to create the final product. He then followed this up with the ingredients needed to create an antidote and Wyn diligently recorded what she would need to find in order to make it, taking particular note of the need to heat it up to boiling point before rapidly cooling it off in order to reach its optimum effectiveness.

The rest of the afternoon followed the same pattern as they went through an array of different poisons and antidotes that had all been created in the field and were things they could probably replicate if required. Having the different ingredients and products to look at kept it interactive and kept the recruits on task, devouring all the information being thrown at them, and by the time they were dismissed for the evening each of them felt a strong sense of satisfaction at the unusual knowledge they now had.

That evening was a fairly subdued affair, as everyone relaxed in the communal area. It had been non-stop since arriving at Special Forces and weekends were a thing of the past, so they had to make the most of every second of downtime they got. They had created a rota for cooking evening meals in pairs, and tonight was Wyn and Cole's turn. It was a good excuse to spend some time together in the kitchenette and, although they weren't completely out of sight of the others, no one batted an eyelid at the joking and messing around going on, putting it down as playful banter. Plus, when he was sure that no one could see, Cole would take it that little bit further by running his hand down Wyn's back, squeezing her hand, or standing just a little bit too close behind her as he reached around to pretend to help her stir. She revelled in getting to see the playful side that he normally covered with his professionalism, and every touch made butterflies dance in Wyn's stomach. Between them they made making a chilli a far more fun affair. Wyn also felt she had something to prove as she tried to remember what she could of how Sister Cariad made chilli. But, when so few of the recruits had any idea when it came to the kitchen, she could tell that Cole was impressed when he tried it, and when they served it up to the rest of the recruits the satisfied noises they received echoed his sentiment.

Chapter 24

After a restful night's sleep, fuelled by good nutrition and an exhausting day, they returned to the lecture theatre ready to continue the subterfuge classes as per their original schedule. S.A. Crianz was there to greet them and was pleased to see that their spontaneous change in timetable the day before had helped and he once again had their full attention as he discussed different torture techniques used in interrogation. By the end of the day the recruits were all feeling comfortable with their basic knowledge on interrogation, and were content that it had been a steady day without the tension and unease of the day before. However, as the session came to an end, S.A. Crianz put a stop to the recruits who were already readying themselves to return to their residential quarters.

"Not so fast lads, you are going to be staying on for an ad hoc meeting this evening. Some of the agents will be along shortly, so just take five until they get here."

The recruits returned to their seats and sat around chatting; anything involving the Special Agents put them all slightly on edge and they speculated about what the agents would be talking to them about.

"I reckon they've got us missions already and we're going to have to be rushed off immediately. They were desperate enough to get us here." Toby was excited by the prospect. He was by far the most desperate of the recruits to be seen as a real Special Agent, being nineteen now and having been in the army for nearly two years without any excitement to show for it.

"I don't think it'll be anything like that yet. We definitely don't know enough to keep ourselves alive, so we would certainly be too much of a risk." Andrew was always the first to bring logic back to the table; Toby looked disappointed at how quickly his theory was shot down.

"Maybe someone isn't up to scratch and they're gathering us all together to make an example of them." Lewis was always ready for some drama and always assumed the worst.

"Whatever it is, we're about to find out." Carter shut down the conversation as the recruits all became aware of the footsteps echoing towards them from the corridor and, sure enough, soon a selection of Special Agents entered the lecture theatre.

S.A. Maddox led the group, followed by fourteen others, most of which the recruits had now met through the time they had spent integrating, and they lined up at the front of the room. S.A. Maddox took to the centre of the floor and smiled widely at the recruits, catching Wyn's eye for just a fraction too long. Wyn sat up a little straighter and the corners of her mouth curled upwards just a little, she had a good feeling about this all of a sudden.

"Good evening! I hope you've all had a very educational day and that S.A. Crianz is keeping you suitably busy." She winked playfully in his direction. This was a far more fun side to her that the recruits had not seen before, she was clearly enthusiastic about whatever they had come to discuss. "Today I have come to you for two reasons. The first is that the army couriers have been and delivered the letters that your families wrote to you yesterday. You will receive these before you leave here this evening, to read in your own time. Secondly, after some conversations about how it would work, we have decided to try something new. Between us, we have a wealth of different knowledge and experiences, some of which we have shared with you already, but we have also been where you are. We know just how much information you need to take in and how we did it, and what tips and tricks we wish we'd known along the way. So, for the first time ever, we are going to pair up so we can give you some one-to-one mentoring." Something clicked in Wyn's head as she realised where this was going. "We have looked at your results from your tests on base and tried to match you up to the agent that is most similar to you in terms of their skills and outlooks, so that they can show you what worked well for them and where best to get help with your weaker areas. But show them your utmost respect—these special agents have all volunteered to help out with this experimental mentoring programme and are giving their free time, so I expect a lot of appreciation to be shown."

There was a ripple of noise from the recruits as they all agreed to these terms and eyed up the agents on parade, wondering who each of them had ended up with.

"So, I'll go first, and I will be mentoring Rigg." S.A. Maddox nodded at Wyn in a gesture intended to solidify this arrangement.

"Ooh, teacher's pet." Lewis teased, but snapped his head back to the front when S.A. Barb called out his name and his mentor was set.

One by one, the special agents announced who they'd been paired with. Comments passed among the recruits in support of each other's mentors and once the last had been announced, everyone went quiet, waiting for the rest of their instructions.

"Okay, so you know who you are paired with and I would recommend having a quick chat before you leave here this evening, so you can arrange your first catch-up. They also have your letters so will be able to give you those. After that, you are then free for the evening." S.A. Maddox dismissed the recruits, who all milled over to their designated agent as instructed.

Wyn held back, allowing her comrades to move in front of her and create space before she clambered past the seats and down to the front of the theatre where S.A. Maddox was waiting expectantly. Wyn tried to walk up to her as nonchalantly as possible – as far as everyone else knew, they didn't know each other outside of the group interactions and she couldn't risk giving it away by being far too enthusiastic about their one-to-ones.

"Rigg, how are you this evening? So, I was thinking we have our first catch-up tomorrow after your subterfuge session for the day is complete?" Wyn nodded in agreement. "Brilliant, I'll give you ten minutes to break out and get a drink, then I'll meet you outside your communal area and we can head to my office. It'll be quiet and we can get a lot done then." S.A. Maddox grinned knowingly as she said it. "Oh, and here's your letter... I think she's proud of you."

As Wyn looked down at the envelope that S.A. Maddox was pushing into her hand, she saw the familiar scrawl of Mrs Clay's on the front and felt the pang of homesickness return; she wasn't sure if she wanted to read it, but S.A. Maddox clearly had. She closed her eyes, thrust the letter into her pocket, and politely excused herself; they would have plenty of time to talk more tomorrow.

She was one of the first to leave the lecture theatre and return to the communal area, where Lewis and Toby had already found corners of sofas to tuck themselves up into and read their letters. One by one the recruits returned and each found their own spot. There was a sombre mood and complete silence as everyone took in what their loved ones had to say, knowing that this may be the only contact they had with them for the next year. Looking at the options, Wyn decided it was all a little bit too open and took herself into the dorm room, where she sat cross-legged on her bunk, readying herself to open the envelope. Once the familiar handwriting was laid open in front of her, she took a deep breath and absorbed the content.

#

Dear Terrell,

Have been thinking about you lots... I hope you're doing okay, wherever you are now, but well done on getting there! When I said to aim for the best, you certainly exceeded my expectations, and this couldn't be better in terms of what we'd hoped for you to achieve. At graduation, they were extremely complimentary and explained how much you all had to impress to get the opportunities you've been given, and we both know you've overcome so much more than them, so hold onto that whenever it gets tough. You're doing amazing so keep it up. But I can't help with when to wait until, because I don't know what you're doing. Whenever you do it, you've already proven yourself so don't worry about that.

I've passed on your love to the right people, and let them know that your opportunities were extended due to showing extra-special promise. They seemed happy with that. They sent their love back and asked me to tell you that they miss you and that they are very proud. They are all doing okay and are all safe and well.

And that couldn't be better news about my long-lost friend. If you can, then tell them I think of them often, and hopefully the fact that they're there means they'll be able to help you.

Love,
Lydia

#

Wyn clutched the paper to her chest. S.A. Maddox was right, Mrs Clay did sound proud, and it was nice to know that she also thought this opportunity was entirely positive in terms of their ambitions and eventual impact. But most important for Wyn was the reassurance that the Brothers and Sisters were all fine and content with the cover story; it was enough to calm her deepest fears and concerns, even though it didn't eliminate the guilt of the deceit. She had buried her worries and longing for them so deep for the last few months that this tiny bit of second-hand contact was comforting, and she reread the words to really absorb the reassurance they held. But the letter hadn't given her the answer she had hoped for—she was no closer to working out when to reveal herself. She would just have to wait and see what S.A. Maddox had to say about it tomorrow and hope that she could give her a solution.

The mood for the rest of the evening remained fairly subdued. Everyone was struggling with tempestuous thoughts—both inspired and comforted by contact from home but feeling lonelier and more fearful for the future than ever. Once she had come to terms with her own words she ventured back out into the communal area and headed over to where Cole and Carter were sat around a table. She slipped alongside Cole and listened to the brotherly heart-to-heart.

"But Cole, mum's letter was so worried and she's right; what if one of us died and never got to go home? Or even both of us could die—what would she do then?"

"Hey, breathe. It would be awful and of course she's going to worry about it – she'd only have Caleb left, and we both know he's not the favourite." Cole chuckled, trying to lighten the mood. "But she's proud of us, she said that outright, and Dad's absolutely over the moon! Signing-up at all was also going to have risk, and yes this has more, but if you really don't want to do it then there is no shame in saying that and going home. I'm worried about them too and don't want to upset them, this was never going to be easy, but we're lucky that we're here with each other."

"No, I can't do that. Then I'd be a real failure and, if I do this and make Dad proud then he might accept me a little bit more when I tell him about me, but then…" Carter trailed off, lost in thought as he mulled over how much easier it would be to just go home. "No, I can't."

Wyn smiled at Cole and the caring way he looked after his brother. She was pleased that she had made Carter speak to him and it had clearly helped bring them closer together; she nudged Cole with her knee under the table in an affectionate sign of solidarity. Using Wyn as an excuse to move off such an emotionally-charged subject, the brothers brought the conversation around to a safer topic and compared the special agents they had been given as mentors. Fortunately, they were all happy with their pairings. Other recruits slowly came to join in the stilted conversation and it was apparent that Carter was not alone in second-guessing his place in Special Forces after reading their letters, so the recruits banded together to try and distract one another from their feelings. Then, after an easy dinner of grilled chicken, jacket potatoes and salad, they all agreed it would probably be best to have an earlier than normal lights out, so they said their goodnights and turned in.

It was clear the next morning that sleep had not reset everyone's emotional stability, with Percy and Toby both considerably quieter than normal, but Wyn knew she had to throw herself back into the lessons so she didn't end up the same as them. They made their way along the corridor and took their seats, waiting for S.A. Crianz to introduce the next topic in the subject: false identities.

"So, false identities are an interesting one because there is so much you can do with them. It can be a remote identity that you just use on the phone or in other forms of communication—then you only need to work out a voice or a writing style to go along with the persona you create. However, you might go undercover and have to create everything from persona to appearance to physicality. It can be quite good fun but it doesn't come naturally to everyone."

Beside her, Carter was sniggering and elbowing her in the ribs. He clearly couldn't see past the fact that this was exactly what Wyn had been doing for months and the irony was certainly not lost on her. S.A. Crianz looked at Carter in alarm as he snorted.

"Everything okay, Reece?"

Carter clammed up and didn't know how to respond to this, so said the only thing he could think of to get the attention off himself.

"Just that Terrell does a brilliant girl impression..."

Wyn's mouth dropped open in horror and anger at this betrayal; she impulsively reached out to punch him in the arm as she seethed. This was certainly not the sort of attention she needed when she still had no idea how long she would have to keep her pretences up.

"Is that right, Rigg? How about you come down to the front and show us?"

"I really don't, I don't know what Carter's talking about."

"Come on, don't be shy – you'll all be coming up with identities and showing them to the class over the next day anyway, so you might as well get it out of the way. If it's good enough, then you can help me judge the others." S.A. Crianz encouraged and Wyn obliged, deciding that if she did a half-hearted version of her real self now, then at least she might be able to avoid having to put herself on the spot again.

As she picked her way along the row to make her way to the front, she tried to run through exactly how much of her real self she should give away. It had been so long since she'd been able to act natural, it almost felt like she would really be putting on a fake persona. Fortunately, only Cole and Carter had ever met her real self and they both knew who she was, so she didn't need to worry about anyone recognising her. However, she still didn't want to be too convincing.

"What is it you want me to do?" she asked, willing S.A. Crianz to change his mind even though she knew it was unlikely.

"Well, Reece said you can do a good female impression and that really would be valuable in the field. So, I want you to come up with a name, walk the length of the room and introduce yourself to me. It's that simple. And then we'll start working on developing the details once everyone has decided on the identity they want to create."

That didn't sound too bad but Wyn still cringed as she headed towards the far wall. Most alarmingly, she found herself scared of getting it wrong; she really had been pretending to be a boy for too long if she'd forgotten how to be her natural self. With a swing in her hips that felt totally alien but completely comfortable all at once, she let her feet fall one in front of the other in her natural feminine gait. She stopped in front of S.A. Crianz, pushed her hip out, set her weight over one leg, and placed her hand on her hip in the most stereotypically female pose she could muster.

"Hi, I'm Kiara, nice to meet you."

S.A. Crianz raised his hands and started a slow clap, looking her up and down incredulously. As soon as she realised that her demonstration was over, Wyn returned to her go-to male pose with her hips and weight centred and her feet further apart; she cringed inside to find that she almost felt more comfortable that way now. The rest of the recruits had joined in the clap and someone wolf-whistled—Wyn was pretty sure it was Carter and decided that she was going to make him pay when this was over.

"Mr Reece was most certainly correct to point this out, Rigg. That was a very good interpretation of the female form. In terms of gait, I would say you are crossing your ankles a bit too far over as you walk. Try to make it a bit more as if you're walking along a tight rope, just to stop the wobbling and make your hip swing a bit more natural, but other than that it was impeccable."

Now Wyn could hear Cole trying to stifle a laugh, but she couldn't deny that it was funny; after all, she was being corrected on how to be a female when she'd spent seventeen years of her life being one. All she wanted to do was bury her face in her hands in a mix of amusement and disbelief, but she took the constructive criticism respectfully and slipped back to the seat the moment she felt she could get away with it.

"Well, I feel that Rigg has got us off to a very good start, and we will most certainly be working further on this character for you!" S.A. Crianz shot another impressed look at Wyn. "Now, the rest of you need to start thinking about the basic outline of the false identity you want to create. Don't get me wrong, what you come up with today is not what you will be sticking to in the field – every situation will call for a different identity and persona. As such, we are first going to run through the top points to take from the situation to decide what false identity you need to create."

S.A. Crianz made his way to the whiteboard at the front of the room and began to list what they needed to consider on a base level to fit with the mission's goals. These were things like ethnicity: you would need to consider both the ethnic groups in the physical location and the group you were wishing to deceive. Also, age: an older figure would be more likely to gain the respect and trust of an enemy, whilst a younger persona could infiltrate the foot soldiers on a social level and maybe get secrets out of them in a far more laidback environment. There were a lot of things to consider but by lunchtime, each recruit had a list of their false identity's age, gender, ethnicity, name, and three personality traits to work on. Despite themselves, everyone was enjoying it; it was a bit of light relief and it was fun to pretend to be someone different for a while, just like playing dress-up as a child.

After a break for lunch, the recruits were instructed to go down to the gym so that they could work on physicality in a bit more space. They were working on standing poses, walking, sitting and finally, voice-work, and S.A. Crianz worked his way around the room to advise each recruit on what specific body language changes they needed to consider to encompass all of the traits they had identified. Wyn was surprised by just how much the personality traits changed the body language and made a mental note to start studying people more closely to see if she could pick up on the differences and learn to read people better. She was also shocked to learn that she was not the only one creating a female identity.

"Terrell, how the hell do you make it look so easy? I feel like I'm squishing all my bits and pieces and about to teeter over with every step." Lewis was falling all over the place as he tried yet another unsuccessful walk from one end of the room to the other, and even S.A. Crianz wasn't hiding his amusement at just how uncoordinated he was. But, despite his initial struggles, Wyn found that by reversing the techniques she had used to walk like a man she could successfully advise Lewis on how to walk more like a woman, and by the end of the session he could walk at least halfway across the room looking sort of feminine if he concentrated precisely on where his feet landed. Despite the embarrassment of just how hard he found it, he was seeing the funny side and the mood among the recruits was lighter and more playful than it had been since they'd arrived. As everyone made the most of the chance to be silly and create over-the-top caricatures of their identities, there was a joviality that was well-needed and much appreciated, and that was strengthening the bond between them. S.A. Crianz was pleased that they were also progressing and developing vital skills despite the fun they were clearly having, each creating a good base to continue to refine the next day. Spirits were high as the class finished for the day with everyone in a collectively good mood.

Chapter 25

Wyn dashed back to the dorm to splash water on her face to reset and refocus before waiting in the corridor for S.A. Maddox to collect her. Together they made their way back up to floor 17#, chatting about Wyn's day as they went. They arrived at S.A. Maddox's office; the glass wall looking out over the blinking lights of the evening city was just as mesmerising to Wyn as it had been the first time and for a moment, she was transfixed. Then she was brought back into the room by S.A. Maddox inviting her to sit at the grand desk.

"So, where shall we start? First of all, is there anything you want to ask me?"

This was like a red rag to a bull, as the intrigue that had surrounded S.A. Maddox since the cadets had first set sights on her all those weeks ago had continued to grow. Wyn didn't know if she would be overstepping the line but thought it was worth asking the question to find out.

"How did you get here? No women are allowed anywhere near the military and then you get such a prestigious role, and I've just been wondering how?"

"I could have guessed that would be the first question." S.A. Maddox laughed, but she didn't look annoyed at Wyn's probing. "Well, it's a long story, and it was definitely not on purpose. Back when I was a teenager, I got involved with a boy called Maximilian. Lydia would probably remember him, she really didn't like him, and I guess I understand why. He was trouble, and I was fed up with the oppression of the government, so I was easily swept up in his rebellion. We even ran protests on the steps of city hall to demand our rights to move freely. One day he decided it was a good idea to break into the government building, but we came across secrets that they would have killed to protect and we got caught and had to run. We left the city that night and travelled across the country to set up somewhere else. We agreed it was too much of a risk to contact home; back then, the government were still trying to scare everyone into submission and they would make an example of anyone who crossed them. We were number one targets for quite a while and they sent out a search party. But we kept quiet so that, in the end, people just assumed us dead—idiotic teenagers who went across the city lines and couldn't hack it."

"I reckon Lydia had an idea. She always blamed the government for you disappearing. She knew it was because of them."

"She knew more about what Max and I did than anyone. I never forgave myself for not getting a message to her that I was okay. But once we established ourselves, we needed money and so Max signed-up and ended up becoming quite a high-ranking Major. He was tasked with creating the first Special Forces but I helped him a lot; I was the more logical of the two of us and a better people person. As a married couple, we lived together in the army residences so it was easy for me to integrate into the process without any of the higher ranks noticing. Between us, we got Special Forces to the top of its game. Unfortunately, Max was murdered on a mission… He was poisoned by the enemy and it corroded him from the inside out – a very unpleasant way to go."

Wyn's heart broke for her in that moment as S.A. Maddox stopped suddenly and desperately tried to maintain her self-control. She had tried not to think about Maximilian for a very long time. Squeezing her eyes shut and drawing in a long breath she refocussed on her story, bringing all her Special Forces training back into play.

"Anyway, that left Special Forces leaderless. However, everyone knew of my involvement and we'd grown close enough that my gender was irrelevant to them. Chief Lint was in control of the military as well as the Government by then and he didn't know what to do when they requested I take over leadership of Special Forces; he tried to contest it and fight them down, but they all threatened to quit if he didn't concede. As a unit, we do so much that the public isn't aware of. We are constantly on missions and it is the intel we gain that guides what all of our other soldiers and units do, so Lint couldn't afford to lose us. He eventually agreed, as long as I was kept on a strict need to know basis, and he has thrown more than one threat my way to try and keep me in line. I have never met anyone who hated women quite so much, but that was eight years ago and I'm still here. I have proven myself and not even he can take that away from me, and I think he would be too scared to try."

Wyn was incredulous at the story she was hearing. No wonder S.A. Maddox had the strength and confidence to rival any Major or General, she had clearly been an irreplaceable asset for the country and Wyn couldn't begin to imagine how amazing that would feel, but hoped that she would one day find out.

"Didn't anyone recognise you though … from when you ran away?"

"Luckily it never came to that. By the time I was known for being Head of Special Forces, the men who had caught us all those years ago had declared us dead and never made the association. I was a scrawny teenager back then and they certainly weren't going to make the connection with a full-grown woman with bright hair and muscle tone. Plus I never used my real name – you have been the first person I've said my real name to in over sixteen years. It feels strange saying it out loud again."

"Why me? Why did you trust me?"

"It wasn't so much about trust when we met… I mean it is now, we both have too much to lose not to trust each other. But I figured that if you decided to discuss our communications but used a name that they thought was completely wrong, then they would just assume you were lying and I could deny any knowledge of who you are. Self-preservation is important to learn when you're alone at the top as long as I have been."

Wyn felt immediately closer to S.A. Maddox, partly through the pride of being allowed into her secret and partly through the empathy that was pouring out at all that she had been through. It made Wyn realise that she had one more person to do this for and that would give her that extra boost of strength to keep going. And now that they had bonded more, it was important to start thinking about the real dilemma facing them.

"So, let's get onto the real reason that I created this mentorship – planning what you're going to do next." S.A. Maddox could feel the lump of emotion threatening to rise up once more so moved the conversation on swiftly. It had been a long time since she had let her guard down quite so much and it was an uncomfortable feeling, she was certainly ready to push the attention back onto Wyn.

"I don't know. I keep going backwards and forwards. Here there isn't somewhere to reveal who I am and make any impact. What if I just got sent home and that was that, all of this for nothing. But I don't know how much longer I can keep it up."

"I've been thinking too, and you're right that it isn't a straightforward position to be in. You have been undercover for a long time and that is an exhausting place to be, but you obviously need to plan when you will make the most impact to make it all worthwhile. And what you've been doing goes hand in hand with the training you've been doing here—you are clearly skilled in your subterfuge topics and utilising you as an undercover woman in the field could be the most valuable asset we have in some missions that are potentially just around the corner. Once you were out there, you wouldn't be around many agents and you would have the perfect excuse to fall back into being a woman without giving yourself away. If you were willing to do it, and went out there and completed a mission in potentially one of the most dangerous and complex situations we have ever faced, then your return would be celebrated. These celebrations involve the highest-ranking figures in the country—government, military and business alike—and that is somewhere that you could really make your moment count. But you'd have to survive the mission first and it would be far from easy. Your life would very much be on the line and you would learn and see things that you would never be able to get out of your memory no matter how hard you tried."

S.A. Maddox was scrutinising Wyn's face, trying to read her reaction. Wyn's mind was racing with the thought.

"You mean, go out properly and be a real special agent? And then reveal myself when I come back?"

"Exactly! Go out and do something that less than 0.5% of the entire armed forces ever do and with far greater importance, then come back a hero and see how much more of an impact that makes when they see that women can make it in one of the most competitive, specialised roles we have. That is success most men only dream of; think of how amazing it would feel when they realise you surpassed them all. Not even Lint could argue with that!"

She was talking with such passion that Wyn could feel her heart already starting to race with the idea of the satisfaction and pride she would feel at proving herself to the world. The nervous-excited butterflies were dancing in her stomach just thinking about it. Despite the risk and the danger, this enthusiasm was infectious, and Wyn knew she was being easily talked round to the idea. Enya was right, this would work.

"Alright…" Wyn could feel the words teetering on the edge of her tongue. She knew that once they were out there was no going back, but the butterflies were fluttering up into her chest and pushed them out. "I'll do it."

S.A. Maddox's face was radiant as it filled with an intensely proud grin which reflected Wyn's own expression back at her, but both of their faces dropped suddenly as they were interrupted by a frantic knocking at the door.

"Come in?" S.A. Maddox was not expecting any interruptions and the panicked nature of the knock was disconcerting.

S.A. Finnell came dashing in, lacking his usual air of untouchable superiority and visibly flapping as he tried to command S.A. Maddox's attention.

"Sorry to bother you. We've had word back from Operation Cascade. Things are worse than we anticipated and we are going to need to reconsider our next step. They asked me to get you immediately whilst they can make contact." His voice jumped as he raced to get the words out.

It was clear to Wyn that the situation was urgent and S.A. Maddox was already gathering herself out of the chair.

"We will have to reconvene again tomorrow evening, in the same format. When we have missions overseas it is often difficult to make contact, so it is essential to talk to them whenever they are available and I need to get to the control room immediately. I am very sorry for the disruption, Terrell."

S.A. Maddox impressed Wyn by how quickly she fell back into their traditional roles, and as she finished speaking she strode out of the room, assuming Wyn to be following behind without even checking. The three of them made it to the lift but Wyn was instructed to wait in the corridor and call it again once it had reached floor 20*, then she could use it to return to her residential quarters.

Wyn spent the rest of the evening wondering what could have been so important to have called S.A. Maddox away, and what sort of excitement and drama was going on overseas. Soon she might even be part of it and being within reach of the secrets was extremely frustrating. She was fixated on what might be happening for the rest of the evening, inciting more than one comment from the other recruits about just how 'away with the fairies' she was, but her daydreams were exciting and she was enjoying being caught up in them. After food and having clambered into her bunk, she lay there hoping that soon she would know just what was going on, without having to imagine. The idea of being a trusted special agent helped to lull her into a sleep filled with exhilarating missions and secrets.

The next morning, the recruits were woken abruptly by S.A. Barb bounding through the dorms and flicking on the lights. Wyn groaned as she sat up, rubbing her eyes and staring around the room in confusion

"Everybody up and to the lecture theatre, army-issue t-shirts are fine. Up and at 'em lads!"

Nobody was ready for his jovial tone at this time in the morning, especially not when he started to pull the blankets off those of them that were showing no sign of stirring. Within twenty minutes, they were all sat in their usual seats facing an array of special agents who all looked intensely serious and were watching the recruits carefully.

"Morning gentleman! Thank you for joining us and apologies for waking you so early. We have gathered here for two reasons today. The first being that two recruits have requested to be removed from the process and I can announce that that request has been granted."

A shocked gasp spread through the recruits, and Wyn could tell by the looks on the faces of some of the agents that this was a surprise to them too. She glanced around at her comrades to see if she could work out who it was, but she had a good idea who it might have been. Toby and Andrew were both still struggling after reading their letters from home and she could tell that both of them had been questioning what they were doing here. S.A. Maddox confirmed her suspicions in her next breath.

"Andrew Freemantle and Tobias Clitheroh, please follow Special Agents Finnell and Crianz and they will complete your exit interviews and paperwork. You will then have a brief opportunity to say goodbye before they escort you to your transport back to your bases."

Wyn sent an empathetic look in Andrew's direction as he walked across the room to where the agents were waiting. It was clear he was embarrassed that his decision had been aired so publicly, and there was something about losing the first friend she had made in this process that made Wyn feel extremely vulnerable. He looked back at her with apologetic eyes. Once both of them had been led out of the room, S.A. Maddox continued with her announcements.

"We are very regretful that we have to lose two recruits who brought a lot of variety to our team, but we fully appreciate their decisions and they will continue to have our support in spirit going forward. Now, onto reason two. Yesterday we received contact from the camp set up by the agents who went out a few weeks ago and, although they are making progress with the individual missions that they are due to undertake, they have also come across far more complications than we anticipated. They are attempting to get through the final barricades to where the enemy control centre and leaders are based but we did not expect the complexity of the surroundings, or how many civilians it could compromise. As such, we have decided to go at this from another angle and this will include some of you."

The recruits all stared back at her in amazement—they'd only been in training less than a fortnight, how could they be considering sending them out into the field already? Trepidation and fear ran through them as they anticipated who would be chosen.

"Lewis Brightcoff, Daniel Edgington, Carter Reece, Cole Reece and Terrell Rigg, please stay behind. The rest of you are dismissed to the common room."

The five of them watched as the others removed themselves from the lecture theatre, watching after them in a mixture of pride and terror. They were all silently questioning why they had been chosen, but were too scared to say a word. However, Wyn had a pretty good idea, following her conversation with S.A. Maddox the day before. They sat staring, waiting for someone to make it make a bit more sense.

"So, as you may have guessed, you have been selected—from your success in the sessions so far and advisement from your mentoring agents, who are also going out on missions—to be the recruits that continue their training in the field. We aren't going to just send you out there to fend for yourselves, we will continue to teach you and refine your skills, and we won't let you do anything that we don't think you're ready for. This is an incredible honour, and is unprecedented in anything we have done before, so be proud of yourselves. Now, go back to the common room and say goodbye to Andrew and Toby, and then someone will bring in some kit bags – you can take only as many personal items and clothing as will fit into it. Later this morning we will come to collect you and further brief you on the plan. By this evening, we will be travelling to our overseas base. You are dismissed."

The recruits were all still in shock and barely said a word as they made their way to the front of the lecture theatre. S.A. Maddox held out her hand and gestured to Wyn to hold back as the others left. Once it was just the two of them, she began to speak.

"Well done, Wyn! Don't think that this is all my influence, you've shown a lot of vital skills—not just your false identity—and it means that you are fully on track to the big reveal that we wanted. And you know what this means, most excitingly?"

Wyn just shook her head, still overwhelmed by the extremely sudden and dramatic change in her direction. But S.A. Maddox was right, this was exactly what she needed for her cause and what she had been aiming for since she got here; underneath the fear-fuelled anxiety was a warming bubble of pride.

"Wyn, congratulations, you are officially a special agent!"